DAUGHTERS OF ASH
BOUND BY ORDER BOOK ONE

DAKOTA MONROE

CONTENTS

ABOUT THE BOOK

Daughters of Ash is the start of an adult series where Mulan meets The Handmaid's Tale. This series is a dark, dystopian fantasy romance that is very slow burn and more plot-centric. In the first installment, we follow Cassia as she infiltrates the Enforcers after hiding the last twenty-six years of her life. Women are property in Dascenia, and they are either kept in a breeding facility from the day they're born, or purchased by a man to be used for anything he wishes. Men have every freedom granted to them, and Cassia is determined to change their world back to what it used to be before the leaders of the Syndicate took over. When she discovers the Syndicate is calling for a new team of Enforcers to take out a rebel group found outside the perimeter, Cassia uses her privilege as an undocumented woman to join this team, learn their secrets, and dismantle them from the inside.

CONTENT WARNINGS

This book is a dark dystopian fantasy, with suggested romance and direct romance in later books. Please note the series is a reverse harem and includes topics that some may find disturbing or triggering.

For a full list of the content warnings, please visit dakotamonroe.com/contentwarnings

BOUND BY UNITY

DASCENIA

FOR THE GREATER ORDER

IDGE

N

W   E

S

ORCER TRAINING CENTER

MAGIC SYSTEM

The magic in this world is called 'power'. Powers are abilities that men are born with, and they each have only one. Most of these powers need physical touch with what they're using the power on, but some people are able to grow their power enough that they can use it without touch. Power is not a huge part of their world and is mostly used by the Enforcers.

Women do not have powers.

Adapters
    Ability: Resilience to environmental extremes.
    Use: Survive in harsh conditions, like extreme heat or cold.

Anchors
    Ability: Shift body density to become heavier or lighter.
    Use: Improve balance, stealth, or resist movement or injury.

Chargers
    Ability: Generate static charges.

Use: Disrupt electronics or deliver shocks.

Clingers
Ability: Adhere to surfaces for climbing or holding objects.

Use: Climb walls, ceilings, or securely carry items.

Concealers
Ability: Shift light to blend into an area.

Use: Enhance stealth and avoid detection in different environments.

Empaths
Ability: Sense and influence others' emotions.

Use: Same as ability.

Remnants
Ability: Gain impressions of recent events on objects or places.

Use: Track or understand past occurrences.

Revealers
Ability: Detect lies from others.

Use: Sense dishonesty without knowing the full truth.

Suppressants
Ability: Dampen physical pain.

Use: Endure injuries or painful conditions.

Telepaths
Ability: Communicate mentally with others.

Use: Silent communication with nearby allies.

Thermics

    Ability: Control temperature.

    Use: Warm or cool objects or people.

For the girls who were told to be quiet, to the women who forgot how loud they can be: Use your voice. Take up space. And never apologize for existing.

CHAPTER ONE

CASSIA

I tell myself this is enough. That safety is worth the silence.

It's a lie I almost believe.

A lie I convince myself to play along with, if only for the people who have sacrificed much to keep me hidden all these years. If not for them, my life would look very, very different.

The knight on the board taunts me as I weigh my options. Each move unfolds in my mind like pages in a well-worn book —familiar paths with predictable endings. The dark and light squares have been my battlefield for as long as I can remember; it's one of the few places I'm allowed to wage war.

"Your move, Cassia," my father mutters, his voice patient but tight with the knowledge of what's coming.

Three potential paths sit before me, but only one leads to victory in five moves. I chew on the worn flesh of my cheek as I consider each option once more, prolonging his misery. Perhaps my methods are unkind, but these small rebellions are all I have to live for.

I slide my bishop diagonally, capturing his rook.

A breath leaves father as his shoulders slump, finally grasping the direction of the game—the inevitable checkmate I set in motion. His king is already dead; the execution just hasn't happened yet.

"I concede," he says, tipping his king with a resigned flick. "That's three in a row, dove."

I smile, not humble in the slightest, warmth radiating through my chest. "I could have won two plays sooner, but I wanted to see if you'd notice a trap."

That's the thing about chess...I do not play to win. I play to witness the moment my opponent realizes their collapse is inescapable, because I've been several steps ahead the entire time. It would be easy to defeat them quickly. To save them the effort of trying.

But I do not wish to conquer just this one battle. I crave to win every one after that, as well. I want my enemy to know who I am before we even step into the ring—already anticipating how fucked they are.

And that sort of reputation is not cultivated by taking the easy way out.

"Of course you did." His head shakes, exasperation softening into pride. "Your memory gives you an unfair advantage. You've memorized every possible scenario by now."

"Not every scenario," I counter, resetting the pieces with practiced grace. The smooth ivory figures—yellowed with age—click against the wooden board. Satisfying. "Just the ones you favor."

What I don't say: I have memorized twenty-three opening strategies he cycles through, documented the exact pressure of his fingers when he's about to sacrifice a piece, tracked the subtle shift in his breathing when he thinks he's discovered a weakness in my defense. Chess isn't about the game; it's about the player. And I've studied my father for twenty-six years, so it should not still come as a surprise to him that I win every time.

Well, nearly every time.

The man wouldn't continue playing with me if I didn't relinquish the game here and there.

A thud from the outer walls snaps the thought in half—dull scraping accompanying it. Every nerve in my body awakens as I stiffen. The map of our house flares in my mind on instinct: three steps to the hallway, seven to my parents' room, three more to the hatch and then down a set of stairs. Father and I listen, breaths held as we determine the rhythm of footsteps. Too slow for a patrol and too uneven for armored Enforcers. A cart rattles past, close to the front window, and a man laughs, the ice in my chest easing a fraction. Not tonight. They won't find me tonight.

It takes monumental effort to force my fingers to unclench from the table and refocus on the board as I pretend my heart isn't still climbing through my throat.

Father says nothing.

In his defense, what is there to say?

The floorboards creak outside the sitting room, followed by the distinctive rhythm of my mother's steps. She appears in the doorway with a wooden tray balanced between steady, lithe hands, steam rising from three bowls. A clip holds back her strawberry hair, allowing her flushed cheeks proper space to breathe.

"Dinner," she announces, voice as warm as the stew she's carrying.

My father rises to assist her, adjusting the tuck of his button down before grabbing the tray and setting it on the small table in the corner. The scent reaches me—root vegetables and herbs from our modest garden, and the protein of some preserved meat. My stomach tightens, angry with the lack of sustenance I've granted it today, demanding I dive into my bowl with the grace of a wild animal.

"Perfect timing," I say, abandoning the chess pieces.

"Father just conceded." My tone adds the *again* I choose not to voice.

Mother's eyes crinkle before she utters my insinuation. "Again?" She knows we can never play just one round. "Pierce, at some point you need to accept that she's better than you."

"Never." His reply is blunt and monotone, but the smile pulling at his lips betrays him.

We settle around the table, our routine as fixed as the walls imprisoning me. My father takes the first bite, humming as he nods his approval—the signal we can begin. These small ceremonies maintain our semblance of normalcy, as if we're just a typical family instead of conspirators in a lifelong crime.

A crime in which the only payment is death.

"How was the library today?" mother asks as she passes a piece of bread.

Father swallows, the worn skin of his throat bobbing before he replies. "Busy. The Syndicate's latest decree about approved reading materials has everyone scrambling to ensure compliance." A flicker of something—anger perhaps—crosses his face before disappearing beneath a veil of calm. "Three more books were added to the restricted list. Something about content potentially *encouraging female independence.*"

The words hang suspended in the air. My fingers tighten around their spoon, but my mouth remains closed.

"Anything else?" mother prompts, her tone forced with a lightness I'm certain she doesn't feel.

It's difficult to feel light at all in the world we're forced to live in.

Father reclines in his chair, grazing a hand over his chin. "Actually, yes. Word is the Syndicate is organizing some new Enforcer group. They're recruiting men from across every province." His brows crease as his dark eyes go distant. "It's not clear why. Enforcer numbers are already at capacity."

The front door swings open before he elaborates, a current of cool air swimming through the house. Heavy footsteps approach—my brother's distinctive gait, slightly favoring his right leg from an old injury.

A smile claims my lips as Lachlan appears in the doorway, his tall frame filling the space. Despite the exhaustion evident in the shadows beneath his eyes, his familiar face brightens when he spots us.

"Perfect timing," he says in a voice a bit deeper than mine, echoing my earlier words. "I'm starving."

Mother pushes from the table, rising to fetch another bowl of stew. "How was your trip?"

Lachlan drops his pack by the door and slumps into the empty seat across from me. "Long. I really hate how cold it gets in the mountains. Ailridge might look pretty from a distance, but the wind cuts right through you up there."

"The delivery went well?" father inquires. He is very good at showing interest in Lachlan's job as a messenger, even when it's anything but.

"As well as can be expected. The Syndicate officials inspected everything twice, but the paperwork was in order." He accepts the bowl my mother offers with a smile, nodding his thanks. "The manufacturing hub in Pyrem is ramping up production for something. No one would say what."

I sit quiet, content to absorb their words while savoring the warmth of the stew. This is my window to the outside world—snippets of information gathered by my father and brother, carefully pieced together in my mind like a mosaic of places I've never seen. Flat images and maps can only offer so much.

What's it like out there? I ask my inner self, repeating the same inquiry I have for thousands of days in a row.

I've constructed elaborate mental images from books and stories, but imagination can only take you so far. I've never felt rain on my face or wind through my hair outside these aging walls. Never walked on streets, entered shops, or stood beneath an open sky without the frame of a window blocking small pieces of it.

I steal glances through the windows sometimes, when no one is looking. Quick peeks at the world—the tall, neighboring buildings Enforcers patrol, scuff marks along the stone ground that change day after day. But these glimpses are like trying to understand an ocean by looking at a single drop of its water. Impossible.

The stack of books my father brought home catches my attention where they rest on a side table. A surge of excitement rushes through me as I spot a worn leather binding with faded gold lettering; a history book, by the look of it. Those are my favorites. My fragments of a past when our world operated by different rules. They may as well be fantasy books for how unthinkable some of the entries are.

I reach for the stack, wheeling the table closer and yanking hard when it catches on an annoying dent in the floor.

"Found some interesting things in the archives today," father muses, following my movements. "That history volume was in the restricted section, so handle it carefully. I'll need to return it without any evidence that it left the library."

I nod, understanding the risk he's taken and beyond thankful for it. "I'll be gentle." And I will. These books will be handled with the care of a newborn baby.

My fingers trace the embossed cover.

A Comprehensive History of the Northern Territories: Pre-Unification Era

My heart beats faster at the title. The pre-unification era— when Dascenia was divided into what they call *states* instead of provinces. When borders were more permeable and rights more universal.

"So," a feminine voice begins, breaking into my thoughts, "what were you saying about this new Enforcer group, Pierce?"

He shrugs. "Not much more to tell. The postings mentioned special assignments outside regular Enforcer duties."

"Outside the perimeter, maybe?" Lachlan suggests in a passive tone. "There have been rumors among the traders about activity beyond the border."

"Escapees?" Mother's voice drops to a whisper, though no one outside can hear us.

"Possibly." Father's expression darkens. "The Syndicate wouldn't mobilize a special unit for nothing."

Glancing between the three of them, I catalog their expressions. The tension in their shoulders, the careful way they choose their words even in the privacy of our home. This is what the Syndicate has done to us—made us afraid in our own sanctuary, trained us to speak in half-truths and implications.

My thoughts stray to the women in the breeding facilities. About the powers they do not carry to fight back, and the laws that bind them to the men who purchase them like cattle. About my mother, who was lucky enough to be bought by a good man, but who still cannot leave this house without him.

And then I think about myself.

I shouldn't exist. An undocumented woman who grew up outside the three facilities. A woman with powers she should not possess. Only men have powers, so why am I different?

My eyes roll before I can stop them. Lachlan is always the answer to anything strange that happens to me—sharing a womb will do that. Sometimes the weight of such knowledge feels like bloated pressure in my chest, pushing against my ribs, begging for release.

"Did you see the market in the city?" mother asks Lach, steering the conversation to safer waters—though I'm not certain our wonderful city of Pyrem is a much safer topic. "Were there fresh vegetables yet?"

He nods, settling his spoon in the now-empty bowl. "Some early greens," he answers. "Prices are high, though. The Syndicate's taking a larger percentage this season."

Discussion continues while my attention turns back to the history book. Its pages are thin and delicate beneath my fingers, containing truths the Syndicate doesn't want remembered. The layers of dust between pages are evidence enough.

I read about a time when the territory now called Dascenia was part of something larger, something called the United States of America. How its states formed a loose coalition with their own governments but united under central principles. How people—*all people*, including their women—could travel freely between them.

Like I said, it may as well be classified as a fantasy book.

I suck in deep, calming breaths as I skim through the pages. The book describes vehicles called *commercial airplanes* that carried people through the sky, metal beasts that somehow defied gravity.

Creases pinch my forehead as I recall what our flying contraptions are called—drones, I think, but as far as I know, they cannot even carry one person.

The text discusses democratic voting, where people chose their leaders instead of submitting to those who stole power. It speaks of women who owned property, ran businesses, and led governments.

It truly sounds like the best fiction. A beautiful, impossible dream.

The conversation flows as I absorb these scraps of history. Eventually, the dishes clear, and I've waited the appropriate amount of time after dinner before I can reasonably excuse myself. I do not want to be disrespectful, but I'm aching to dive further into these pages.

"I think I'll head to my room," I announce to no one in particular, gathering the thick stack of books.

Father nods, reaching to muss my hair, smiling when I groan and pull away. "Don't stay up too late, dove."

"I won't," I promise, already calculating how much reading I can fit in before sleep claims me.

The hallway to my bedroom—*our bedroom*—is short and narrow. The house isn't large, but it's been home my entire life. Sometimes I wonder if I should feel more confined, more desperate to escape. But how can you miss what you've never known? Still, there are moments when the walls contract, when I find myself staring at the ceiling and imagining what lies beyond our small corner in Pyrem.

The door to the room I share with Lachlan pushes open easily. Two narrow beds against opposite walls, a small dresser between them, a bookshelf crammed with volumes I've read and reread until their spines have cracked. It's not much, but it's mine.

Ours.

Sometimes I wish for my own space. Not because I mind sharing with my twin brother—he's my closest friend, the keeper of my existence—but because privacy feels like a luxury I've never tasted. Even on the nights he's away, traveling for his job.

In this world where I must remain hidden, where my very presence is a crime punishable by death for my entire family, having a corner that's just mine seems like an unattainable indulgence.

But I understand the necessity. If Enforcers were to raid our house, having a single bedroom for the *only child* makes our deception more believable. And in the grand calculation of risks versus comforts, this small sacrifice hardly registers.

I grunt as my body settles on the bed before scooting back against the wall and revealing the insides of the history book with reverent hands. The soft crack of the spine reminds me once again to be careful—this book doesn't belong to me and must return undamaged.

Well, time has damaged it enough. But wear from hands is far different than that of darkness and gravity.

The pages reveal more wonders from the past: structures called movie theaters, where people gathered to watch stories projected on walls larger than our entire house. My head tilts as I try to imagine it—sitting in darkness with strangers, all facing the same enormous image, sharing laughter or tears of fear. Our small television, one of my father's prized finds, seems pitiful in comparison.

"Remember that," I whisper to myself, employing the technique I discovered as a child.

When I concentrate on a piece of information and instruct myself to remember it, it dwells in my mind with perfect clarity. Not just the information itself, but the context —where I was sitting, what the page looked like, how the light fell across each word. It's as if my mind takes a photograph and files it away where I can access it whenever it's needed.

Technically, my brain stores everything it processes, but I utter those two words to myself when I want them to remain in my active memory, instead of stored to only be recalled when the topic presents itself.

This ability has been both a blessing and a curse. I never forget a chess move, a conversation, a pattern. But I also never forget the pain in my mother's eyes when she speaks of the facility where she grew up—Riverton—or the too close sounds of Enforcers' boots on our street that forced my father to build the hatch when I was seven.

I reach for my notebook, hidden between the mattress and wall. It's not that I need to write things down to remember them—I don't—but there's something satisfying about creating a physical record of the things I find most interesting. I enjoy knowing that even when I'm gone, unknown by the entire world outside the three people in my family, there will be a piece of me left here.

It makes me feel like my existence isn't completely worthless.

The notebook is worn, its pages filled with my small, neat handwriting documenting lost things from the past. I add a new entry:

Movie theater. Large public building where people watched films on screens as big as walls. Strangers sat together in darkness, sharing the experience collectively. Imagine our television, but twenty times larger. Everyone could attend, regardless of gender or status. Admission price was small. Early versions opened in the 1900s and lasted until the Collapse.

My fingers run along the indented words, my mind wondering what it would be like to sit in such a place, surrounded by others as we all focus on the same story.

To exist without fear.

The door creaks open, and I slide the notebook back into hiding with practiced speed. But it's only Lachlan, brunette hair damp and mussed.

"Still awake?" he asks in a quiet voice, dropping onto his own bed. The frame squeaks beneath his weight.

"Just reading." I gesture to the book, tapping the edge.

He nods, watching me with careful attention, a habit I hate he's formed. "How are you doing, Cass? We haven't talked in a bit, with how busy work is."

The question lingers between us, heavier than its simple words suggest. He asks this often, especially after returning from his travels—as if checking whether my confinement has finally broken me in his absence.

"I'm fine," I mumble, offering the automatic response. Then, because it's Lachlan and he deserves more, I add, "Restless. Curious. The usual."

He smiles, the expression so similar to my own it's like looking in a mirror. We share the same dark hair, though his rests just below his shoulders while mine falls to waist-level. The same observant eyes and pointed chin. If I cut my hair and wore his clothes, we'd be nearly indistinguishable—a fact that has crossed my mind more than once over the years.

"Brought you something." He reaches into his pocket, pulling out a small package wrapped in cloth.

My heart lifts along with my brows. This is our ritual—Lachlan bringing back small treasures from his trips, tangible pieces of the world I cannot see. I've never been able to truly express just how much these little gifts mean to me.

I unwrap it carefully. Inside is a small, carved figure of a mountain cat, its body graceful even in stillness. The wood is dark and smooth. Polished by experienced hands.

"It's beautiful," I breathe, fingers caressing the soft curves.

"Made by a craftsman in Ailridge. Said the mountain cats used to roam freely through the terrain before the Syndicate's hunting parties decimated them." His voice drops lower. "They're making a comeback, though. Breeding in the high valleys where Enforcers don't patrol."

I understand the subtle subtext: nature finding a way despite oppression. Life persisting in hidden places. Something that made Lachlan think of his sister.

A small smile graces my face in offering. "Thank you," I say, placing the figure on my small shelf alongside the other gifts he's brought me over the years—a polished stone from a river in Ofin, a tiny glass vial of red sand from the deserts of Belken, a dried flower from Vinford.

My collection of the mysterious world.

Lachlan yawns, stretching his long frame. "I should sleep. The journey back was long."

"Of course," I reply, adjusting my position to something more comfortable. "Thanks again for the cat." He nods, already drifting away beneath his blanket. Within minutes, his breathing deepens and slows.

I watch him for a moment, this brother who is my mirror and my shield. Without him, I would have been confiscated at birth like all female infants—removed from my mother's arms and shipped to a breeding facility, raised to accept submission as natural. I would either be breeding stock by now, bearing children for the greater order of the Syndicate, or some man's property, used for whatever he desires.

Instead, I snuck into this world undetected as my mother birthed only a son before the midwives could arrive, according to the official records. And I'm still here. Hidden. Free, in a limited sense.

Alive in ways other women could never hope to be.

It's a blessing I try never to take for granted; I know just how lucky I am. *And yet...*

Sometimes I hate myself for the restlessness that gnaws at me; the selfish desire to see more, do more, be more. My mother and father have sacrificed everything to keep me safe. Even Lachlan has given much of himself for my welfare. I should be grateful for the small freedoms I have—to read, learn, and exist without a man's ownership.

But I have knowledge. And power—my Empath ability. I could be helping others instead of hiding. I could be making a difference instead of playing chess and reading about a time of the past that only exists in the minds of the oldest in our society.

Lachlan's soft snores fill the room as his brows twitch. Out of habit, I free my power to check that he's not having a nightmare. Only excited, impatient emotions drift from him, and I chuckle to myself as I slip from bed and crack the door, allowing a sliver of light from the hallway to illuminate my book. My parents are in their bedroom by now, and the house will be quiet until morning.

I settle back on my bed, the history volume heavy in my lap. For now, this is my rebellion—learning what the Syndicate doesn't want known. Preserving the memory of freedoms lost. My chest squeezes.

One day, perhaps, I'll find a way to do more.

But for tonight, I read by the thin line of light, absorbing the knowledge of when women walked freely under open skies. I turn each page with care, mindful of my father's warning.

There's a small, gleeful resistance in these actions—in learning what I'm not supposed to know. Developing the mind they would have stunted, and honing abilities they would have suppressed.

The words blur as my eyes grow heavy. I fight the drowsiness, determined to finish at least one more chapter before sleep steals my mind away. But eventually the book slips to rest against my chest, and I drift into dreams of a place where my existence isn't a capital crime. Where I can walk beside my brother in the sunlight instead of hiding in his shadow.

In my dreams, I'm free. And that will have to be enough until I can find a way to make those dreams a reality.

CHAPTER TWO
CASSIA

The thick paste of the wooden bowl shifts from a muddy brown to a pale green as I stir slowly. The transformation happens in streaks, and my eyes lock in on the ribbons of color swirling as I introduce sage oil drop by drop. The scent fills my small workspace—a corner of my bedroom—earthy and sharp, with the underlying sweetness of the birchweed sap I'd ask mother to collect from our garden last week.

"Almost there," I mutter to my invisible audience, reaching for the powdered sealwort root.

My fingertips brush the small clay jar, its texture grainy against my skin. It slides to the edge of the table, stopping just to the side of me. Precision matters most in these final steps. Too much sealwort and the mixture becomes rigid and cracks; too little it slides off the skin like oil in water. I've failed in both directions more times than I care to count.

Frustrating, but inevitable.

I tip the smallest pinch of the fine powder onto my palm, gently blowing half of it into the mixture. I don't want to risk overdoing it...again. The paste bubbles faintly, tiny air pockets rising to the surface and bursting in slow motion, indicating that if I cease movement for a moment, the mixture will begin boiling. I continue stirring, counting under my breath. One hundred clockwise rotations, then the same in reverse, breaking any pockets that form.

This is my nineteenth attempt at creating a wound sealant—a transparent second skin that would encourage the perfect environment for healing. I've read accounts of similar things in old medical texts, descriptions of liquid bandages that protected injuries while allowing them to breathe. If I could replicate it, even crudely, it would aid my mother when she cuts herself in the kitchen. Or Lachlan when he returns from his travels with scraped knuckles and mysterious bruises.

It could mean something beyond these walls.

The paste thickens as I work, clinging to the wooden spoon. I hum, tampering the flutter in my stomach. That's promising. The last batch was too liquidy, dripping down wounds instead of sealing them. Adding another pinch of sealwort, I hold my breath as it's stirred in, praying to the stars this is finally it.

A soft knock at my door breaks the hardness of my gaze, though I remain still and continue to stir.

"Cassia?" My mother's voice, gentle but insistent.

"Come in," I answer, not looking her way as the handle twists. The mixture is at a critical stage—the ideal balance between each of my previous failures. Maybe this is the one.

The door creaks open, and I catch my mother's reflection in the small mirror propped against the wall. She's always had a calming presence about her. It settles my nerves without any effort on her part, even when I'm severely stressed over something as small as the dish in front of me. Her eyes scan my face before drifting to the bowl, a familiar mix of curiosity and concern in her expression.

"Still working on your healing paste?" she asks, shifting to stand next to me. Notes of my favorite meal fall from her linen skirt, coated in the essence of warm bread.

Salmon. Not a meal we often get the privilege of, and is usually only reserved for particular occasions. I don't question her, though, instead focusing on my answer while she works up the courage to tell me whatever is creasing the skin on her forehead.

I nod, giving the mixture one final stir before setting the spoon aside. "I think I've almost got it this time."

She makes a soft humming sound, her way of expressing approval without saying it outright. Living in secrecy teaches you to speak in body language and expressions—I could have an entire conversation with each person in my family without ever uttering a word.

A rare privilege to experience, some would say.

"What's the new ingredient?" She leans closer, crinkling her nose as her eyes study my work.

"Sealwort. Ground it finer than before." I tap the tiny jar with my fingernail. "The last batch was too liquidy, so I think the powder will help it set without hardening completely, if dosed in micro-increments." She smiles at that, her hand finding my shoulder and squeezing gently. I lean into her touch, accepting the way in which she prefers to express her love.

"I need you to clean up soon," she says, her voice dropping lower as she clears her throat. "Your father's boss is coming for dinner tonight."

My stomach tightens. Vague memories of disgust wash through me from his previous visits. "Hardan? Tonight?" I already know it's him, but I need her to confirm it. Not knowing for sure will just increase my anxious thoughts.

"I'm afraid so. You know how he insists on these dinners twice a year."

I do know. Hardan Lesson, my father's supervisor at the library, uses these *social visits* to remind my father of his place —to reinforce the hierarchy that keeps every man looking over his shoulder and every woman staring at the floor in submission.

"He's bringing Eliana?" She nods, and my lip curls at knowing I'll have to listen to the man berate and dehumanize his wife for the entirety of their visit.

I've never met Eliana—or anyone for that matter—but I've heard her voice through the floor in the past. I rage over the careful way she speaks, always waiting for her husband to finish spewing his nonsense before offering the most innocuous of comments. The flat cadence of her words, devoid of anything that might provoke a reaction, is almost enough to yank me from hiding so her husband can learn what blood tastes like.

I hate him for what he's reduced her to.

But I keep my mouth closed from the violence, instead saying, "I'll be ready," before turning back to my workstation, dismissing my mother.

I don't mean to be rude, but I'd rather ignore her presence than say all the things spiraling through my head. She's too kind for my brand of hate.

She hovers for a moment longer, her eyes on the small collection of jars and bowls that represent my modest laboratory. I know what she's thinking—that I take too many risks, that my experiments could raise questions we can't answer if an Enforcer were to demand a random inspection.

But she says nothing of this. She understands what these small creations mean to me.

"Don't take too long. I am just finishing up the preparations." She presses a light kiss to the top of my head before leaving me alone once again.

When the door closes, I examine the pale green paste in my bowl. It's thickened to the consistency I've been aiming for—not solid, but not flowing like water. I dip a fingertip in, smiling at the texture. It's smooth, almost silky, with a cooling sensation as it clings to my skin.

Hope flutters in my chest, a feeling I've learned to temper with caution. I've been here many times before...thinking I'd finally solved the puzzle, only to watch my creation fail in new and frustrating ways. I understand that's the nature of everything—retrying until something works or until you die—but it's frustrating all the same. I want things to work the *first* time, not the twentieth.

I scoff at my naive thoughts. As if.

Wiping my finger on a scrap of cloth, I reach for a small vial. Using a thin wooden spatula, I transfer a portion of the paste into the vial for later testing. If this batch works, I'll need to be meticulous in documenting every step I took to create it.

Dipping the same spatula back into the bowl, I scoop out a generous amount and consider where to apply it. Usually, I'd make a small cut on my inner arm—controlled and easy to hide—but today I decide to try it on unbroken skin first. If it burns or causes irritation, better to find out before introducing it to an open wound.

My hand carefully applies the paste to the outside of my wrist, spreading it into a thin layer. The cooling sensation intensifies—a mild tingling that's not unpleasant. The paste adheres well, neither dripping nor smearing, and I watch with fascination and unsteady anticipation as it begins to lose its green tint, becoming more translucent by the second.

"Please work," I whisper to every star that will listen, holding my arm steady.

The transformation continues, each moment of suspended

silence prickling my skin as I wait impatiently. The paste thins further, molding to the contours of my skin. For a moment—one perfect, hopeful moment—I think I've succeeded. It appears exactly as I'd imagined: a transparent second skin, flexible and protective.

But of course my dreams stop there.

The tingling intensifies, sharpening into discomfort. Fingernails dig into my palms as the layer continues to harden, growing rigid instead of flexible. My skin beneath it whitens as the paste contracts, pinching and pulling from every direction.

"No, no, no..." I tap the edge of the hardening film, wincing when a tiny crack appears. Then another. And another. The lines spider through the entire layer and, within seconds, pieces begin flaking off, leaving behind redness and a coppery taste in my mouth. I should really stop biting my cheek when I get angry.

Managing a few deep breaths, I finally sigh before brushing the remaining fragments into my palm. Twenty attempts, twenty failures. What did that man once say about doing the same thing over and over again?

It doesn't matter, regardless that I change minute things each time. This one came closer than the others at least. The paste adhered well initially, and the transparency was perfect. Perhaps a few granules less of sealwort will be the magic attempt? Or maybe adding some rendered pine resin for flexibility?

I make a mental note to try these modifications, though it will have to wait. For now, I need to prepare for an evening of darkness, erasing myself even further from existence for a few hours so my family can maintain our collective lie.

My hands go through the motions of cleaning my workspace methodically, wiping surfaces and returning ingredients to their proper places. The failed paste goes into a basket with the others—every failure contains a lesson if you're patient enough to find it.

Once everything is tidy, I fetch my *hideout supplies*, as I like to call them—a worn blanket that smells of cedar from its storage chest, a small reading light with a clip attachment, and one of the new books my father brought home. This one is about ancient agricultural practices; not particularly exciting, but educational in its own way, and that's better than nothing when you're left in a hole with only your thoughts for hours.

Shoving everything in the blanket and holding it to my chest, I wander to my parents' bedroom, where my father is already waiting. He stands by the far wall with a warm smile I'm sure he's forcing out just for me, where a section of floorboards has been pulled back to reveal a narrow opening.

"Ready, sweetheart?" He kneels beside the opening, waiting for my go ahead.

"Yes." I say it with more confidence than I possess; I'm never truly ready for the hatch—the dark, cold, crushing sense of confinement lingers with me for days each time I experience it.

My father reaches into the opening and tugs on a heavy, brass ring, lifting a hinged section of the floor that reveals a second, deeper entrance. The wood is stained dark and fitted with metal brackets, ensuring invisibility when closed while being sturdy enough to support weight from above. The craftsmanship is impressive. Father spent months perfecting this hideout, ensuring the seams disappear completely when closed, as if the double protection would keep the Enforcers out if they ever raided our house.

It's the thought that counts, I suppose. It makes all of us feel just a little less anxious about it.

I groan as my eyes study the narrow steps descending into pitch black. The space was originally a root cellar dug beneath the house, but my father repurposed it when I was seven, knowing the days would come that I would need to be hidden in a better place than the small area under his and mother's bed. He reinforced the walls, added ventilation through a disguised pipe, and furnished it with a small stool and shelf that barely fit, but they're enough for me.

My prison. My sanctuary. The reason I still exist.

"It shouldn't be long today," he remarks, his voice softened with the guilt he always carries about this necessity. "Hardan mentioned a meeting later in the evening, so I hope he'll insist on leaving quickly."

"It's fine, dad." My attempt at sounding nonchalant is weak, but he doesn't comment on it. "I have my book."

My feet begin the plunge into the hatch, not pausing at the creaks caused by my weight. The air shifts as I move deeper—more cool and damp, carrying the stagnant scent of soil and stone. At the bottom, I crane my neck to peer at my father, whose face is now mostly a silhouette framed by the square opening.

"I love you, dove," he says, a comforting exchange of words we never skip.

We never know if this will be the last time we're together. The Enforcers could be walking toward our house at this very moment, as far as any of us are aware.

"Love you, too." My throat sinks. I hate goodbyes; and even though he's not going anywhere, it still chokes me up.

He blows me a kiss and slowly lowers the inner hatch. The brass hinges, which he oils religiously to prevent squeaking, mutter only the softest sound as the heavy lid closes. The final click of the latch engaging feels like a period at the end of a sentence. One written in pen.

Darkness envelops me completely.

Blowing air through pursed lips, I count to ten in my head while my eyes adjust to the blackness before switching on my reading light. Its glow is meager, illuminating only a small circle around me, but it's far better than imagining the strange shapes that somehow always form in the dark.

This space is as familiar to me as my and Lachlan's bedroom. Roughly four feet square, with a height that allows me to stand if I hunch a bit. The walls are packed earth, the floor bare dirt covered by the world's thinnest rug. The shelf contains emergency supplies like water, canned food, a chamber pot—as if I would *ever* use that—and a set of matches.

The hatch is neither comfortable nor truly uncomfortable. Just simply...necessary.

The price of my existence.

I settle onto the stool, arranging the blanket over my shoulders against the chill. Clipping the reading light to the back cover of my book, I position it to illuminate the pages without wasting its limited battery. Given how dim it is, it will need new ones soon.

My gaze snaps up when muffled voices indicate the sounds of life continuing without me. Footsteps scraping across the floor mask the faint murmur of my parents' voices as they prepare for their guests. Ordinary domestic sounds that emphasize the normalcy I will never get to experience.

Time passes strangely in the hatch. Minutes stretch into what feel like hours, then collapse when I emerge to discover barely any time has passed at all. I concentrate on losing myself in the book, soaking in words about crop rotation and soil management in civilizations long dead, but after just a few pages, the sound of the front door grabs my attention. The grating noise as it opens reverberates through the structure of the house. It's only a moment before the heavy tread of unfamiliar boots sounds, followed by the lighter steps of someone who's not my mother. My lip curls at the boisterous laugh of Hardan Lesson, too loud and forced, like everything must be about him.

Sometimes I'm thankful I do not have to meet the guests that visit our home.

I've never seen the man, but I detest him with a clarity that surprises me. I loathe how he treats my father, how he speaks about women as if they're possessions and not people sitting directly next to him. How he embodies everything corrupt about the Syndicate's rule without having the self-awareness to recognize it.

Maybe he does, though, and just cannot be bothered to care. Why would he? Our world was made to cater to his kind... of course he wouldn't fight it, or at the bare minimum, speak on its faults.

And I despise how he treats his wife with my whole being; how he speaks over her, cuts her off, belittles her with casual cruelty disguised as the humor of men. I know this not from observation, but from the silence that follows his barbed comments. I imagine Eliana is a bird with clipped wings, kept in a rotting cage and told she should be grateful for the bars that imprison her as the only other option is surely much worse.

That's the life of a woman in Dascenia: bad or worse.

If I had been born to his household instead of my father's, I would have been sent to a facility before my first breath cooled on my lips. Men like Hardan don't risk their standing by harboring illegal daughters.

I'm lucky. I know this. But luck is an artificial comfort when you're buried alive.

I close my book, knowing I won't be able to focus any longer. Instead, I listen. My brain tracks the movements above by the brief thuds of footsteps and voices. I count the steps—

one, two, three, four—and map them against my mental floor plan. They're in the main room now, likely standing near the fireplace where my father keeps his collection of approved books prominently displayed.

Five, six, seven. They're moving to the dining table, and I'm proven correct a moment later when chairs scrape against the floor.

When they settle into dinner conversation, I attempt to read the book again, finding my place with difficulty. The words blur before my eyes, meaningless shapes that refuse to resolve into sense. It's frustrating.

Then a phrase cuts through my distraction. "...new Enforcer group..."

My head rises, attention instantly diverted from my book—not that it's such a hard feat to accomplish. Hardan's voice continues, ever louder than necessary, "I spoke with Captain Daren this morning. The situation is more serious than they initially thought." He pauses, likely for dramatic effect. "They've discovered an entire community hiding beyond the perimeter. Women, children, the works. Living out there like rabid animals." My father makes a noncommittal sound as my lip curls.

"The Syndicate's forming a special unit," the man continues. "Best of the best. They'll train over at the center, then head out to deal with these vermin once and for all."

"When will they deploy?" my father asks, his voice a careful neutral that tells me he has many opinions about this subject but will keep them hidden.

"Don't know exactly. Few weeks, maybe a month. They're recruiting now—any able-bodied man between twenty and thirty-five. Preferences given to those with useful powers, of course." Hardan groans before speaking again. "I tried to convince Easton to join, but the boy continues to defy me. He'll never become a man at this rate. Fucking waste."

My pulse quickens at his words, pushing out the hatred he carries for his son.

Father mentioned this yesterday...an Enforcer group formed specifically to hunt people living freely beyond our borders? How did they escape?

"The interesting thing," my eyes roll at Hardan's voice again, though I no longer want to vomit at the sound, too interested in his words, "is this unit won't be assigned to a specific province afterward. They'll be mobile, responding wherever they're needed. Directly under Syndicate control."

"That's...unusual," my father responds.

"It's brilliant," his boss counters. "No provincial loyalties, no local entanglements, or restrictions. Pure enforcement of Syndicate law, wherever required." His boisterous laughter makes me cringe. "Recruits are to meet at their respective Halls before dawn tomorrow, so hopefully they'll figure this shit out soon and we can go back to normal."

I bite my tongue a little too hard when my mother speaks. "Wonderful news, Hardan, though I am curious why you are providing Pierce with the details?" I'm expecting him to lash out at her like he does his wife, but to my surprise he chuckles and answers her question.

"Well for Pierce's son, of course." I scoff, the sound melting into the damp surroundings. Of course he would refer to Lachlan as my father's son, as if my mother didn't make and birth him. "I figured the boy would appreciate something better for his career than being a mere messenger."

Mom doesn't respond, and my father quickly shifts the conversation to other topics—trade quotas, new library restrictions, the Founding Festival. It's disgusting there's a day to celebrate the Syndicate's founding, but that train of thought disappears as I'm no longer listening to them.

My mind races, caught on this single piece of information.

A mobile Enforcer group. Unattached to any province or station. Free to travel across Dascenia.

Something stirs in my gut—a wild, impossible thought I immediately try to dismiss.

But it lingers.

What exists beyond the perimeter? I've been told it's wasteland—barren expanses of land and water, devoid of resources and civilization. Each province specializes in producing different necessities, trading with each other through official channels. Pyrem provides administrative services and manufacturing, Ailridge specializes in mining and stonework, Ofin grows most of our food, and so on. A perfect system of interdependence, carefully controlled by the Syndicate.

But if there are people living beyond the perimeter, thriving enough to form communities...

Sometimes, I watch Enforcers through our windows, during the night when all lights are off and ensure my parents are sleeping. They all wear the same uniform, the same one Lachlan is made to wear when traveling between provinces. Black tactical clothing with reinforced panels, heavy boots, and those masks—full-face coverings with only a narrow slit for the eyes. I've never seen an Enforcer's face; their identities remain hidden even from each other when on duty. Not that I'd have much of a chance to, with the smallest opening in my curtain the only view I have of the outside.

But curiosity has always been my weakness, especially where Lachlan is involved. Seeing him in uniform for the first time sent me spiraling down a path of learning the Enforcer code, along with random texts dripping in military idealization.

Because of this, I know their masks are not just for intimidation.

They're for anonymity.

A thought forms, so outrageous I almost laugh aloud.

What if a woman joined them?

Ridiculous. They'd know immediately...the physical differences alone would give them away within minutes.

But would they?

I think of my brother and me, mirror images with subtle distinctions. We have the same dark hair, the same angular features and observant eyes. His jaw is sharper, his shoulders broader—but not dramatically so. We're both thin, on the smaller side for our age.

If I pulled my hair back in a tight bun like he wears his, if I bound my chest and pitched my voice lower...

Could I pass as Lachlan?

And I have powers. The Empath ability I've kept hidden; the same one I likely have because I shared a womb with my twin. I can sense emotions and influence them with concentration. Only men are supposed to have powers...my ability would be undeniable proof of my sex.

I breathe out a long bout of air, stirring little particles of dust in the muted light.

What am I thinking? This is pure insanity. I've spent twenty-six years hiding in this house, never once setting foot even in our garden. I know nothing of the outside world beyond what I've read in books and glimpsed through windows.

And yet...

What am I doing *here*? Hiding in a hole, testing failed ointments, reading about worlds and culture long lost. Protecting myself while women are captured and imprisoned, their bodies used as breeding stock, their children taken from them, their lives controlled in every aspect.

I have a unique opportunity. I am invisible to the Syndicate. Undocumented. Identical to my brother, possessed of powers that shouldn't be mine. If I could slip into this Enforcer group, what might I discover? What information could I gather?

What small sabotages might I undertake?

Could I make a difference, even a small one?

The Provincial Hall in Pyrem is not too far from my house, and the Enforcer Training Center is located in this province near the perimeter, if I remember correctly. Hardan said anyone interested in joining this new unit is to report to the Hall before dawn, and I assume they will transport them to the Center. It would be a relatively quick journey for me, though I imagine the recruits from other provinces left days ago.

But they'd surely check backgrounds? Perhaps identification, proof of citizenship, or documentation of previous employment.

I pause. What would they care for physical identification if masks are not permitted to be removed?

My brother's uniform is exactly as I've seen on other Enforcers, so if I appeared already wearing it, looking the part, and display a little of my power, they would have to let me through.

I shake my head as if I could physically dislodge these dangerous thoughts. It's madness. Inevitable suicide. I'd be caught within days, if not hours. And then what would happen to my family? They'd be executed for harboring me and deceiving the Syndicate.

But if I succeeded—if I could blend in, collect information, perhaps even help just *one* person...

The voices above grow louder, more animated. Dinner must be finished and they've shifted to the more social portion of the evening. Hardan's laugh blares through the floorboards, making me flinch.

I return to my book out of habit, but it all swims before my eyes, a puzzle of my own making. My mind is caught in a loop, sifting through possibilities and probabilities, weighing risks against potential rewards.

Twenty-six years of safety versus one chance to *finally* do something of importance.

Twenty-six years of watching from windows versus stepping into the world for the first time.

Twenty-six years of being no one versus becoming someone who matters.

The next hour passes in this tormented contemplation. Eventually, the front door clicks and I stretch my neck as heavy footsteps retreat down the porch. The hatch opens a few minutes later, flooding the space with warm light. My father's face appears, concern etched around his eyes.

"All clear, dove," he says, extending a hand. "You okay? You look a little pale."

"Just cold." I spin to gather my blanket and book to hide the lie written across my face. I've never been very good at hiding my physical emotions. "And a little stiff."

He pulls me up easily, his grip firm and reassuring. When I'm standing beside him, he tugs me into a quick hug and my tense muscles relax.

"I'm sorry about tonight—all of this."

"It's not your fault." The words come automatically, my usual response to his traditional apology after these visits.

He rewards me with a warm smile, one I try to reciprocate, but inside, something has shifted. A decision forming—not yet fully acknowledged but taking shape nonetheless.

After cleaning with my mother and bidding my parents

goodnight, I find myself in the bathroom, staring at my reflection in the small mirror above the sink.

I study my face with new intensity, cataloging the features I share with my twin and those that differ. My jaw is softer, lips a smidge fuller. But our eyes are identical—the same deep violet. My hair falls past my waist , neverending it seems, though Lachlan's is cut a bit shorter and usually tied back.

Could I truly pass as my brother? As a *man?*

The differences seem suddenly surmountable. A slimmer face could be explained away as recent illness. A softer voice as a throat condition. The only real challenge would be my eyes—not their appearance, but what they might reveal. They would need to project confidence. Authority and familiarity when I've never known either.

But Lachlan wouldn't know their world either...not really.

Shit, I'm actually considering this. Stepping outside after decades of hiding to infiltrate the very organization that would have me raped and milked if they discovered my true identity.

It's madness. Complete, blatant madness.

My shoulders jolt at a sudden knock on the door. "Cass?" Lachlan's voice, heavy with sleep. "You've been in there a while. Everything okay?"

I clear my throat, staring at my eyes as I answer. "Fine, just thinking."

"Well, think in bed. Some of us need to use the bathroom before morning." He doesn't sound annoyed, and I smile despite myself.

"Give me a minute, and I'll be out."

"One single minute," he warns, but the warmth in his tone belies any real irritation.

I splash water on my face as the pressure in my head continues to rise. I wouldn't last a day as a man.

But as I open the door and pass my yawning brother, I can't

shake the feeling that something fundamental has changed tonight. A possibility has presented itself, and now that I've seen it, I can't unsee it.

My eyes are immediately drawn to Lachlan's uniform hanging in the open closet of our bedroom. The darkness behind the slit in the mask calls to a part of me I've wanted to let loose for so long.

My decision is made before I fully realize it.

I'm going to do this. I'm going to become an Enforcer.

And then I'm going to destroy them from within.

CHAPTER THREE
CASSIA

I shoot upright in bed, my nightshirt clinging to each part of my skin from the copious amount of sweat. My heart hammers against my ribs like it's attempting to break free from the danger I'm about to put it in. My body feels like it's burning despite the room's chill, and I shove away the blanket that's tangled around my legs.

Darkness squeezes me, the familiar shapes of my bedroom transformed into looming shadows. Across from me, Lachlan's steady breathing fills the tingling silence. He sleeps soundly, unaware his life—our entire family's lives—are about to change because of the decision I've made.

I haven't slept. Not a moment. My mind refused to quiet as it spun through scenarios and calculated risks, imagining outcomes both triumphant and disastrous. The hours crawled by as I stared at the bare ceiling, waiting for the time I'd need to rise, half-hoping I would lose my nerve.

If anything, I'm only more determined.

Careful to not make a sound, I slip from beneath my covers and place my feet on the cold floor. My limbs droop with exhaustion, but my mind is sharp, focused by a cocktail of fear and resolve that burns through my veins.

I glance at my brother once more before grabbing the small pack I prepared last night from beneath my bed. My hand flails until I feel what I'm looking for, dragging it slowly to the surface. Peering behind me, Lachlan's face is still peaceful in sleep. I didn't expect to wake him, he sleeps like the dead, but every sound feels like a bomb exploding. I don't even trust he couldn't hear my heart if he were awake.

Will he understand I couldn't bear another day of living through books and windows? Will he hate me when he realizes what I've done?

I hope not. Even if I am being selfish.

But at the same time, I hope he does. Perhaps it will be easier for him to accept my betrayal if he loathes me for it. I will shoulder his hate if it makes this better for him.

The floor creaks beneath my weight as I walk to the door, and my eyes widen as I curse my stupidity. I know how to avoid every weak spot in this house; so giving myself away from naive distraction is unacceptable. I freeze, tilting my head to listen for any change in Lachlan's breathing, but it remains steady. Once in the hallway, I pause again to aid my ears in catching any sign that my parents are awake. Nothing but the familiar groaning of an old house and the distant ticking of a clock in the main room.

I should want one of them to wake in time to stop me. To unknowingly keep me from a fate that will surely lead to nothing but pain and emptiness.

And yet I don't want that.

Both hinges on the bathroom door protest quietly as it pushes open, and I wince. Once the door closes with a gentle click, I lean against the edge of the sink, sucking in a few deep breaths before flipping on the small light above me. My reflection stares back, pale and wide-eyed. For a moment, I don't recognize myself—this version of Cassia who's about to walk into the ranks of the Enforcers. Who's about to shed her skin and become someone else.

My lip curls as I strip from my nightclothes, fear and sweat still clinging to my pores. I yearn for a proper shower, but the pipes would groan and wake my family. Instead, I settle for the next best thing: a wet washcloth I scrub over my body. The chilled water raises goosebumps across my skin, making me shiver every few seconds. This is certainly a poor substitute to a full wash, but it will have to do. I cannot risk this one chance for the sake of cleanliness, especially as the majority of it would be to sate my mental state.

My fingers squeeze and release in a quick pattern before I shove the anxiety away and grab Lachlan's uniform from my pack. The dark fabric catches the light in certain places, almost appearing as though it's smiling; taunting every moment I continue readying myself. As if it doesn't believe I will succeed, and it's happy to watch me fail.

I pull it apart piece by piece, laying each item on the counter with reverent care. Before long, I'm staring down at black tactical pants with reinforced knees, a long-sleeved shirt with its stiff collar, and a heavy jacket with a missing Enforcer insignia indicating rank. Lachlan once explained it's a common practice for him and the other messengers to remove their insignias when traveling between provinces—something about discourse amongst officers.

Remarkable system we have if Enforcers from different provinces cannot even work together like adults.

I glance out the window, my face pinching at the slightest change in tint, indicating dawn is quickly approaching. I slide on the uniform, the fabric much heavier than I expected. The boots are unwieldy on my feet, strange as I'm certain Lachlan and I are the same size. But that's not what gives me pause—no, it's the smell. The faint notes of my brother; the soap he washes with, the slight musk that clings to his clothes. It's comforting and unsettling at the same time.

At least I'll have something familiar with me out there, even if it is just a scent.

I'm struck by yet another wave of panic as I button the jacket. *What are you doing, Cassia?* I've never even left our house, and now I'm planning to join the most dangerous organization in Dascenia? I'm going to get caught. Then killed.

I'm going to get my entire family killed.

"Stop being a baby," I whisper-shout to my reflection, my voice barely audible. "Just do it. This is what you've always wanted and prayed for."

My lungs suck in a shaky breath as I reach for the scissors I'd placed in the pack, my fingers trembling at the sight.

This is going to be the most difficult part. My hair has been with me my entire life. One of the few things that's truly mine, that I have complete control over. The one thing that really separates me from Lachlan and allows me to be an actual person in my secluded, hidden world.

Something hot skims my cheek—I'm crying.

It's just hair, I tell myself. *It will grow back.*

It's not just hair, though...it's the last piece of Cassia I'm about to cut away. After this, I will be Lachlan. I will be a man. An Enforcer trained to do the bidding of the Syndicate, working to suppress the very things I unashamedly hold close to my heart: autonomy. Freedom. Equality.

Such notions will not do for the Syndicate if I leave this house.

They want obedience. Submission. A quiet, faceless soldier who never questions why the world was built to keep their women caged.

But I was never meant to be quiet.

And I sure as hell was never meant to stay in a cage.

Blowing out the last bit of air coursing through my body, my eyelids flutter closed as I make the first cut.

The sound of the blades slicing through each strand is deafening in the small bathroom. Weight falls from my head in thick chunks, tickling my senses as they tumble down. Something shifts in my chest—not pain, but a peculiar lightness. I open my eyes and stare at the long tress in my hand, then at my reflection.

The person looking back at me is already different. Half my hair still hangs to my waist, but the other half is jagged and short, barely brushing the underside of one shoulder. It's wild and unfinished.

Caught between identities.

Will it be difficult to keep Cassia alive while I live as Lachlan?

The next cut comes faster, almost eager. My lips twitch as more hair falls across the sink and onto the floor, covering my feet. When it's done, my breathing is hard and ragged.

I look different. Not quite like my brother, but no longer like myself either. The face staring back at me is a stranger's— sharp featured, hollow-eyed from lack of sleep, with wild eyes that drip with a strange sort of excitement.

I allow myself a few more seconds before gathering the fallen hair, carefully wrapping it in a towel. I'll need to dispose the evidence of my transformation where my family won't immediately find it.

After tying the remaining locks into a tight bun at the nape of my neck, I tuck several extra ties into my pack. My heart skips as I reach for the final piece of my disguise: the mask.

The Enforcer mask is made of a rigid synthetic material, black and featureless except for where the eyes are shown. It covers the entire face, from forehead to chin, wrapping around to secure at the back of the head.

Faceless, indeed.

My fingers brush across the smooth surface with open disdain. This is the point of no return. Once I put on this mask and step outside the front door, I cannot come back. Not as Cassia. Perhaps not at all.

With trembling hands, I lift it to my face and slide it into place.

The transformation is immediate and jarring. The world narrows to what's observable through the slit, while my breathing is oddly loud inside the enclosed space, creating a warm and damp environment. The hardened material presses against my skin, uncomfortable but not painful. The material is unyielding, forcing my face into neutrality.

I stare at my reflection, and a perfect soldier stares back. My eyes are the only recognizable part of me now, and even they appear different. They make me want to hide. To rip this uniform off and crawl back into the safety of my bed, only to spend another day wondering if things will ever change.

I know they won't. Someone needs to stand up for the rest, and I'm done being a bystander. No longer will I wait for others to give me what I've never had.

So I lift my chin and square my shoulders like I've seen Lachlan do. I need to carry myself differently now, doing away with the subtle, contained movements I've become accustomed to. I need to take up space, project confidence and strength.

I nod to myself before gathering my things. It's only when I leave the bathroom that I grasp I need to leave some explanation; my family deserves that much, at least.

Staring at the blank piece of paper I grabbed from my notebook, I struggle to find words that could possibly explain what I'm doing. Or why.

How do I tell them I love them but need more? Or explain their protection has become a prison, though it's kept me safe and alive all these years? How do I make them understand I need to do *something*, not just hide forever?

I write out a dozen versions, each attempt insufficient before I settle for the simple truth.

I'm sorry, I have to try. I love you.

Before I can think better of it, I place the note on my bed and hurry to the front door. I allow myself to pause for only a moment as I wheeze through pursed lips, the air in my lungs suddenly weighing too much.

For a second, fear overwhelms me. I could turn around, slip off the mask, dispose of the evidence, and pretend I never considered this madness. But at what cost?

I'm done questioning myself. The lock flips before my fingers tug the door open. Cool, fresh air rushes in, carrying scents I've only briefly been exposed to before. The predawn sky stretches above me, a twinkling canvas of deep blue fading to the first hints of light.

My foot steps across the threshold.

I'm outside.

I'm outside.

For the first time in my entire life, I'm outside.

The sensation is disorienting. Dizzying. There's no ceiling above me, no walls caging me in—just open space stretching in all directions. It's a vulnerable feeling, and hairs rise along my arms at how exposed I am. And yet...I'm exhilarated. My heart pounds so loudly I'm certain anyone within city limits must hear, but perhaps not over the ragged breathing I'm failing to control.

There's no one around. The street is empty; silent in the early morning hours, and my senses pick up no active emotion, only lingering remnants of others who occupied this street in the late hours of the night.

I thought there would be others heading to the Hall, eager

to join this new team, but there's not a soul in sight. There must be some men coming, right? They likely live within the inner parts of Pyrem, so I'll see them soon enough.

But still I pause, uncertain. Is it the right day? Did I misunderstand what Hardan said?

No, I heard correctly. I'm certain of it. The others are just taking different routes or don't wish to join a group that hunts women who've managed to escape.

I chuckle to myself. Like that would ever happen.

Peering left, I orient my mind toward the city center as planned. The route is burned into my memory—two blocks east, four north, then west one block. Easy. I can do this.

My first steps are awkward as Lachlan's boots stomp heavily on the paved street. Am I moving wrong? It feels as though anyone who sees me will instantly know I'm not what I appear to be. Each attempt to walk as my twin does is strange, with longer strides and a slight swing to my arms. It feels unnatural, but I persist.

As I advance deeper into the city, buildings grow taller and more imposing. Many are constructed of black glass and steel, reflecting the emerging dawn in streaks of orange and purple. These are the administrative towers, where officials work and some men live. Small apartments stacked one on top of another like the shelves of our bookcase at home.

I'm struck by a wave of gratitude for our modest house. How could anyone have hidden me in one of these glass towers? The thought fires shivering fear through me. If not for my parents' home, with its humbly renovated underground hatch, I would have been discovered years ago. Or more likely, never given the chance to exist as anything but a usable hole and breeding stock.

"North on Basin Street," I whisper to myself, reciting the

directions continuously as I walk. "Four blocks. Then west on Syndicate Avenue. One block."

The quiet repetition keeps my mind focused, preventing me from spiraling into lingering panic. I pass darkened storefronts, their windows displaying goods I've seen only on television. Clothing shops with mannequins dressed in men's attire. An electronic store with devices whose purpose I cannot even guess. A grocer with fresh produce artfully arranged, the bright colors muted by the night. There are streaks of blue at the edge of one building, as if someone attempted to wipe something away.

Each turn I feel more awed and enraged. This simple act of walking down a street, of seeing shops and buildings up close, burns away any hesitation I clung to since leaving my bed—this basic freedom has been denied to half the population.

My pace quickens, renewed anger fueling each step. *This* is why I'm leaving. *This* is why the risk is worth taking.

Pyrem Hall looms ahead, a massive structure of black stone and tinted glass. Unlike the other buildings, which gleam with polish and care, this one projects an intentional austerity. It's meant to intimidate—to remind citizens of the Syndicate's power.

It's working.

My gait falters as I approach the final block. In front of the building, a line of Enforcers stands at attention on the wide steps. Their masks catch the growing light, always cold and featureless. Two large vehicles wait at the curb, hoarding my attention as I study their angular body with narrow windows. They are reminiscent of the slits in our masks, effectively blocking much of their surroundings, but leaving just enough of an opening to peek through. The sides are sleek, black with no indents for handles or other features. Is that to keep others from getting in? Is there a special device that only allows certain Enforcers to open the doors?

It's only logical to assume they hold the same internal setup, enclosing their occupants inside the steel walls until someone with enough authority deigns to free them.

Muscles in my throat tighten. My heart's somewhere between my ribs and teeth, beating loud enough to out me on the spot. I should turn around. Run. Get under my blanket and pretend I never even thought about this level of idiocy.

As the thought forms, another figure approaches from a side street. A man walking with purpose, advancing directly toward the line of Enforcers. He's also in full uniform, and his determined stride suggests he's here for the same reason I am.

Great. Now if I bolt, it's not brave. It's suspicious.

I force a breath in, spine straightening like I've got steel in it instead of soup, mimicking the confident posture I've seen my brother adopt. Chin up.

Be Lachlan. Be confident. Be someone whose heart isn't threatening to explode across Syndicate Avenue.

These boots feel wrong. The mask is suffocating. And I'm seconds away from collapsing into a puddle of fear.

But I walk forward anyway. Because if I don't, this whole plan dies right here.

CHAPTER FOUR

CASSIA

As I reach the bottom steps, I catalog how tall they each are. How broad. I'm not small, but compared to these men, I feel diminutive. My gaze remains steady, though, focusing on who I assume is the lead Enforcer as he turns his attention to me and the second recruit. My theory was correct; the patch on his shoulder confirms his rank amongst the men—a single line, parallel to the ground. Captain.

Lachlan has the lowest rank, a simple circle, indicating his position isn't even that of a recruit. One he cannot wear if he's traveling between provinces. I'm sure others condemn that frequently.

The captain steps forward, his posture indicating authority and impatience.

"State your purpose," he barks, his voice slightly muffled by the mask.

The man beside me speaks immediately. "Reporting for the new Enforcer unit, sir. From the eastern quarter."

Shit, I should have prepared a response. Why didn't I prepare what I should say? My mind races, straining to formulate an answer that won't sound feminine or uncertain.

The Enforcer turns to me, waiting. His eyes burn my confidence as he glares. Assessing, evaluating.

"And you?" My breath catches at his harsh tone, but I manage to hold still. "I won't ask again." I've been silent too long, lost in my thoughts. Panic flutters through my stomach again, and I open my mouth out of desperation, but no sound comes out.

He's going to figure it out. The other recruit didn't hesitate to answer, and I'm here sputtering like an idiot who has something to hide.

I've killed my family before even leaving the city. I don't know why I thought I could do this...

"Are you here for the new unit or not, recruit?" The Enforcer steps once in my direction, and it takes everything in me to not flinch back.

I manage a quick nod, more than grateful that hard, opaque material hides the fear I know must be written across my features. I pray to the stars he cannot find it in my eyes.

The man stares at me for an eternity, in which time I do not even dare swallow the mounds of saliva pooling in my mouth. I attempt to keep my gaze level; to emit confidence rather than the terror threatening to choke me. My heart pounds so frantically I'm convinced the stiff front of my uniform must be visibly moving with each beat. If not for the reinforced material and banding, the outline of my small breasts would surely be noticeable in the ascending light.

Finally, fucking finally, the Enforcer gives a curt nod.

"Fine. Both of you in the first transport." He gestures to the nearest vehicle.

I exhale slowly, through the smallest hole in my lips, careful to not let my shoulders drop from immense relief. The first test is passed, but there will be hundreds more. Thousands, perhaps, before this is finished.

If it ever is.

The other recruit swivels to the vehicle without a second thought. I follow his confident lead, matching his pace but keeping a respectful distance. He moves with an effortless stride, carries himself with the conviction of someone who belongs here. He's several inches taller than me, but my limbs lock to mirror his without being obvious. He pushes a random spot on the back door, my eyes widening as a piece of steel gives to his fingers before the door pops open. There's no key or device in his hand, so perhaps the handles are hidden merely for aesthetic purposes.

I slide over one of the benches facing each other, the leather material cool and slick beneath me. The other recruit settles into the opposite bench, clasping his hands as he peers through the small window. We sit in silence, not looking at each other or speaking. I'm grateful for this small mercy. I'm not ready for casual conversation; not confident in my ability to deepen my voice convincingly.

A moment later the front doors open with a pop, and two Enforcers enter the transport. Neither regards us as they prepare themselves. There's a series of mechanical sounds before the vehicle hums to life beneath us. The sensation is unexpected—a gentle vibration that travels through the floor, up my boots, into my bones. When the transport begins to move, I fail to contain a small squeak of surprise at the sudden forward momentum.

Stupid, stupid, stupid. What kind of reaction is that from a grown man?

My cheeks heat, and I face the window regardless that no one can see my cheeks burn, hoping neither the Enforcers nor my fellow recruit noticed my response. Outside, the buildings slide past as we accelerate, beams of light shining across different angles as the city wakes to the rising sun.

"Looks like it's just us," the man across from me says, his voice low but friendly. "Haven't been in a vehicle before?"

I glance at him, surprised by the leisurely tone. After the terse exchange with the captain, I expected a stoic silence for the journey. His voice is pleasant, though—a light baritone with a hint of an accent I can't place. He did mention he was from the eastern quarter, but that means nothing to me in terms of his home place.

"No," I reply, keeping my words clipped and my voice as low as I can manage without cracking or sounding unnatural. "First time."

He hums, seemingly unconcerned by my lack of experience. "They're uncommon outside official capacity. I don't ride in them often myself."

I nod, unsure if he expects a response. How do men talk to each other? My only reference is my father and brother, but their conversations are colored by familiarity and the comfortability of family. This is different—we're strangers, evaluating each other, establishing some strange hierarchical relationship.

The recruit seems content with the silence for a while, gazing out at the city as it gives way to the more industrial outskirts of Pyrem. Factories and warehouses replace sleek buildings, their utilitarian designs a strange contrast to the polished city center. Clearly this part of the city is not as cared for.

Eventually, he speaks again. "What's your name?"

The question catches me off guard, though it shouldn't. That's a normal thing to ask, especially since we'll be training together. I open my mouth and Cassia is almost the first sound to emerge before I catch myself.

"Lachlan." The name is strange on my tongue when applied to myself. "Ashford," I include after a moment. Lach usually refers to his work peers by their last names, so I'm not certain if he was asking for that.

I adjust my hips to address him properly for the first time. He's watching me with curious eyes, the only part of his face visible—forest green, intelligent, observant. He nods, satisfied with my answer.

"Elias," he responds, though I idiotically didn't return the courtesy of asking, and my pulse jumps. Was that rude of me? Perhaps, though he doesn't sound offended.

One thing I've not gleaned from books and experience is the emotional weight of conversing with others. Talking with my family is natural, because that's all I've known, and I thought I was prepared to speak to others in the same manner, but it's clear expectations between men are something wholly different than I'm used to.

"You're very quiet," he notes, head tilting slightly. "That's not a bad thing. Most people talk too much when they're nervous."

My teeth gnaw along my bottom lip, no response gracing the front of my mind. Does he think I'm nervous? Can he tell I'm not what I appear to be?

I pause. Oh—*oh*. Is he an Empath as well? Has he been noting the volatile shift of emotions I've experienced since we stood together in front of the hall?

I should be doing the same...using my power to know how he's feeling about me—

"What did you do before this?" His tone is conversational, but I open my awareness toward him a little, not wanting to be blasted with the emotions of everyone in the car, and I'm immediately swallowed by curiosity. Not suspiciously so, but I get the sense I intrigue him. "Based on your reaction to the transport, I'm guessing not Syndicate work?"

I shake my head, keeping my gestures brisk and masculine. "No. Private sector."

He hums. Something sweet drifts around me, the taste of his amusement. What did I say that was funny?

"What part of the private sector?"

I contemplate my words, forming each carefully. "Messenger services, primarily. Some administration." It's close enough to what Lachlan does that I can speak about it with some confidence if pressed. Though I'm cursing myself for all those times I tuned out his stories of travel; I could have learned much more about his position.

Elias settles further into his seat, squeaking the tight leather as his arms cross. "And what brought you to the Enforcers? This new group, particularly?"

I consider the safest answer, swallowing around the thickness in my throat. It was close to drowning me a mere hour ago, but it's dry as a desert now. "Change. Purpose." I shrug, the movement feeling unnatural but necessary. "Opportunity to see more of Dascenia."

It's not a lie, though it's far from the complete truth.

But that's how I need to play my role. As close to the truth as I can be without giving myself away. The more lies I spin, the harder it will be to keep up with my story.

"Fair enough," Elias remarks, and to my relief, he doesn't press for more details. Instead, he offers some information about himself, though it's vague enough that I can't piece together much about him.

He's been an Enforcer for several years. He specializes in adaptive tactics. He was personally selected for this unit by someone he refers to as the Commander.

His manner is reserved but not cold; loosely professional without being rigid. It's not what I expected from another

Enforcer, though I'm not sure why I didn't think they would be more casual with each other than they are with leadership and civilians. There's an intelligence in his eyes that makes me uneasy—not because it's threatening, but because it seems too perceptive. More observant than I want to deal with.

I'll have to keep a safe distance from him.

My responses remain brief as I maintain what I hope passes for male stoicism rather than suspicious reticence. As the minutes stretch into hours, the ache in my shoulders deepens from the rigid posture I've adopted. My back is straight, legs positioned at what I hope is a natural, relaxed angle. The mask, which was only uncomfortable at first, now suffocates me, the air inside hot and stale. How the hell do they wear these all day?

Outside the window to my right, the landscape shifts from industrial zones to agricultural fields, before the more desolate regions near the perimeter appear. We're moving much faster than I anticipated, the vehicle eating up distance at a speed I find both exhilarating and unsettling. My stomach lurches occasionally when we graze uneven patches of road, but I swallow the nausea and maintain calm.

"How far away is the Training Center?" I blurt, interrupting whatever Elias was saying about protocol. The moment the words leave my mouth, I wish I could take them back. I should have waited for a natural pause in the conversation.

Or better yet, remained silent.

If the other recruit is annoyed by my interruption, he doesn't show it. "Not too far now," he answers. "Six hours or so. We're making good time. Our section of the city is closer to the center, so it's a relatively easy drive."

I nod and turn back to the window. I'm exhausted already, and all I've done is spoken to one person for a few hours. The strain of maintaining myself as Lachlan and my lack of sleep are catching up with me all at once.

Great start to your stupid idea, Cassia.

"Not much for conversation, are you, Ashford?" Elias says, and there's something in his voice I can't quite identify. Not mockery, exactly, but something lighter than his previous demeanor. "That's alright. You'll have plenty of time to get to know everyone once we arrive."

I manage another nod, not trusting myself to form coherent sentences anymore. My eyelids are heavy, thoughts blurring at the edges. The rhythmic sound of the transport on the road and gentle vibration beneath me are oddly soothing.

I shouldn't sleep. I need to stay alert, aware of my surroundings. What if I relax too much and my posture gives me away? What if I talk in my sleep?

Despite my best efforts, my eyes flutter closed. The last thing I see before slipping into unconsciousness is Elias, watching me with those thoughtful eyes.

I JOLT awake when the transport halts abruptly, my head snapping forward before I catch myself. For a disorienting moment, I have no idea where I am or why my face feels so hot and confined. There's a weight on my chest that doesn't belong there, pressing in, restricting my breathing—

Then memory floods back: the uniform, the mask, the transport, Elias.

I straighten my spine, heart racing as I reorient myself. The interior of the transport is brighter, regardless that the overhead lights darkened at some point, as afternoon approaches outside the windows.

I fell asleep. *I fell asleep in front of three men whose whole life is to hunt women like me.*

I let my guard down completely. If I'd talked, shifted wrong, if my mask had slipped—I'm such a fool.

But none of that happened. Elias is still seated across from me, though he's now facing the front of the transport where one of the other Enforcers speaks in low tones.

I swallow around the rock in my throat, wishing I'd thought to bring a canteen of water.

Too quickly does reality sink into me: it's too late to change what I've done. My parents must know I'm gone by now, no doubt having found my note. They're probably frantic, keeping Lachlan home to avoid questions, trying to figure out where I've gone and why.

A wave of guilt-ridden nausea washes through me. I've put them in an impossible position...if they come after me, they risk revealing my existence. If they don't, they'll be sick with worry, imagining all the terrible things that could happen to me.

But there's nothing I can do about it now. I made my choice when I donned this uniform.

I can't turn back.

Grabbing my pack, I tug it onto my lap, needing its weight. The few possessions I have—Lachlan's sleep clothes, my notebook of lost things, a few essentials—is both comforting and a reminder of how little I was able to bring into this new life.

Elias stands, stretching slightly before looking at me. "Welcome to the Enforcer Training Center, Ashford," he says, his voice neutral.

His steps pull him from the transport without waiting for a response. After a steadying breath, I follow, stepping from the vehicle into my new reality.

Whatever happens next, I've crossed an inescapable threshold—not just the one that separated me from the outside world this morning, but one that divides my life into before and after. Cassia Ashford, the hidden girl who watched the world through windows and books, is gone.

In her place stands Lachlan Ashford, Enforcer recruit.

I hope I'm strong enough to be him.

CHAPTER FIVE
CASSIA

My stomach churns—not from motion sickness, but the oppressive brick of fear and uncertainty pressing on every nerve ending. I reach to adjust my mask under the guise of comfort, but in truth, I'm trying to steady my trembling hands before anyone notices. The synthetic material feels alien against my skin, trapping my breath in humid pockets that smell of my own sweat and anxiety.

Ahead of us, the Training Center looms like something from a nightmare. Its massive, merciless structure displays a sharp silhouette against the pale afternoon sky. The stone walls, fortified with gleaming steel, swallow the weak sunlight rather than reflect it, casting a foreboding shadow over the surrounding area.

This place was not built to welcome. It was built to intimidate.

I follow Elias, lengthening my strides as much as I dare to mimic his. He moves with the easy familiarity of someone returning home, while every step I take feels like a trespass into forbidden territory. Like I may as well scream my true name for everyone to hear.

My shoulders ache from hours of sitting stiffly in the transport, muscles tense and sore. I don't dare roll them for relief. Everything about my movements must scream *ordinary* and blend seamlessly with the men around me.

But even before we reach the building's entrance, I realize I have no idea what ordinary means in this context. Doubt creeps in, cold and insidious.

The air here is warmer than in the city, but I feel cold to my marrow. A shiver threatens to collapse my body as we're herded into a large open courtyard. I suppress it viciously, snarling at it from within. Enforcers don't shiver. Enforcers don't show weakness.

Other vehicles were in line before Elias' and mine, and more arrived behind us. I count nineteen other recruits walking ahead of me. Elias has already stopped near the entrance, speaking with someone whose posture suggests authority. I can tell which ones are new recruits like me—we all carry small packs and lack weapons the established Enforcers wear with such casual menace.

The perimeter of the courtyard is lined with silent Enforcers, their faces turned toward our group with the unnerving attention of predators assessing potential threats. Or prey.

And I'm willingly walking into their ranks.

"Line up," barks a sharp voice, cutting through the quiet murmuring.

I jolt and move into formation with the others, counting my breaths to keep calm.

One in, two out, three in, four out.

The man addressing us has imposing, broad shoulders, his posture rigid with the kind of command that expects immediate obedience. Even through the space filled with bodies, the weight of his gaze is heavy as it sweeps across us.

"You will be tested," he begins, pacing the line with measured steps. It's clear he's accustomed to being heard and obeyed without question. "Your strength, endurance, and intelligence will determine whether you are fit to wear this uniform. Fail, and you will be dismissed. Succeed, and you will earn your place among us."

He introduces himself as Arayik, the Commander, and continues outlining rules and expectations with ruthless efficiency.

This must be the man that selected Elias to be in our group—

I stall, my attention snagging on the two Enforcers standing behind the Commander. The one on the right, standing where Elias was a few minutes ago, stares across our group with calculating eyes.

Fuck me. He's not a recruit. I was stupid to not check his ranking in the vehicle, but I can easily make it out right here. Two arrows pointing downward—a lieutenant.

I silently curse myself. Of course, the one person I was borderline rude to during our journey turns out to be one of our leaders. Perfect. My ability to sabotage myself remains unmatched.

Arayik introduces the other two as Elias, his second, and Kellen, his third. I'm so frustrated with myself for not taking in every detail, for immediately getting off on the wrong foot with leadership. When Arayik directs us to follow him, I linger at the back of the line. The heat of Elias' gaze tracks me, and I'm hyperaware of every step I take. No wonder he was so curious about me.

I wish there had been time to practice walking. I can't just keep changing my gait. They'd either kick me out for being suspicious or for looking like a damn idiot.

I decide to keep my walk as normal as I would move, just

with longer strides. That should be easy enough to maintain, regardless of how awkward and forced it feels.

We follow the Commander through a grove of trees, and my jaw drops when we emerge at what can only be an obstacle course. It's unlike anything I've ever seen outside of the forbidden books my father brings home. There's a towering wall with strange shapes sticking from it, thin beams suspended over what look like deadly drops, followed by a series of tunnels and obstacles that appear designed to break the human body rather than test it.

Arayik barks at us to drop our packs and line up to begin. My heart hammers against my ribs. I didn't expect this—not on day one, after traveling for ten hours. I thought there would be some kind of orientation...an introduction to the facility, or at least a chance to get our bearings before being thrown into physical trials.

No, we're diving directly into the flames without so much as a safety briefing.

Commander announces with cold clarity that this isn't merely an assessment. Anyone who fails to complete the course will be sent home immediately. He doesn't even want to learn our names until we prove ourselves worthy of his attention.

"You're not worth the effort if you can't handle the most basic training you'll do here," he states, the contempt slicing through his voice thick.

Sweat trickles down my back and builds in my mask. I'm certain I look as terrified as a cornered animal facing a pack of hungry wolves.

When several recruits, including myself, hesitate to move after being instructed to begin, Arayik snarls another command and I jolt into action, running to catch up with the others. I glance to where the leaders stand, Elias' head tilted in my direction. But I remind myself I'm just one of many recruits. There's no reason he'd be focusing on me specifically —no way I could have done anything so egregious already to warrant special attention. They can't possibly know my secret.

My blood thickens, pounding through my body so hard that remnants of it push through my temples. As I wait for my turn on the first test, I watch the others carefully, analyzing their approaches. It's obvious brute strength—which I decidedly lack —will not be enough to get me through. I'll need to rely on my mind, balance, and whatever scrap of physical endurance I can muster.

Conditioning my muscles all these years to prevent atrophy will be of no aid to me today.

When I step to the beginning, the Enforcer overseeing this section of the course watches me with disdain. Perhaps he can already tell I'm physically weaker than the others. Or more likely that's just how they all regard recruits—as if we're insects they would love nothing more than to squash.

"Go," he commands, his tone almost taunting when I hesitate.

Then I'm moving.

The first hurdle is a climb—a towering wall with thick, knotted ropes hanging from its peak. I'm not muscular by any means, especially in my upper body, but I am thin and lithe. I silently pray to any star that might listen that I can lift my own body weight. Being sent home on the first day would be humiliating and terrifying in equal measure—somehow worse than being killed for identity theft.

Or for being a woman.

I leap for the nearest rope, my hands burning instantly as the rough fibers drag along my skin. Pain shoots up my arms as I haul myself upward. Every single muscle screams in protest, unused to this kind of exertion. It's more difficult than I imagined, and I doubt the added weight of the Enforcer gear is doing me any favors as it threatens to drag me back to the dirt.

Nearby, one of the other recruits yelps as he slips from his rope. The leaders laugh, a sound that chills my bones despite how hot I am. I will *not* be the next source of their amusement.

My nails dig into the rope, several snapping against the coarse fiber, and pull myself up with renewed determination. Pain becomes secondary to survival. My arms shake with the strain, but somehow I manage to reach the top of the wall.

At the summit, I allow myself half a second to scan the next challenge ahead. It's a narrow beam, slick with water, hovering above a pit so deep light barely penetrates its depths. Fall there and I would die—or suffer injuries severe enough to wish I had. What kind of training facility intentionally risks lethal injury? Are they trying to kill us before we even begin?

A steadying breath whistles through my teeth when I notice I'm the last in line, and all three leaders are watching me as if I'm the evening's entertainment. Their scrutiny ignites something in me—not fear, but anger. How dare they set us up to fail and then watch with delight? The flash of indignation gives me a burst of much needed confidence.

I steady myself before stepping onto the beam, focusing on keeping my center of gravity low. My balance wavers but never fails. A lifetime of confinement taught me how to move—quick, quiet, invisible—lest an inadvertent sound or vibration alert someone to my existence. Years of working with delicate concoctions for my experiments trained my hands and body to remain steady under pressure. For once, my sheltered life has given me an advantage.

The course continues with more obstacles—rope swings over mud pits, a tunnel crawl through jagged rocks, and a climbing net that leaves my hands bloody and raw. Each element is designed not just to challenge, but hurt; to weed out the weak through physical trauma rather than mere difficulty.

I catch sight of the leaders as I navigate the course, noticing the definition in their muscles, the way they carry themselves with the conviction of men who've tested their bodies against impossible tasks and emerged victorious. They didn't get those muscles from easy training. This brutality has purpose, even if I find it barbaric.

By the time I collapse at the finish line, my lungs feel like they've been scorched from the inside out. Every breath burns. But I don't let the pain show in my eyes, instead forcing my body to straighten and meeting the gaze of the Commander as he walks past, observing each of us with clinical detachment. I try to project the same stoic indifference the other recruits display.

Perhaps not the best idea, as the lack of oxygen in my blood creates black spots in my vision.

He moves on quickly, pointing at two men who struggled more visibly than the rest. "You and you. Leave. You're done."

My stomach drops. I hadn't realized he was being entirely serious about immediate dismissal. There's no second chance or opportunity to improve. One failure equals immediate dismissal.

The next test comes without pause—a mental challenge designed to assess strategic thinking and problem-solving under pressure. We're ushered to tables set with various objects that appear innocuous enough until Arayik's third—Kellen, I think —explains our task: disarm a mock explosive using logic and deductive reasoning.

A timer is set, and my hands uncharacteristically shake as I work through the puzzle. But while my body may be failing me, my mind remains sharp. At least the bleeding wounds from the rope clotted quickly.

I dig into my head and recall a passage I read years ago about circuit mechanics and apply the principle here, my fingers manipulating the components with growing confidence. When the timer buzzes, my device is successfully dismantled.

One recruit isn't so fortunate. He's dismissed with the same flick of a wrist as the first two.

The final round tests our power. Each recruit must demonstrate their ability and the leaders will determine if it's useful enough to warrant keeping us. My stomach flutters—I'm actually excited about this part. I've been practicing for years, pushing myself further each time. I must take a moment to thank whatever twist of fate gave me power when I was born—without it, this is where my deception would fall apart.

Elias instructs everyone to partner up, but I hang back at first, not confident enough to approach any of the others. He notices my hesitation and beckons me forward.

"Ashford, come here. You can demonstrate on us directly."

Wonderful...just what I needed.

I cross my heels and spin to approach the three men, ignoring the forming lump in my throat. The Commander asks my name, and I stutter so badly that Elias answers for me.

"This is Lachlan Ashford." Is he being helpful or is he already suspicious of me?

His superior nods before inquiring about my power. I clear my throat, opening the back of it to deepen the sound. "I'm an Empath," I answer, meeting his hard gaze.

Light shines from behind me, illuminating his eyes through the opening in his mask. They're dark, almost black, and utterly devoid of warmth—the kind of eyes that have witnessed cruelty and participated in it without remorse.

He doesn't act pleased with my answer, but at least it doesn't trigger any additional hostility. Empaths aren't the most valued power type among Enforcers, from what I've gathered.

They prefer more offensive abilities, where the user doesn't need to touch another person to use power on them.

"Influence one of us," he commands, giving no further instruction as he holds out a hand.

I don't need further instruction, nor do I reach to grab his hand. This is my moment to prove my worth, and I cannot afford to be timid. I've wanted this for too long. Still, I consider holding back—showing too much skill might draw unwanted attention.

Being sent home would be worse than a little scrutiny.

It's decided, then. I reach into my core and focus my energy, doing something I've never attempted on aware strangers before—I influence all three leaders simultaneously, sending a tangy emotional current to each.

Most individuals require physical contact to use their power. Chargers need to touch what they're electrifying. Thermics must make contact with what they heat or cool. Revealers can detect lies when they touch the speaker. But I've pushed my ability further, practicing relentlessly in the solitude of our home, never having the privilege of using my powers physically.

A small blessing, I realize.

The second and third chuckle beneath their uniform, Elias grabbing his stomach while Kellen shakes himself free. I could probably keep them laughing for a while, but I sent only a trickle of feeling to them. The Commander is more difficult, not wanting to budge, so I increase his current, pouring more emotion into him.

He laughs—a short, startled sound that dies instantly, as if he's horrified at his own reaction. The noise is so unexpected that several recruits whirl to stare. I've never heard such a cold laugh before, and judging by the way his muscles immediately hardens, neither has he. At least not recently.

Before my connection to him cuts off, raging heat forces me to step back. At the same time, a high-pitched ringing blooms inside my skull, sharp and demanding, like my ears are bleeding on the inside. My balance wavers, vision speckling at the edges. I bite down on the sound clawing through me, refusing to give him the satisfaction of seeing me falter.

He's pissed.

He leans forward, towering above me as I shove my power far away, not wanting to feel a moment more of his anger. How does he live with himself? It's all-consuming, and I'd only had a taste.

I hold myself still as he bends so close our masks clink, the heat of his breath grazing my lashes. It's terrifying. This man could crush me with a single thought, and there is nothing I could do about it.

"I should have sent you home after the first phase," he growls. "You're weak, slow, and physically useless."

I freeze, uncertain how to respond. Has my demonstration backfired? Did I push too far?

After a tense moment, he straightens, his eyes not leaving mine. "But I've only met one other Empath who could influence without touch like that. You can stay." His voice drops lower, whether to keep his words between us or sound scarier, I do not care. "For now. But the moment you cease to be useful, you're gone."

My throat tightens, and I walk away without saying anything, sweet relief trickling into my bones. Kellen dismisses one more recruit, leaving fifteen others plus me, along with the three leaders. He explains we're here to train for a special assignment, but we do not need to know the specifics yet.

"Trust your superiors or leave," he remarks in a flat tone when one recruit questions our forced ignorance. "Those are your options."

I already know why our team was formed—to hunt the rumored group of escapees outside the perimeter. It was the very information that spurred me to make such a rash, out of character decision. Had I not heard Hardan mention the specifics, it would have been quite the shock to learn later that I'd be expected to capture women who managed to free themselves. I wouldn't be able to do it.

I'm not sure I can, even knowing the truth.

The leaders briefly summarize our schedules and responsibilities. Each one will focus on different skills; Arayik will handle tactical discipline, physical fitness, and combat readiness. Elias plans to teach mental and empathetic flexibility, situational awareness, and adaptability in high-stress environments, further solidifying my theory that he is also an Empath. Kellen will teach analytical and strategic skills, training recruits to think several steps ahead and adapt plans based on new intelligence.

Arayik raises a brow to add, "And remember this—if one of you screws up, you all pay. That's how the team works." Cryptic, though understandable.

As they speak, I bristle at the time I will be spending with the cold leader, given how poor my performance was in the physical tests compared to the mental ones. I'll also need time with Elias, since I hesitated repeatedly today. I need to learn to remain calm and focused in every situation.

A skill I will gladly accept instruction on.

The level of thought put into their training surprises me. I wonder why they need such sophisticated skills when their job is primarily to enforce laws and raid houses to capture women who are far weaker than they are. Empathy training? For what purpose? I've never once heard of an Enforcer showing empathy to anyone. The thought makes me sick because that's how things should be, but they aren't...

The Syndicate doesn't want compassionate soldiers; it wants efficient, loyal ones.

Arayik concludes with a final announcement. "The Syndicate values privacy," he says, and I almost laugh. They value privacy for men. "If anyone requires a private room, speak now. I do not give a shit if you sleep in the mud each night, but I'm obligated to offer."

I raise my hand without hesitation. There's no way I'm sharing sleeping quarters with more than a dozen men if I have another option. I'd never have a moment of true privacy, and I absolutely cannot risk being discovered while changing or sleeping.

The leaders stare at me, and someone in the group of recruits barks out a laugh. I bite my tongue as I'm the only one with my hand raised.

The Commander stalks toward me, stopping intimidatingly close. "Why do you need a private room?"

I blurt out the first excuse that comes to mind. "Medical reasons." I quickly adjust my claim, knowing how that's likely to backfire on me. "They don't affect my performance, but I would prefer some privacy for them."

It's not a direct lie, I suppose. Being a woman in a facility full of men who would kill me for existing could be considered a medical condition.

"What medical reason?" he presses, and I falter. Fuck.

I have no idea what to say, my head whirling with a thousand thoughts before I recall a passage from Syndicate law I read years ago. According to regulation, no one is allowed to demand another man's medical history unless said man voluntarily shares the information.

I'm in a predicament. Again. Citing this law will likely antagonize him further, but I cannot share a room with the others.

The risk is worth taking.

"I'm not required to disclose that information," I say with as steady a voice as I can manage. Then, just to reinforce it, I recite the exact wording from the law, "Section fourteen, paragraph three of the Syndicate Health Code states that no citizen may demand medical information from another without explicit consent, and no position of authority grants exception to this privacy protection."

Arayik's answering laugh chills every hair on my body. He bends forward until his mask nearly touches mine, his voice dropping to a whisper meant for me alone. "You have no idea the things I can do with no one batting an eye. Watch yourself, Ashford."

Then he straightens before announcing, "Ashford gets a private room. Everyone else will bunk together."

Dizziness floods through me so powerfully I almost stagger. It feels like the first real breath I've taken since sitting in the hole under my parents' room last night.

The leaders show us to the main building without further comment. As I walk through the door, a faint zipping rings above me, which is strange, but I'm too overwhelmed to investigate. No one else seems bothered by it.

The interior is exactly what I would expect from a facility designed to break and rebuild men into weapons. Everything is black and gray metal, the walls and floors gleaming under harsh lighting. There's nothing soft or welcoming about the space. It feels detached. Impersonal. Much like the masks we all wear, I suppose. A physical manifestation of the emotional distance the Syndicate requires of its Enforcers.

Throughout the rest of the day, I keep my empathy abilities tightly controlled, using them sparingly to gauge the emotions of those around me without drawing attention. There's a mix of nervousness and determination from the other recruits—feelings which mirror my own internal chaos. Unlike them, however, my legs are shaking and need a long break. Perhaps I should have performed more squats over the years, regardless of how much I loathe them.

Kellen directs us to our quarters with a nod. My private room is small but functional. With just enough space for a bed, a storage unit, and a small desk and chair. After dropping off our packs, he leads us through the facility with haste, loosely explaining various protocols.

The bathroom and shower arrangements surprise me. They're communal spaces with stalls for toilets and showers. Thank the stars for the minimal seclusion of the stalls, but I had hoped for my own bathroom. I won't dare push my luck, though.

The third ranking leader explains meal times in the cafeteria, warning that if we miss scheduled meals, we don't eat until the next designated time. "This facility doesn't cater to individual schedules," he explains, pinning each of us with a hard stare. "You will adapt to ours, or you will leave."

Something about Kellen's speaking style draws me in. He reminds me of myself—someone who stores vast knowledge but carefully measures how much to share, holding back to avoid overwhelming others. There's an alertness in his eyes that suggests he sees far more than he reveals.

After a few more halls, we reach an indoor training area. The space is open, with lines marking the outer perimeter. I recognize their oval shape, commonly used for running exercises. Though I don't understand why they need painted lines when the walls were built to define the space. It cannot be so difficult to run near them?

Shaking my head and ignoring the rumbling in my abdomen, I scan the rest of the room. There's various equipment spread throughout the space—weights, a climbing apparatus on one wall, combat rings, and a specialized area for power-practice. It's a section enclosed in clear glass, and inside, two Enforcers are using their abilities against each other. One creates small electrical charges between him and his opponent while the other dodges with preternatural speed.

The two missing leaders join us in the training area, their postures and builds immediately identifying them even behind identical masks. I shouldn't have been worried in my ability to distinguish them from the others. Even in this short time, I've gotten better at recognizing specific gaits and movements—another reminder of home.

"The remainder of today will be spent here," the Commander announces. "We will assess where each of you needs the most training." His voice hardens, and I swear the air around him tightens. "I will not tolerate weakness in my team. Every member will be equally proficient in all necessary skills, or they're gone. I have no time or sympathy for anything less than excellence."

What follows is a grueling series of assessments—strength tests, reflex exercises, combat drills, and power demonstrations. I perform dismally in most physical challenges but excel in the mental ones. My power allows me to anticipate intentions and reactions, giving me a much-needed edge in combat that partially compensates for my lack of strength.

Barely, but they haven't kicked me out yet so I'll consider it a win.

By the day's end, I'm certain I've been dragged across the entire perimeter and hung out to bake in the sun. Every muscle aches with a depth of pain I've never experienced. My mind spins with exhaustion and the relief-filled anxiety of having survived the first day.

It's a feat to make it to the dining hall, but I manage and grab a simple dinner—two hard boiled eggs and an apple. I'm no longer hungry, my stomach knotted and sour, but I know my body needs protein and carbohydrates to recover and prepare for the coming days. I will force myself to eat mechanically in private, promising my poor body I'll do better tomorrow. Today was just about survival.

And survive I barely did.

I sneak from the hall and make it to the sleeping quarters without further incident. Though I desperately want to shower, I decide it's too risky tonight. I'm too exhausted to maintain proper vigilance in a communal space. Instead, I just use the bathroom quickly before locking myself in my room.

Alone at last. Trembling hands lift to remove my mask before I collapse onto the narrow bed. The cool, stale air feels like heaven against the grime on my face after hours of confined breathing.

Silent tears track down my cheeks as the full truth of what I've done finally sinks in.

I'm overwhelmed. Terrified. Uncertain whether I'm being brave or suicidally foolish. My body aches in places I didn't know could feel pain, and I'm mentally drained from the constant attention required to maintain my disguise.

How am I going to do this every day? How did I ever think I could pull this off? I've willingly walked into the lion's den and painted a target on my back.

But as the pressure behind my eyes pulls me toward sleep, one thought rings clear amid the chaos: I made it through the first day.

I made it through the first day.

One day at a time is okay if that's all I can manage.

CHAPTER SIX

CASSIA

The training room is dim as I creep into its walls well before dawn. The air still clings to the chill of night, and there's a peace I wouldn't expect to find anywhere on these grounds. My footsteps thud against concrete floors, the hollow sounds bouncing back to me like unwanted company. Though welcomed, the vast emptiness in the room is eerie. As if it's holding its breath, keeping from blurting out the threat I know surrounds me.

At least I'm alone.

I need this solitude. My muscles scream from yesterday's training, each movement a groan-worthy reminder of how unprepared my body is for this charade. It's embarrassing and unacceptable.

But it's my mind that truly refuses rest. Behind my locked door last night, I'd stared at the ceiling until the darkness became a canvas for my fears—abstract images of all the ways I could fail or die.

All the ways they could kill my family.

Things I'd only ever seen in the hatch. I'm so selfish for doing this.

The floor is cool beneath my legs as I slide down the wall

and stretch them out before me. The uniform is heavier today, tugging what little energy I possess to the ground I rest on. My lips curl from the rigid material pressing against them—I truly hate the way the mask traps my breath and creates such uncomfortable humidity. But I'd never risk removing it, not here. That's a luxury reserved for my bed.

The trouble is Lachlan's been accused of being a woman before by people who didn't know better. If that happened to him—with his deeper voice—what chance do I have if anyone glimpses my face? Would Lachlan's record and my power be enough to convince them?

I could probably talk my way out of mild suspicion. I am an Empath, after all.

Sighing, my head drops back to the wall. I have a backstory that checks out, but one thorough inspection would end everything. I have this creeping fear they'd make me remove my shirt to prove I'm male. Or my pants. That is not something I could hide no matter how powerful I am.

My empathy trickles to the surface like the lightest sprinkling of rain. I've held it back to preserve my sanity—trying to process my own emotions while filtering through everyone else's is overwhelming. But alone in this empty room, I can finally let the tightly wound coil of my power loosen. I sigh as my head drops back against the wall.

The release is exquisite.

My awareness extends cautiously, brushing against emotional residue in the space—anxiety, pride, frustration—remnants of those who trained here recently. It's strange, because these impressions shouldn't linger; Empaths usually need physical contact to sense emotions, and even then, only present ones. After decades of nothing to do but experiment with my abilities, I still discover nuances that contradict the official understanding.

For a woman, at least, because of course every piece of literature on the subject refers to the male body.

Then there's the other limitation I've stretched: touching only one subject at a time. Yesterday, I influenced all three leaders simultaneously. The threat in Arayik's eyes when I made him laugh will haunt my nightmares for years. I'd caught a glimpse of something dangerous...like I'd dragged a private part of him into the light against his will, and now he wants to punish me for it.

Perhaps I'll try such experiments more often on him, if he's going to hurt me anyway. Discover how he enjoys having his body taken from him and used for the enjoyment of someone else.

My lip curls. Less than a day around new people and I've already shrunk to such drama-infested pettiness.

Stars, the same burning question flicks through my mind for the hundredth time this morning: what am I doing? I have no concrete plan. Learn about the internal workings of the Syndicate, discover how exactly they maintain the breeding facilities. I know why women are kept there, but understanding the logistics might reveal weaknesses.

This was an impulsive, foolish decision.

Something snaps in my mind—I'm getting ahead of myself again. I won't be able to do any of that unless I survive this training, learn their ways, and remain inconspicuous enough to gather such information. Then, *maybe*, I can finally do something good with my life.

I exhale shakily and shift my focus inward once more. My empathy is a delicate thread; something to be drawn taut or loosened as needed. But if left untouched or coiled too tight, the fabric of it weakens, like a neglected muscle. So I practice wrapping it tightly around myself, muting its influence. I imagine constructing a wall between myself and the surrounding emotions—something impermeable and unyielding. Then, as slow as I can manage, I loosen its hold until it flutters about aimlessly.

Control is everything.

My hands flex as I concentrate, sending the power out in different directions, expanding and thinning the tendrils at will. The process drains me further than I care to acknowledge, and my control slips more often than I'd prefer.

A flash of something—distant but sharp—jolts through me, and I jerk forward. The rage burns so potent it makes my skin flush with instant heat. This is not my anger. I flinch, pulling back hard, and the sudden emotional emptiness dizzies my senses.

"What the fuck was that?" I whisper.

My temples ache, a familiar pain of overextending my power. I've been here for hours now, pushing my limits, and while I'm pleased with the progress, I know it's not enough.

Faint voices echo from the corridor outside—must be breakfast hour already. My stomach twists at the thought of food, but it will have to deal. I need to eat.

I stand even as my legs protest, and ensure my mask is secure. My reflection in nearby glass catches me off guard. Expressive, revealing eyes stare back at me, wide and uncertain. I shove the feelings away, suck in a deep breath, and empty the life from my gaze before leaving the room.

As I approach the dining hall, the cacophony makes me pause at the threshold, utterly shocked.

Are these the same disciplined men from yesterday's training? Enforcers crowd the long rectangular tables that fill the room, their masks either off or tipped up enough to reveal their mouths. But that's not what stopped me. The noise and behavior is overwhelming—they shout across tables, laugh with mouths full of food, spray crumbs as they argue and joke. I grimace at the display.

How does one prioritize which aspect of this chaos to process first? The sheer volume assaults my ears as much as the lack of discipline confounds me. Do men always act so childish when not on duty?

They exhibit none of the rigid control shown during training. Fists slam on tables for emphasis as they throw bits of food at each other and belch without apology. The energy in this room is so frenetic that if I could bottle it up and consume it, I'd never need to eat or sleep again.

Then there's the revelation that they're showing their faces to one another—something I knew they were permitted to do, but hadn't anticipated. Did they do the same last night?

I wouldn't be able to identify who is who just yet, but that's not the issue.

I didn't consider how I'm supposed to eat meals outside dinner.

I can't just tip up my mask...I'll have to take everything back to my room, which is unfortunate, assuming that is even admissible during the day. It would also help to become accustomed to this wild, unfiltered behavior. I'm already too stiff and formal by comparison, though I see no other choice.

I study them as I walk, vowing I'll never act in such a manner. There are far more men here than just our team; this must be the central hub for all Enforcers, not just recruits in training. This knowledge pushes me to focus on my walk, placing each foot with deliberate heaviness, allowing my shoulders the slightest swing. I have to push through the center of the room to reach the food stations, and though no one is actually looking at me, a hundredweight of eyes track my movement.

I've never felt so damn self-conscious. Not from embarrassment, but hyperawareness. Every breath and small gesture becomes a calculation, and I have to wonder if I'm the only Enforcer to ever feel this way.

Eventually, I grab a tray and gather what my body needs, down to specific vegetables for micronutrients that will aid in muscle recovery.

Whirling to the exit, my shoulders dip as I confirm not a single person has paid me any attention. Just a short walk and I can eat in peace, without the terror of removing my mask.

I'm mere feet from the door when a voice cuts through the din.

"Ashford!"

I recognize the commanding tone immediately and pivot to address Arayik, flanked by Elias and Kellen, seated at their own table near the entrance. Elias beckons me over with a casual wave. Their masks are firmly in place, no food lingering in front of them. Do they not eat? Or perhaps they're like me and prefer privacy for their meals.

I approach reluctantly, stopping before their table with my tray clutched in tight fingers.

"Where the fuck do you think you're going?" the Commander demands, his shadowed eyes narrowing.

"To my room," I answer, keeping my voice low and steady.

"You can't eat here with everyone else?" His head tilts. "Or is this part of your *medical issue* again?"

The condescending bite in his tone ignites something hot and dangerous in my chest. Why does he have to be such a dickhead? I've done nothing to warrant this targeted harassment, except use my power exactly how he instructed me to.

"It isn't," I reply, unable to keep the edge from my tone. "But would it matter if it was? Do you have something against those with health conditions, *Commander?*"

The title is a joke. Of course he has problems with anyone

different from himself. This man and his kind use women for pleasure and stock, stripping away their humanity, reducing them to reproductive vessels. They're no better than farm animals, and the parallel is sickening. Women are selected for their fertility, kept in rusty cages, made to produce children until their bodies wear out and are disposed of. At least cattle are fed properly and given basic care. From what I've gathered in my mother's careful words, women in those places are treated only as resources, not living beings.

My face seethes with heat as Arayik glares at me. Elias clears his throat, the sound uncomfortable. Kellen simply observes, his posture betraying neither approval nor disapproval. I file that information away—maybe they're not as loyal to the Commander as they first appeared.

Any potential division among leadership could be useful.

"Actually, I do, Ashford," Arayik remarks after a tense moment, not elaborating on his admission. "Let's hear why you can't eat with the group."

I grip the tray tighter, knuckles straining against their stretched skin. "We're on Syndicate grounds, as I assume you're aware. I understand the necessity to remove our masks to eat. However, I do not wish to remove mine while on grounds. So I will eat in my room." I pause, then add, "Is that acceptable to you, *sir*, or must you continue interrogating me?"

I mentally curse myself. I shouldn't push patience today, but something about his piss poor attitude drives me crazy. He embodies everything I despise—the cold authority, the never-ending cruelty, the unquestioned enforcement of Syndicate laws and desires.

He doesn't deserve my kindness, and certainly not my respect, if this is how he treats his supposed equals. I can't even imagine how brutally he'd treat me if he knew I was a woman.

No, that's a lie.

Of course I can imagine it—he'd tear my head from my body after raping me without so much as allowing a spoken explanation.

Arayik's anger manifests physically; veins standing out on his forearms as his fists flex. Elias shifts his weight to one hip, as if preparing to intervene. A strange heat flutters through my abdomen at the intensity of the rage directed toward me, but before I can analyze the sensation, the Commander stands, pushing into my tray until it's the only thing separating our bodies.

I hadn't the time to fully appreciate his height yesterday, but now, with him looming over me, I am acutely aware of how easily he could overpower me. It's terrifying, and I want nothing more than to run from this room and vomit until there's nothing left of me. But I force my eyes to remain neutral and will my limbs to stiffen as if they are stone.

I will not give him the satisfaction of my fear.

Hands seize mine, squeezing with crushing force. Pain radiates through my arms, but I swallow my verbal reaction, clenching my jaw hard enough to sprout a migraine. Every other woman suffers far worse than this daily. I can endure this small altercation.

"You're really getting on my fucking nerves, Ashford," he growls, the sound low but intense. "Tell me why I shouldn't kick you out right the fuck now and be done with you? I don't need some insubordinate on my team."

Dramatic much? What an excessive reaction for such a minor issue. The man clearly needs a therapist.

Despite the pain in my hands and the very real threat of expulsion, I maintain eye contract, refusing to back down. "Because I'll have no problem taking news of your mediocre leadership skills straight to the Syndicate and letting them know that you single recruits out because of some ridiculous superiority complex." I suck in a shaky breath. "Section twelve, paragraph seven of the Enforcer Code explicitly states that those in leadership positions must remain objective, as every man is to be treated equally unless they have broken established laws."

His eyes narrow to burning slits, searing my insides with every second he stares, and his grip tightens beyond what should be physically possible. My suspicion crystallizes—is he an Anchor?

"Remove your hands. Now." My voice drops, turning cold and sharp. Fuck this asshole. From my peripheral, Elias shifts again, more noticeably this time. "Use your power against me again without consent, and you'll be reported before you can even think about apologizing." I'm taking a huge risk accusing him like this, but his response tells me exactly what I feared.

"Apologize? To the likes of you?" he hisses, his fingers twitching. "You're literally nothing here."

I laugh, a dark sound that startles me. "Then why can't you seem to keep your attention off me, Commander?"

Elias releases a soft chuckle, causing Arayik's head to jerk in his Second's direction, though his eyes never leave mine. Something in his posture changes—his shoulders loosening a fraction, grip finally easing on my hands.

"Get out. Now," he barks before stepping back.

I don't wait for him to repeat the command, nearly sprinting from the dining hall as my head pounds frantically, adrenaline making my steps unsteady on the race back to my room.

Why do I do this to myself? I could keep my head down, submit to whatever he demands, and make myself invisible. It would be safer. Smarter.

But I know why. I'll find myself trapped dead before I willingly submit to a man. Arayik and every other Enforcer in the cafeteria uphold the very laws that kept my mother and me prisoners in our own home. They're the reason I've never felt the sun on my face or grass beneath my feet until now.

They're monsters. And no matter how badly I'm desperate to remain unnoticed, I cannot let them—*any of them*—walk all over me. It feels fundamentally wrong, and a betrayal of everything I am.

I can only push back so much without risking exposure, but my disgust and rage need somewhere to go. If verbal sparring with Arayik provides that outlet, then so be it—even if having his full attention is the most appalling thing.

CHAPTER SEVEN

CASSIA

The clatter of boots echoes through the corridor as I follow the rest of my group to the training room, a dull ache settling deep in the crevices of my muscles with every step. My body will never be used to this kind of exertion, but I force it to stand straighter regardless.

The doors slide open with a mechanical whoosh, revealing the space I left not long ago. Our three leaders stand in formation at the center, their identical black uniforms and expressionless masks making them seem like extensions of the same entity rather than three separate men.

I suppose they are.

My stomach twists as I catch sight of Arayik's hands, weaved under each arm from their crossing. My fingers still hurt where his grip held me, and I'd bet my position here there are bruises marring my skin. An Anchor's strength lies in his ability to control his own destiny—to make himself immovable or unnaturally heavy and resolute. I've read about them of course, but experiencing one firsthand was terrifying.

The fifteen remaining recruits form a line, shoulders squared, heads forward. I find my place, mimicking their stance.

Blend in. Become invisible.

Arayik holds a small electronic notepad, studying it as his tongue clicks. I should add my observations about men's behavior to my notebook later. Their pack mentality in the dining hall and their deference to hierarchy despite their bluster. The obsession with displays of strength. It's all interesting, if not useful.

"Step forward when your name is called," the Third announces, his voice sharp and precise. Each syllable carries a weight, demanding immediate compliance.

The saliva in my mouth withers to nothing as they begin listing names. Though nothing about the process seems punitive, my body reacts as if I'm being sentenced. Each recruit that steps forward is assigned to a training schedule split between the three leaders. Some receive schedules heavy with Elias' sessions, others with Kellen's. My stomach knots tighter with each name that isn't mine. What if they've discovered me already? Are they just taunting me, and this organization is just a formality before they drag me to a facility?

No. You're just being paranoid.

"Ashford."

I jolt at my family name, creaks sounding from my stiff joints. Willing my legs to move, I step forward with hopeful grace. My boots stick to the floor with each step.

"Mornings with Elias and Kellen," Arayik says with a flat look. "Afternoons with me."

Of course. Just my luck. Hours every day with the man who already despises me. I expected this, knowing my physical strength, stamina, and skill are lacking horribly, but I still don't want to accept it. Suppressing a sigh, I nod once and step back into line. At least he didn't single me out for further harassment. Small mercies.

As the remaining assignments are distributed, I mentally

count each one. Four others will join me in Elias' first morning group. Five will train with Kellen while I'm with Elias, the rest with Arayik, then we'll switch. And in the afternoons, just three others will share my personal hell with our sunshine of a Commander.

Brenner is among them—a hulking man with a permanent sneer visible even through his mask. He's a Charger, capable of generating electric currents with his touch. I'd witnessed him demonstrating yesterday, sending arcs of blue light between his fingertips. The others are Finnick, an Adapter who can withstand extreme environmental conditions, and Calder, a Thermic.

Powerful, physical abilities. Unlike my empathic talents, which Arayik clearly regards with disdain.

And yet I made him laugh without so much as a thought.

Kellen steps forward once the assignments are complete, detailing our daily schedule. Breakfast at six, training at seven, group transitions at nine. Lunch at eleven, followed by an hour of blessed downtime before afternoon sessions from one until five. Can't wait.

"If you're late, you're out. If you're absent without prior authorization, you're out," he states, taking time to examine each of us. "We are encouraged to remove anyone from the team at any time, for any reason."

Arayik fixes his gaze directly on me. "So you'd all do well to listen and shut the fuck up unless told otherwise."

A few recruits snicker, and my ears burn. They must have witnessed our confrontation earlier. Wonderful—now I'm marked as a troublemaker by my teammates.

After explanations of where to meet, more rules follow, blending together in a stream of restrictions and expectations. We can't leave the grounds without permission; fighting among recruits is forbidden; any disputes we can't resolve ourselves go to the leaders, but bringing up such complaints means automatic dismissal.

"Any questions?" The Commander's tone suggests he's ready to dismiss anyone who opens their mouth.

My mind floods with them instantly, regardless. Why are underground levels restricted? How many women are kept in each facility? Do the Enforcers ever remove their masks when executing missions? Why do they uphold the Syndicate's laws at the expense of half the population? How many people have escaped beyond the perimeter?

But my lips remain firmly shut. One confrontation per day is enough.

"Dismissed. You have ten minutes until training begins."

The recruits disperse, following their designated leaders. I fall in line with Vito, Malcolm, Brenner, and Pax behind Elias, my heart finally slowing now that our great leader isn't glaring at me. The Second guides us through a series of halls I hadn't seen yesterday, eventually reaching an elevator that requires his handprint to activate.

"This is a restricted access route," he explains as the doors slide closed. "Only leadership and authorized personnel can use these elevators." Good to know.

The same restriction doesn't apply to the stairwell.

The descent to a lower level is smooth, though my stomach's rolling would disagree. Three floors, then four, then five. I hadn't realized the facility extended so deep below the surface. I'm curious what lies in these hidden spaces...more training rooms? Weapons? Prisoners?

I all but leap from the elevator when the doors open at the sixth underground level, and follow Elias through another hall. The lighting here is different—colder, with a bluish tint that makes the metal walls appear almost liquid. Our footsteps vary too, suggesting thicker walls or ones made from contrasting materials compared to the main floor.

Elias speaks, filling the silent squeaking of our walk. "This is a special instruction room. What you experience here stays here—the technology is classified."

Doors part on a whisper, revealing a vast, empty space. The room must be fifty meters across, with ceilings high enough to house two stories. A continuous sheet of metal makes up the floor, unbroken by seams or panels. All four walls display a dull matte gray that somehow both absorbs and reflects the light overhead.

"This," Elias remarks with a hint of pride, "is the simulation chamber."

The deeper I walk into the room, the more detail I notice. Subtle patterns caress the floor's surface, intricate designs etched at a microscopic level that catch the light when viewed from certain angles. Whatever technology this room contains, it's far beyond anything I've ever seen or read about.

"Today we focus on threat assessment and quick-decision-making. Each of you will enter a simulation individually, where a scenario will test your ability to identify hostiles, protect civilians, and neutralize threats with minimal casualties." Something pulses in my throat. "You'll wear these," he continues, holding a thin metal circle. I cannot tell where it is supposed to fit, but it appears uncomfortable. "They allow you to perceive the simulation as if it were real. You'll feel impact, temperature changes, and limited pain without actual injury."

Ah, it's a necklace of sorts. Its oval shape makes more sense as Elias demonstrates how to wear it, positioning it at the base of his skull, where the mask ends, tucking it under the seat of his throat. I watch closely, memorizing the placement for when my turn comes, desperate to limit the amount of embarrassment I experience in one day.

Vito—the lean, quiet man who demonstrated Clinger abilities during the assessment—is called first, striding to where Elias gestures at the center of the room before settling his device into place. "The rest of you, stand against the wall. You'll be able to observe without interfering. Your objective is to determine who is hostile and who is civilian," he continues in a louder voice. "Once identified, secure the civilians and attempt to reason with the hostiles if possible. If that fails, neutralize them. Use everything at your disposal, including your power."

Elias taps something on a control panel near the door, and the air shimmers. A translucent cube forms, encasing most of the room, a small boundary for us left just outside. We can see through it clearly, but the shimmering is curious...would it zap me if I touched it? Or is it just a visual effect?

Vito's head begins to turn as if he's seeing something completely different from the empty room. A large image appears on one surface of the cube, showing us what the recruit must be observing: a bustling street lined with shops and crowds of people moving in all directions.

"The band transmits visual and auditory information directly to the brain," Elias whispers to our group while staring at the screen. "His body remains here, but his senses perceive the simulation."

I huff a breath, my lips quirking. The technology is astounding. From my limited knowledge of before the Collapse, nothing this advanced existed. Absurd that the Syndicate has made so much progress in this, even as they've regressed in nearly everything else.

We watch as Vito navigates through the simulated street, eventually encountering a standoff in a small plaza. Six men hold weapons on a group of cowering civilians—mostly women and a few children. A hand slides to his hip, drawing a weapon he does not possess in the real room. He raises some sort of gun —thinner than those the Enforcers normally carry, with a faintly luminescent core visible through transparent chamber sections.

Vito approaches with obvious caution, speaking to who he's dubbed as the leader of the hostile group. The simulation transmits audio, which only adds to my awe. They demand release of prisoners, threatening to harm the hostages if Vito doesn't comply, which sours his attempts at negotiation.

I spend a moment observing the women. All apparent civilians. All terrified. All in need of male protection. The imagery is nauseating and reinforces the idea that women are weak, helpless, and incapable of self-defense or authority.

Or autonomy.

Vito focuses so intently on the male leader that he fails to notice one of the female hostages slowly rising from her crouched position. While his attention is elsewhere, she pulls a knife from beneath her torn dress and lunges, slicing Vito's throat from behind.

His hands fly to the simulated wound, though nothing appears beneath his fingers, the clanking of his gun ringing through the open space. The simulation flickers before dissipating, leaving our group in an eerily quiet space once more. The shimmering cube remains, but there is no longer a projected image along the side.

Vito remains in his position, appearing stunned as his hands continue to press against his uninjured throat. He staggers, and Elias moves forward to steady him before answering the question in his eyes.

"The sensation feels real. The pain registers, but as I said, no physical damage occurs." He focuses fully on Vito. "What did you miss?"

"I..." The recruit's voice is hoarse, as if he still feels the phantom wound, before his throat clears. "I didn't consider the hostages might be plants."

"Exactly. You made assumptions based on appearances. The woman in the blue dress showed multiple indicators—her positioning, the way she tracked your movements with her eyes, her controlled breathing pattern. All signs she wasn't the frightened hostage she appeared to be."

I can't help but scoff at the irony. A woman deceiving a man by exploiting his assumptions about female inadequacy. The similarity to my situation is too close for comfort. But I'm also disturbed by the portrayal; the deceptive, murderous woman as the ultimate villain in the scenario. It cements the idea that women who don't conform to expected roles are treacherous and dangerous.

Stars forbid a woman just wants to live in peace without the influence of a man by her side.

I pause. Would *I* be considered dangerous right now?

Vito's shoulders quake, hands flexing as they press against a wound that isn't there. The sound of his shaky breaths grates at the inside of my skull, threatening to bury his panic in me the way fear sometimes does when I'm careless. Without thinking, I brush the edge of his emotions, sending out a thread of calm. His breathing evens, shoulders dropping a moment later.

Relief should follow, but it doesn't. Instead I pause as my forehead creases. *Was that really for him...or for me?* I didn't want him to cry. Didn't want to feel the rough edge of his fear clawing at the barrier of my power. Influencing him was easier, though now I'm questioning if it was the right choice. What gives me the power to manipulate others' emotions just because the urge strikes me? The thought curdles in my stomach.

Malcom steps into the cube next, facing a completely different scenario—an ambush in a narrow alley. Unlike Vito, he reacts with instant violence, firing at anyone who moves. He survives but fails the mission by killing several civilians in his indiscriminate attack. Elias is calm but firm in his critique, emphasizing precision over brute force.

Pax follows with a hostage exchange gone wrong. He manages better than the first two, using his telepathic abilities to communicate silently with one of the civilians and coordinate an escape. Still, he misses a hidden attacker and takes a bullet to the spine before the simulation ends.

Brenner's turn involves a complex betrayal scenario where someone posing as an informant leads him into a trap. He responds with calculated violence, using his Charger abilities to electrocute multiple attackers at once. It's effective but lacks finesse, and Elias notes several moments where de-escalation might have been possible.

Then it's my turn.

Deep breath.

My mouth dries as I step forward to accept the metal band from my leader. Our fingers brush briefly, and his green eyes flick to mine. I ignore him, positioning the band carefully at the base of my skull, making sure my hair remains tucked securely under my mask.

It wouldn't be the end of me if I let it down, being the same length as Lachlan's, but I'd rather not have something else to explain. I procure too many questioning glances as is.

"Center of the room, Ashford," Elias directs, drifting back to his spot against the wall.

I walk to the indicated spot, my heart hammering. Is it normal to taste the blood beating rapidly through my body?

Focus, Cas.

This simulation is different from the tests we endured yesterday. Those were straightforward while this requires swift thinking, decision-making, and potentially speaking to people who won't hesitate to kill me. What would Lachlan do if he were here?

I chuckle to myself; he wouldn't have come in the first place.

Before I can spiral further, the world shifts. Gray walls fade, replaced by the interior of an opulent building unlike anything I've ever seen. Marble floors stretch beneath my feet, polished to a mirror shine. Pillars of some dark stone rise to support a vaulted ceiling adorned with intricate frescoes. Crystal chandeliers hang like frozen waterfalls, shading the area in prismatic light.

And to fuck with my head all the more, I even smell traces of perfume and warm food.

I'm in the entrance hall of what must be an important government building or wealthy private residence. The space is crowded with people in formal attire. Men in dark suits mingle with one another while women in flowing dresses hang on their arms. Others circulate with trays of drinks while music plays softly from an unseen source.

I have no instructions beyond what Elias gave the others: identify threats, protect civilians, and neutralize hostiles if necessary.

But how do I identify threats in this sea of unfamiliar faces? I've only ever interacted with three people who weren't wearing masks, and now I'm supposed to read dozens of strangers?

I should be grateful for the opportunity to learn such a skill, but it's nauseating.

The crowd shifts as I move cautiously, studying faces and postures. My limited knowledge of psychology and body language becomes my only guide. I watch for micro-expressions, for anomalies in movement patterns, or hands that hover too close to potential weapons.

Everyone looks suspicious to me. That woman's smile doesn't reach her eyes; that man keeps glancing at his time-piece. There is a server who avoids a particular section of the room.

Paralysis by analysis. If everyone is suspicious, then I have no useful information.

I need *something*. What is the purpose of this gathering? What am I supposedly doing here?

Glancing down, I'm wearing an Enforcer uniform, but more formal than the standard issue. A ceremonial guard, perhaps? In a nearby reflection, a mask confirms my disguise remains intact.

The conversations grow increasingly tense, voices rising at a steady pace as the thrill of alcohol and dancing take effect. Something is happening. But what?

Irritated, I push through the crowd toward a source of disturbance. Near a large set of double doors at the far end of the hall, several men argue. Their gestures become more agitated as I approach. I can't make out what they're saying at first, but as I draw closer, the words form.

"...cannot allow this to continue," one man insists, his face flushed with anger. "The Syndicate has gone too far."

"Lower your fucking voice. We're surrounded by loyalists." The three peer around nervously before one notices my approach and falls silent, nudging his companions. All eyes turn to me.

The situation crystallizes in my mind. These men are planning something against the Syndicate...and I'm meant to be a loyal Enforcer.

They are the threat. *I* am the law.

Or are they? What if this is a test of my loyalty rather than my threat assessment? What if the real danger is elsewhere, and these men are a distraction. Will I fail if I leave them, or must they be held accountable either way?

No, I will be expected to neutralize any perceived issue arising outside the Syndicate's rule. And I don't have time to analyze further, or ask questions about what they're planning, in hopes I could use the same tactics. Elias' eyes burn through my uniform, watching every small movement and hesitation I make.

One of the men reaches into his jacket, forcing instinct to take over. I draw the weapon holstered at my hip—a sleek pistol similar to the one Vito used. The weight is wrong in my hand, the grip too large for my fingers, but I aim it steadily at the man reaching for whatever he deems important.

"Hands where I can see them," I order, deepening my voice just enough to sound authoritative without overcompensating.

Instead of complying, the man pulls out a small device and presses something on its surface. "Now!" he shouts.

Chaos erupts. The other men draw weapons, gunfire exploding from multiple directions across the hall. Civilians scream and drop to the floor. I duck to roll behind a pillar, everything in my body howling for me to run. This isn't a small threat—it's a coordinated attack. Assessing the situation in fragments between bursts of bullets, I count at least eight armed individuals among the crowd, all targeting what I assume are Syndicate officials.

I peek out from cover and fire at the nearest attacker, a lucky shot striking him in the shoulder. The impact knocks us both back, but he doesn't fall as I do. Shit, I wouldn't have expected guns to be so forceful. Before he can lift a weapon to me, I aim from my position on the ground, higher than the armor he must be wearing. Focusing on his exposed neck, I fire, and this time he drops.

I actually hit him!

A sharp pain explodes in my shoulder, pinning me back to the ground. Gritting my teeth, I push to face my attacker—a woman in server's attire, now holding a compact weapon instead of a tray. The first I've seen aside from my mother. A finger hovers just above the trigger as a battle rages through my head. What did I come here for if I'm just going to harm the same people I'm trying to help?

No, that isn't right. This isn't real, I remind myself. *You are one of them in here. You can't save her.*

Tossing aside every instinct I hold close to my heart, I raise my gun and fire twice, catching her once in the arm and chest. As she falls, I shift to new cover, determined to make sense of the situation. I need to identify the number of hostiles and if any are disguised as cowering civilians.

The moment I release my empathy, I'm stunned into stillness. I'm receiving feedback...I can sense the emotional climate of the room as if it were real. Just how advanced is this thing?

The emotions themselves feel dull, compared to what I'm used to, but it's enough to help me distinguish between genuine terror and determination.

From a better vantage point behind an overturned table, I survey the room. The hostile emotions cluster in the crowd, little islands of deadly intent amid unending waves of fear. I count twelve in total. Four are already down; the three I encountered initially and the server I shot. Eight remain.

One hovers near the main entry, guarding the exit. Two are methodically gathering the Syndicate officials while the others are scattered throughout the crowd, picking off anyone who attempts escape or retribution.

I can't take them all directly, not without killing myself and others. There has to be a better approach.

My eyes lock with an attacker across the room—a large man with a rigid manner who subtly directs the others. This is just like chess...focusing on the key player is my way out. Our gazes meet, and in that moment I don't think, I just push my power *hard*, focusing all my will on him.

Kill your allies. They're going to turn on you any moment.

I pour the paranoia into him, wrapping it in emotions centered around betrayal, suspicion, and rage. I make him feel as though his companions have deceived him—that they plan to eliminate him once the attack is complete.

His eyes widen. The weapon in his hand, previously aimed at a weeping official, shakily swings toward the nearest allied attacker. My jaw locks with the effort it takes to keep him feeling how I need as liquid drenches my lashes, splashing over both cheeks. I am wholly unused to others fighting my presence in their body, but he is wrestling with everything he has to gain back control.

After some struggle, I finally manage to tear through his last strand of defiance, and he fires three times in rapid succession, catching his companion in the back. Before the others can react, he swings to the next, ending their life.

Perfect. My arm lifts to wipe my brow before the rivulets of sweat completely blur my vision, only for me to remember I'm wearing this stupid mask. I hate this thing.

Shaking my head, I maintain control of the man, keeping his emotional pressure steady as he redirects his rage, eliminating his team one by one. Four down by his hand now, four more left, including him.

I'm so focused on my controlled attacker, I miss the movement to my left. Pain explodes through my skull as something impacts the side of my head, and my vision splits into fragments. My connection to the man snaps as I fall backward, causing a torrent of nausea to slam into me.

The barrel of a gun points at my face moments before a flash of light and absolute searing pain—

Then nothing.

I gasp for breath as the simulation ends abruptly, finding myself on my back in the familiar gray room. My head throbs with phantom pain that's already fading. I blink rapidly, desperate to reorient myself to reality after the violent end of the simulation.

A few of the others applaud, and someone lets out an appreciative whistle. Pushing to my feet, my body fights a wave of dizziness as I repeatedly swallow the vomit my stomach attempts to purge. The band made the simulation so real that my body is struggling to recognize no actual harm occurred.

"Interesting approach," Elias remarks, stopping in front of me and blocking the rest of the recruits from sight. "Using your empathy to turn an enemy against his allies was creative. Why did you choose him? There were others much closer to you that would have been easier for you to handle."

I nod, working up an acceptable answer through my convulsing abdomen. "He was their leader." Elias' head tilts, and I take it as an eyebrow raised in question. Swallowing, I continue, "If I chose one of the others, the leader would have directed the rest of his people through their next move. I didn't want them to get away, and I wanted them confused. Choosing him meant there was no one to give order, which caused chaos among their group and took the focus off civilians."

The man in front of me hums, crossing his arms. I don't think I'll be able to explain further if he asks, my head still reeling from how impossibly real the simulation felt. From the cold marble to the acrid smell of gunpowder to the searing pain of bullets...it's horrifying and fascinating what can be done in this room. I wonder if they use it as a torture device...

"Take a moment to recover. Simulation sickness affects everyone differently, but the symptoms will pass."

As I step back to join the others, Brenner is called forward for another scenario. I lean against the wall, breathing slow and deep to quell the raging nausea. Eventually the dizziness subsides, though a dull headache lingers. I have a feeling it will stick with me the entire day.

Malcolm leans toward me from his place on my left. "That was impressive with the whole mind control thing," he murmurs, knocking my arm in a strange gesture of comradeship. "Never seen an Empath do that without physical contact." I shrug noncommittally, not wanting to draw attention to my abilities. The less they know about the full extent of what I can do, the better.

The next simulation begins, but my thoughts drift to my experience. The scenario didn't feel random; it's possible it was based on real events. Or perhaps this is just a way for the Syndicate to enforce the importance of their protection above everyone else.

And the woman...

Is it an acknowledgment that women can be dangerous despite being systematically oppressed? Or is it simply meant to emphasize that any woman who steps outside her assigned role becomes a threat to be eliminated?

I shake away the nonsense, refocusing on the present. One thing is crystal clear: this training is designed to create flawless weapons of the Syndicate—Enforcers who react instantly, who perceive threats everywhere, and who eliminate without hesitation.

The perfect soldiers.

And somehow, I need to become one of them without becoming like them. I need to learn their methods without adopting their mindset. Gain their trust while hoping for their downfall.

These men before me have been conditioned from birth to believe in their unity. The greater order. They've never questioned the system that benefits them. How can I hope to under-stand them enough to push back on the Syndicate's will without losing myself in the process?

The headache intensifies, a physical manifestation of the mental strain I'm under.

I will continue to learn and adapt.

And when the time comes, I will use everything they teach me to piss in the face of their *greater order*.

CHAPTER EIGHT
CASSIA

After Elias' training ends, I trail behind the others as we file along the stairwell. My head still throbs from the simulation, though even with the discomfort, I count the steps taken on our journey to the surface and memorize the route. This place feels like a fortress built on secrets—each hallway potentially hiding information that could help me understand what I'm up against.

When we reach the landing, I pause as if catching my breath—a reasonable excuse given my dismal performance in physical training yesterday. From here, I inspect the railings to the lower levels. It's difficult to discern how many floors there are due to the lack of lighting, but there's definitely more than I had thought.

A voice drifts from somewhere below, too distant to make out words. The sound sinks into the concrete, creating a hollow echo that struggles to crawl up the stairwell. I strain to catch more, but Vito clears his throat behind me, indicating I've lingered too long.

"Move it, Ashford."

I nod once before ascending. By the time we reach the main floor, my lungs are heaving and the others have already dispersed to their next training. The time on the wall taunts me, indicating a mere three minutes before I must be in Kellen's classroom. My legs protest as their pace quickens, navigating the maze of corridors with efficiency.

Kellen stands alone in the classroom, rearranging some materials on a central podium, unaware of my presence. For a moment, I'm frozen in the doorway, staring at his broad back and the precise, deliberate movements of his hands. There's something fascinating about watching people when they don't realize they're being observed—the small habits and gestures they display reveal more about them than their public personas ever could.

This is the first time I've seen any of the leaders without other recruits around. It's an opportunity to examine, but it's also dangerous to be caught staring, so I step into the room, ensuring my footfalls are audible enough to announce my presence.

The leader's gaze flicks up, his eyes finding mine through the narrow slits in our masks. "Ashford," he acknowledges with a slight nod. "Early."

"Yes, sir." Early? There isn't one minute left before everyone is expected to be here.

The lecture hall is cavernous compared to our small group size—a wide semicircle of tiered seating built into concrete, rising from a central area. There are no desks, just seats molded into the risers with not even a finger width of space between them. The ceiling soars at least twenty feet overhead, and soft panels line the walls.

I choose a seat in the front row, directly facing the podium. From this position, I'll have the clearest view of whatever Kellen presents, and—more importantly—the rest of the group will sit behind me where I won't be bothered by their scrutiny.

Hyperawareness settles in my hands as I sit. The setting is

a bit awkward; while I'm forced to lean in a relaxed position, the atmosphere suggests that more rigid posture is required. But I've no idea how to balance the two...Perhaps I should have sat behind the others.

I try setting them on my legs, then shift them to my sides, then back to my legs, unable to find something comfortable that doesn't scream lazy and inattentive. Each movement feels unnatural.

Most of the men at breakfast had lounged back with an easy confidence, arms crossed or stretched wide, legs spread an annoying distance from each other. Sucking in a cool breath, I mimic the casual sprawl.

Yuck.

It's exposing—as if my only purpose is taking up more space than my body needs. Like I'm screaming my presence at every bystander rather than trying to disappear into it. But before I can cringe and adjust for the ninth time, I remind myself this is natural for males, even in other species; where they expose themselves, marking territory and establishing dominance through the most basic displays. This bizarre body language must serve a similar purpose for human men too, as an assertion of space and importance.

Strange creatures, men. I don't recall these patterns with my father or Lachlan, but I'm quickly accepting that nothing I learned about social etiquette in my home will apply to this new world I've leaped into. There was no competition in our home, no hierarchy to maintain, solidifying my dread that I need to stop comparing the two and find my own way here.

Tapping a heel to ease the electricity buzzing through me, I watch Kellen as he continues arranging his materials, the silence stretching taut between us. Much like with Elias in the transport, the quiet is almost comforting in the absence of forced conversation. Familiar, even.

Footsteps echo from the hallway, and moments later the other recruits file in: Nash, Darius, Brenner, Corin, and Silas. They enter as a pack, informal words flowing between them as if they've known each other for years rather than a couple days. They likely bonded over dinner last night, which is not something I'm going to achieve unless I skip some meals.

Befriending others will not keep me here, though, so what is the point in making the effort? I'm content to be on the outside of their bubble for now.

Instead of spreading throughout the available seating, they cluster together in the middle rows, leaving a conspicuous gap around me. Not one of them chooses to sit beside or even near me. I want to feel embarrassed, but I'm only relieved. On one hand, their avoidance stings the deepest parts of my heart. On the other, it means fewer opportunities to notice something wrong about me.

Kellen peers up, his eyes briefly meeting mine before scanning the rest of the group. I think he mutters 'never change' under his breath, but the words are so soft I can't be certain my ears aren't fooling me.

"Fundamentals of mission planning," he begins without preamble, his voice carrying effortlessly through the space. "Analyzing intelligence. Risk assessment." Each phrase drifts with the burden of experience behind it. "Before I begin, I want to gauge what you already know about these topics, so I can tailor our training accordingly."

His arms cross, and I'm suddenly fixated on how the uniform fabric stretches across his shoulders, how it tapers at his waist. The muscles in his forearms tense visibly when he focuses on the back of the room, where the others have begun whispering among themselves like children.

A strange sensation flutters through my abdomen, a tight pressure that spreads warmth along my neck. I shift in my seat, uncomfortable with the feeling yet unable to ignore it. The physiological response suggests attraction, with subtle changes in my heartrate and blood flow, but experiencing it is bizarre.

I've touched myself before, exploring sensations described in the forbidden romance novels I love. Those books were always more thrilling than the bland approved texts—full of emotions and physical experiences I could only imagine. Those reactions were not this, though; more curiosity sated by clinical exploration of my own body's responses.

I study Kellen carefully, noting details I hadn't registered before. His hair is close-cropped at the back where a portion of it is visible, dark but not black. His eyes reflect a deep gray each time he raises them where the light can catch—cool like a storm, but sharp and intelligent. He's rolled his sleeves a bit, exposing the map of veins rising along his arms, more pronounced in his current position.

It's an odd thing to find attractive, yet my mind does. There's something fascinating about those lines, about the evidence of blood and life flowing just beneath the surface.

Would his skin be rougher than mine? Warmer? My finger-tips tingle at the idea of running them through his hair. I've never felt the texture of a stranger's skin or warmth of their body heat—

These thoughts are dangerous. Inappropriate. And yet they flow through my mind unbidden, impossible to contain.

"ASHFORD!"

I jolt in my seat, heart pounding as reality crashes back. Kellen stands directly in front of me, close enough that I have to tilt my head back to see him. My mouth dries. Was I just fanta-sizing about my instructor while he was speaking? Right in front of him?

Yes. Yes, I was.

Laughter ripples from behind me, and someone calls out,

"Sleeping with your eyes open, Ashford?" More snickers follow.

I ignore them, focusing on my leader's impassive mask. His head tilts to one side, and I imagine his brow raising behind the black barrier.

"Were you paying attention?" he asks, voice measured and low.

I should lie. Nod and repeat whatever he just said; but my mind is blank, and I'm lost in the strange sensation of being caught in such an intimate daydream. So I swallow thick saliva and shake my head mutely.

He leans closer, voice dropping further until only a breath of a whisper greets my ears. "What were you paying attention to, then, recruit?"

Stars kill me. I would be surprised if he didn't already know the answer...his voice captures something rough and primal, a shiver racing through my spine that has nothing to do with fear. My heart hammers against each rib, blood rushing to my face beneath the blessed mask. There's no way I'm admitting I was mentally cataloging his body like some specimen to study.

My head shakes again, words failing me.

His arms uncross as he shifts to grip the armrests on either side of my chair, inclining his body until we're a mere inch from each other. This close, I catch his scent—clean sweat and something sharper, like pine and metal melded together. Little obsidian flecks near his pupils catch my attention before he speaks again.

"Let your thoughts stray again and you're out," he mumbles just barely above a whisper.

I manage a single nod, holding my breath to steady it.

Kellen straightens, addressing me at normal volume. "Ashford, what do you know about today's topics?"

I scramble through the library of my mind, searching for

something—*anything*—suitable to say. My thoughts are still scattered, thrown into disarray by the proximity of his body to mine and the lingering embarrassment of before. The recruits behind me keep muttering, their commentary a distracting buzz that makes focus impossible.

I'm furious with myself. This is the kind of training I should excel at—mental exercises, strategic thinking, the application of knowledge. Instead, I'm sitting here like an idiot, speechless, because I can't control my physical responses to a man I barely know and who cannot ever know me in return.

Then it dawns on me—this is part of his lesson. Focus under pressure. The ability to think clearly while distracted or intimidated. Perhaps my incapability to answer is exactly what Kellen wants to demonstrate.

I speak before my head flusters more. "I cannot think of any relevant information at this time, sir." Though not confident, my voice is steady and unwavering.

Kellen goes still, as if my response surprised him. After a moment, he hums and steps back to his podium.

The men behind me erupt in fresh laughter, and a metallic taste stains my tongue from where I'm biting it hard enough to pierce through. "Do you know fucking anything?" one of them shouts. "Why are you even here?"

I remain silent, my cheeks burning so bad I'm worried the skin there will have scorch marks later. This is worse than I'd anticipated. Not only am I failing to blend in, I'm actively making myself a target for ridicule.

Our leader mercifully shifts his attention, addressing the group at large. "Who else can offer some insight into mission planning basics?"

The others volunteer answers I should have identified immediately. From simple security protocols, information verification methods, and risk mitigation strategies; I berate myself for each one I missed.

As Kellen launches into his lecture, I force myself to focus, mentally recording every word. He covers useful topics, and his teaching style is direct but thorough, building complex concepts from simple foundations.

Despite my earlier humiliation, I'm drawn to the material. There's a certain elegance to the way Kellen deconstructs strategic thinking into its component parts, demonstrating how seemingly disparate pieces of information can be assembled into a cohesive approach.

I'm particularly fascinated by his explanation of intelligence analysis—how to distinguish reliable information from misinformation and identify patterns across multiple reports. Basically, how to recognize what isn't being said as much as what is. These are skills I'll need if I'm to gather useful information during my time here.

The stress that had been building in my chest gradually eases as I sink into the familiar comfort of learning. Absorbing knowledge and processing information is something I know how to do. Something I'm good at.

After an hour of lecture, Kellen shifts the class structure. "Now for some practical application," he announces. "I'm going to divide you into pairs and present a scenario. Your task is to develop a mission plan based on what you know while accounting for what you don't."

He assigns our pairs, poor Darius drawing the short stick to be stuck with me. I glance at my new partner, trying to read his reaction behind the mask. His shoulders tighten, but he doesn't openly protest.

Kellen distributes tablets containing the scenario details, and we split off to work. Darius reluctantly sits beside me, maintaining as much distance as the seats allow.

"Let's just get this over with," he mutters, leaning away from me as if proximity might be contagious of something deadly.

I scan our tablet, noting our case: a suspected rebel hideout in an abandoned mining facility near the border between Pyrem and Ailridge. The objective is to confirm the presence of rebels, assess their numbers and resources, and if possible, capture their leader for interrogation. The complication is the facility has only been partially mapped, with unknown numbers of access points and escape routes.

"We should start by—"

"I know how to plan a mission," Darius cuts me off.

I bite back a sharp retort. This isn't about my pride; it's about surviving to accomplish what I came here for. My reply is even. "Fine. What's your approach?"

To my surprise, Darius' plan is logical and thorough. He suggests a nighttime operation to maximize the element of surprise, with scouts positioned at known exits while a small team infiltrates through the main entrance. It's solid, conventional thinking.

But something about the scenario nags at me. "Why would rebels hide in a location that's already on Enforcer maps? Even partially mapped seems too risky."

My partner pauses. "Good point."

We spend the next twenty minutes developing our plan, and I'm pleasantly surprised to find we agree on most aspects. Darius isn't the mindless brute I initially took him for. His approach is methodical, with a clear preference for logic over emotional reactions. He considers my suggestions with genuine attention, nodding when I make an argument he hadn't considered.

By the time Kellen calls for us to present our plans, we've developed an approach that differs significantly from conventional tactics. When the other two groups share their strategies —both involving direct assaults through the main entrance—I mark the flaws immediately. They've taken the scenario at face value, missing the subtle cues embedded within.

When it's our turn, Darius nudges me. "You explain it. It was mostly your idea anyway," he says in a neutral tone.

I clear my throat, uncertain how to pitch my voice low while remaining loud enough for the room to hear. "We determined the scenario itself contains a misdirection," I begin, proud that my tone holds without cracking. "The mapped portion of the facility is likely a trap—the fact that Enforcers know about the location at all suggests the rebels want us to invade that spot."

I explain our theory, how the real rebel base is elsewhere, with the mining facility serving as either a decoy or an ambush site. Our plan focuses on extensive reconnaissance before any infiltration, followed by a minimal-presence operation designed to gather information rather than engage directly.

"The objective isn't to capture the threat, it's to find where they're actually hiding by tracking their movements to and from this decoy location."

When I finish, Kellen sits for a long moment. "Why did your team take this approach?"

I explain, "The scenario had inconsistencies. This sentence mentions recent activity but doesn't specify what kind. This paragraph discusses the mining facility's history but omits *when* it was abandoned. And this map shows six known exits, but the text only references four. These discrepancies suggest deliberate misinformation—either from rebel sources or within the intelligence chain itself."

The leader nods slowly. "Good," he states before discussing the scenario in more depth.

That single word of approval sends an unexpected thrill

through me. It's ridiculous how much I suddenly crave his recognition, but I can't deny the warm satisfaction settling in my bones. Even if it's just one word, it's more approval than I've received from anyone since arriving here.

My satisfaction lasts precisely until the end of our session, when knowledge of what comes next reappears: four hours of physical training with the Commander.

The afternoon sun lashes down mercilessly as I stand at the edge of the outdoor yard, staring at the course laid before me. Yesterday's was difficult; this one is impossible. The walls are higher, the beams narrower, and the pits beneath them are bottomless in the harsh shadows cast by midday sun.

Between obstacles, large open spaces are marked for running, and stacks of weights sit ominously at either end of a central balance beam that spans a pit of mud. My stomach lurches at the sight, regretting the lunch it consumed.

A grim thought occurs—what happens if I vomit? We're not permitted to remove our masks here, and I doubt I could make it to a bathroom in time. The mental image of being sick inside my mask makes me gag, which only strengthens the fear of vomiting. Disgusting.

Arayik strides into the yard, every line of his large body radiating the fury I keep my power from exploring. I shouldn't be shocked at this point...rage seems his natural state of being.

The three other recruits assigned to his afternoon group—Finnick, Calder, and Brenner—arrive shortly after me, standing with the wary alertness of prey animals in predator territory.

"Today we're doing high-intensity interval training," the Commander announces. The three men groan in unison while I stand silent, having not one idea what this kind of training entails. If these hardened recruits are griping, it must be brutal —though I've noticed these men complain about everything from lukewarm food to slightly damp towels, so perhaps their discomfort isn't the most reliable gauge.

Arayik doesn't wait for response, stomping to the head of the obstacle course before beginning. His movements are fluid and powerful as he scales the first wall, using the rope as leverage rather than relying solely on his arms. He crosses the narrow beams with precision, navigates the tunnels with efficient grace, and completes the running section with long, measured strides.

When he reaches the weights, he squats, bending from the knees rather than the hips, and lifts two bulky disks as if they weigh nothing. His balance on the beam is once again perfect— each foot placed deliberately in front of the other as he traverses the twenty feet of it, mud gurgling beneath.

The entire demonstration takes less than five minutes, and Arayik isn't even winded when he finishes. I marked each point of his technique, knowing I will not match his strength or endurance, but I can mimic his form, and focus on efficiency over power.

"You will complete this course as many times as possible in the next two hours. Begin."

My mouth drops. The entire course? Multiple times? *For two hours...*

There's no possible chance I will make it through the day. I couldn't even finish one circuit yesterday without wheezing like I was dying.

I'm going to be kicked out today. I'm about to fail so thoroughly that even Arayik's fascination with tormenting me won't be enough to keep me here. I'll be sent home in disgrace, back to hiding in my parents' house, reading about a world that will never know change.

The thought fills me with a different kind of fire. I didn't leave my family, cut my damn hair, and risk everything just to fail now. I'm here for a purpose.

And if my mother could endure being violated and dehumanized in a facility for years and still find ways to smile, then I can endure this.

Plus, I need information. Who the people are outside the perimeter; how many women they've helped escape; how they're evading Enforcer surveillance. I know this building must contain things that could aid their operation more efficiently. I just need to stay long enough to find it.

"Move!" Arayik's voice cracks across the yard, stabbing through my head.

My body responds before my mind fully registers the command. I sprint toward the first wall, dust kicking up beneath my boots. Yesterday's training has left my muscles sore and stiff, but I push through the pain, focusing on the rope dangling from the top of the wall. Leaping for it, my hands wrap around the rough fiber and pull with everything they have. Both arms scream in protest, but I haul myself up inch by painful inch, imitating Arayik's technique of walking the wall as I pull.

When I grunt and scramble over the top corner, I pause to catch my breath, surveying the course ahead. The others are advancing through the obstacles with varying degrees of skill. My eyes widen as Finnick slips on a balance beam and plummets into the pit below with a startled yelp.

Nope, nope, nope. Not falling in there today. "Focus," I mutter to myself, the word muffled.

Each obstacle needs to be approached with calculated precision. Where I lack raw physical strength, I make up for in strategy. The Commander's demonstration provided a template, and I follow it as closely as possible, adjusting for my smaller frame and limited muscle mass. At one point, I slow my pace, allowing Calder to overtake me. It's better to appear average than to draw attention by excelling or failing compared to the others. I need Arayik to forget me.

After completing the climbing, crawling, and balancing sections, I reach the running portion. The open field that looked manageable from a distance stretches before me like an endless nightmare. My lungs already burn, and the prospect of running makes my legs tremble.

I begin at what I think is a reasonable pace, only to remember I've never ran before. Not properly. The times I moved with speed through my home were brief sprints, nothing like sustained running over a distance. I've made a critical error in beginning too fast. Pacing is necessary during endurance activities, though I know even that wouldn't have helped me as my lungs are gasping for breath after a mere minute. Shit, *it burns.*

Sure, I make it through the required laps, but by that time I'm wheezing so hard I can barely stand. Dropping to my knees, hands brace against the packed earth as I fight to control my breathing. The mask traps much of my exhaled breaths as they come and go too quickly, creating an environment that makes each inhalation feel inadequate.

"Move it, stragglers!" Arayik barks from somewhere nearby. He doesn't single me out by name, but I know the command is directed primarily at me.

My arms quiver as I rise, the muscles above my breasts blazing with fatigue. I stagger to the final portion of the course —the balance beam with its impossible weights. I don't think I could even walk across the beam without them right now. Another recruit is midway on the beam, with the only sets of weights remaining on the other side. I'll have to circle to the opposite end and wait for him to finish.

Finally, some reprieve.

Everyone else has finished, staring in this direction, waiting for me to struggle across. I'm determined to make it through, but muscle fatigue and determination do not fuel each other, and the probability of me falling flat on my face in the nasty mud is high.

When Brenner steps off, I position myself at the end. The weights sit on either side of me, the number forty displayed on each. I can assume what that means, but at this point, I don't care...I do not wish to lift forty *anything* at the moment.

Bend at the knees. Don't pull a muscle. And absolutely do not fall.

Simple.

Spine straight, I lower myself, engaging my core as both hands grip the weights. After three breaths, I heave upward.

The weights barely budge.

My teeth creak when I pull harder, straining until my vision spots at the edges. Slowly, painfully, the weights rise from the ground. My entire body shakes with effort, but I manage to lift them to waist height, whimpering behind the safety of my mask.

I can't do this.

I have to do this.

My mind blanks, blocking out everything else. There is only the beam, the weights, and the next step forward.

By some stars-given miracle, I reach the midpoint of the beam. A surge of triumph floods through me, distracting me just enough that I lose focus for half a second. My foot slips sideways as both knees surrender, and suddenly I'm falling.

The world spins as I plummet into the squelching pit, landing hard with a cry when one of the weights strikes my ribs. The impact drives every bit of air from my lungs in a painful woosh, leaving me gasping for the smallest of breaths. Mud coats my mask, pressing against my mouth when it slides inside, my poor eyes suffocating under a layer of the goo.

I roll onto my back, groaning and swiping a hand through my eyes, only to find my view of the sky blocked by a looming figure. The Commander stands at the edge of the pit, watching me. With the sun behind him, I can't discern whether he's angry or amused.

He answers my internal question a moment later. "You're slow and weak."

The comment is so matter-of-fact, so perfectly aligned with my own self-assessment, that I can't help it—I laugh. The sound bubbles from somewhere beneath the pain and exhaustion, surprising me as much as it seems to surprise him. It's a genuine laugh, albeit slightly hysterical, the kind that hurts my dry throat and shakes my aching ribs.

When I finally contain myself, my arms drop limply to the mud. "Yeah, well, we can't all be you, buddy."

Collecting every last drop of will I have, I push myself to a sitting position before clambering to my feet. Fuck, my uniform has transformed to a rusty brown instead of black. I'll need to wash it—and myself—thoroughly before training tomorrow. The prospect of navigating the communal showers is a dreadful one.

"Do you find something funny?" Arayik asks, his voice tight with unsuppressed irritation.

"Actually, yes," I reply on a staggered breath, not deigning to elaborate further. The vagueness is petty, yet it's impossible to resist needling him. His entire body tenses, muscles coiling like springs under his uniform.

"I buried my sister because of someone who was as slow and weak as you, so I'm failing to understand what you think is amusing. Care to explain?" What does it say about me that hearing each clipped syllable makes me happier than I've been all day?

Then there's the comment about his sister...quite untasteful for him to bring that up when I'm finally enjoying myself. The human part of me wants to offer sympathies, but I can offer them to her myself. In private. He doesn't deserve anything of the sort.

"No, thanks," I answer, allowing a hint of cheerfulness to color my tone. If he's going to kick me out, I could care less about how I speak to him.

I've never considered myself particularly rebellious. With my parents, obedience was a given, as I was always grateful for the risks they shouldered to keep me safe. But something about this pain-in-the-ass man drags out a defiant streak I didn't know I possessed.

Well, my parents never lowered themselves to the subjugation of women or the expected cruelty of upholding a system that values control over humanity.

Every organ in my body cringes when his eyes narrow. "Tell me, Ashford—what's the scan sequence when traveling through a provincial checkpoint?"

My stomach flips. What an odd question. I was under the impression Elias and Kellen managed all our mental training, but I do understand why it would be important during physical efforts as well.

I assume this is something any traveling Enforcer—or messenger, I realize—should know. Lachlan would tease me for days for not immediately knowing the answer.

But I do know... "Badge swipe, obviously," I answer.

Arayik's features flatten as he stands silent for a moment, heat radiating from his body, before spinning on his heel and walking away. Relief mingles with a strange sense of victory—

I've managed to irritate him without crossing the line into insubordination severe enough to warrant dismissal.

I'm playing a dangerous game; trying to prove my worth as a recruit while maintaining just enough resistance to preserve my sense of self. Strange, though, that he's thrown others from the team for less...perhaps I'm not as useless as he would have me believe. My power may be the only thing keeping me here right now.

Wheezing in a deep breath full of mud and sweat, I scoop the area around my eyes again, cleaning it the best I can and begin the long trudge back to the start of the course. There are still hours of training ahead before I can rest.

My body protests every movement, muscles trembling with fatigue and overexertion. But a flame burns steady in my chest —determination fueled by rage at the system I'm infiltrating and hope for what I might accomplish within it.

I will survive this. I will learn from it. Then I will use everything they teach me against them.

CHAPTER NINE

CASSIA

The drop to my bunk is like sinking in thick tar—not that I would know what that's like—every muscle crying out in protest. My body feels like a patchwork of bruises sewn together with threads of unending exhaustion. I'm a marionette with frayed strings, a vessel filled with elastic pain that snaps with each tiny movement.

Stars above, I never knew a person could hurt this much and still be conscious. Or alive.

Sleep beckons me, promising sweet oblivion from this agony, regardless that the mattress might as well be made from rocks for all the comfort it provides my battered muscles. I want nothing more than to surrender to it.

Unfortunately, I must shower first.

The thought alone requires more effort than I can muster. Showering means standing upright. Standing upright means engaging muscles that are currently staging a full rebellion against their owner.

Not to mention the risk of encountering other recruits. Men. Naked. The thought sends a fresh wave of anxiety through my already overtaxed system.

I can only delay so long. The now-dried grime on my skin is

like a second layer of clothing, one that's gradually bonding to my actual flesh. My best chance at privacy will be to wait until the others have retired for the night, so that's what I'll do.

At least they gave us soap—simple, unscented bars that do the job. Enforcer efficiency extends even to personal hygiene.

Shifting to more appropriate activities, I scan the food I've hauled back. It's a veritable feast by my standards—double portions of the protein stew they were serving, three bread rolls dense enough to be used as weapons, and a small mountain of steamed vegetables that smell a bit medicinal. Plus extra water.

With a groan that sounds more animal than human, I force myself vertical. The room spins a moment before stabilizing, and I drink half the water in desperate gulps. As I eat, I admire the items I managed to sneak out of the dining hall.

The best thing about having no companions means others are rarely looking for or at me.

I'd noticed a small container of ice wrapped in cloth near where the meals are prepared. I pilfered a handful of mint leaves, two small spoonfuls of salt, and a single slice of aloe from a potted plant in the corner. The staff would have noticed if I'd taken more, but these items are exactly what I need to prepare a simple salve.

My fingers, clumsy with fatigue, work to prepare what my mother taught me years ago.

"Mint contains menthol," I murmur to myself, grinding the leaves between the back of a stolen fork at the bottom of my water cup. "Menthol activates cold-sensitive TRPM8 receptors in skin cells, producing a cooling sensation that blocks pain signals." The mint releases oils, encasing my small room with a sharp, clean scent that calms my nerves. I melt just enough ice to create a paste with the mint. "Salt draws out inflammation," I continue, adding a precise amount to my mixture. "It creates an osmotic gradient that pulls excess fluid from swollen tissues."

The aloe enters last. "Aloe contains ecemannan, a complex carbohydrate with anti-inflammatory properties, plus enzymes that reduce swelling and stimulate blood flow to damaged tissues." I really need to stop talking to myself.

After stirring the mixture, it thickens—not the ideal salve, but it will serve.

The process drags up unwanted thoughts of home. It's not that I don't wish to think about my family, it's that it *hurts*.

What has their reality been like since I left? They must be worried sick while keeping Lachlan hidden, afraid he'll be seen and reveal there are two of him. What story would they have concocted to explain his absence to neighbors or his employer? I didn't specify where I was leaving to, only that I was...

And my mother. Stars, I'd be surprised if she was sleeping at all. I imagine her lying awake at night envisioning all the terrible fates that might befall her daughter.

I press the heels of my palms against my eyes, stuffing away the pressure that's built behind them. I knew leaving would be hard for me. I didn't fully accept how it would devastate them, and the horror of that realization settles over me, causing a tear to slip free. Followed by another.

I swipe at them angrily. This is pointless. I'm tired and overwhelmed, my emotions bubbling too close to the surface after suppressing them so hard. When I'm stressed or overstimulated, these feelings rise like flooding water, threatening to drown me. I've always been this way, though I don't have the time for this right now.

I suppose it's better to let it out here, instead of risking a breakdown in front of the others. I allow myself a few more silent tears, vexed at my weakness while acknowledging its necessity.

My head whips around to a sharp knock at my door.

I freeze, my heart suddenly hammering against my ribs. For an endless moment, I can't move, can't breathe or think.

The knock comes again, louder this time.

"Open up, recruit," a voice demands. Elias?

My mind races through possibilities, each worse than the last. Room inspection? I've been too careless and someone saw me take the supplies for my salve, so he's here to drag me away. Shit.

My hands scramble to hide the evidence of my identity—shoving my notebook and the salve under my blanket, wiping my face dry, and gathering my hair into bun.

The mask goes on last, and I yell, "One moment," the sound strained.

Everything's in order. Nothing feminine visible. Just a recruit's sparse quarters, messy like any other male's would be.

Oh stars, they know I'm not Lachlan. I'm never going to hug my family again; I'll be tagged and forced to breed, my body used until it breaks.

But there's nowhere to escape...the only exit is the door I desperately do not want to open.

My hand trembles as I unlock it and yank the handle before I can change my mind. Best to just get it over with quickly before the leaders' rough hands break the door down.

Except there's only Elias standing in the corridor, arms at his sides in a non-threatening posture. He's not flanked by guards or holding restraints. He's just...waiting.

The relief nearly buckles my knees.

His eyes survey me bottom to top, glimpsing over my shoulder before meeting mine. I'm not large enough to block his view without looking like a lunatic.

"I wanted to check on you," he remarks, his voice carrying a light note of concern. "You seemed frantic back in the dining hall."

Did I? I thought I'd maintained my composure reasonably well, given I was surrounded by hundreds of unmasked men and terrified of discovery.

"I'm not fond of crowds." I shrug, hoping the gesture reads as masculine nonchalance rather than a nervous tick.

He hums, head tilting as he studies me once more. His arms cross over his broad chest, the material of his uniform pulling taught across his shoulders. I sense he's debating whether to ask something.

"How are you finding your accommodations?" he finally asks.

What an odd question. Is this some kind of test?

My answer is brief and direct. "Fine."

Elias' brow rises behind the mask. "Do you ever take your mask off?"

The question scratches at my sternum. So he does know... He's been baiting me, waiting for me to make a mistake, and now he's caught me.

My hesitation stretches a heartbeat too long as panic bubbles in my throat.

But the leader nods toward my room before surprising me. "You are permitted to remove it in your quarters."

Oh. *Oh.*

"Yes," I blurt, sounding far too eager. I moderate my tone. "I had it off before you knocked."

He hums again, allowing more silence to stretch between us. I'm not sure whether to think I'm done for or just accept that I'm projecting my fears onto his neutral observation.

"Take a walk with me, Ashford."

It's not a request. But is it an invitation or a trap? Something tells me Elias doesn't play with his kills, and if he hasn't apprehended me yet, I don't believe that's what he's here for.

Stop being so fucking delusional.

With a nod, my feet carry me forward as I pull the door closed behind me. The room locks automatically with my thumbprint—a small mercy, as it means no one can search my quarters while I'm gone. Unless they have some way to override the lock, which they probably do. These are Enforcers, after all.

The illusion of privacy is just that.

Elias whirls the opposite direction from the training areas, forcing me to stumble before following. Trailing behind one of my leaders to an unknown destination is more intimidating than being surrounded by hundreds of men in the dining hall. As much as I hate the crowd, it's easy to be anonymous there. Here, I'm alone with a man who has the power to destroy everything in my life with a single word.

"How are you adapting to training?" He glances at me, his pace unhurried.

What's with all the questions?

He needs an answer, though I'm careful not to elaborate too much. "It's challenging."

"Most find it so," he agrees with a nod. "Especially those without prior military or combat experience." A pointed remark about my performance, I'm sure. "The Commander has high expectations, and he doesn't lower them for anyone."

"I've noticed."

Elias chuckles, the sound warm and unexpectedly genuine. "Arayik's methods are harsh, but effective. Those who survive his training emerge stronger."

If they survive. I allow the implication to hang between us unspoken.

We enter a corridor I haven't yet seen, this one less traveled by the lack of scuff marks. I'm led to a stairwell, one more narrow than the one we used for the simulation this morning.

"These stairs are reserved for leadership," he explains as we begin descending. "Don't mention them to anyone."

My mouth speaks before my brain can stop it. "I don't talk to anyone."

My companion only laughs softly. "I've noticed."

We move the stairs in silence for several moments, my muscles screaming, broken by Elias' need for more conversation. "Your abilities during training today were impressive. I've rarely seen an Empath project their power without physical contact until you, but to project it across such distance to multiple subjects simultaneously is outstanding."

I tense. This is dangerous territory.

"When did you discover you could do that?" he asks with a genuine curiosity.

I hadn't prepared an explanation for this. The truth is I've had decades of solitude to practice, with nothing to do but read and experiment with my power.

I can't say that out loud.

"I practiced a lot in my free time." A partial truth. "I just... tried projecting it one day, and it worked. So I kept pushing, strengthening it like a muscle."

My eyes nearly weep when we reach a landing and he leads me through a door into a dark, empty hallway. Our footsteps sound unnaturally loud, mine more so. It's impossible to hide the toll today has taken on me.

"Your thought process during the simulation was especially notable," Elias continues. "Getting a hostile to turn on his own allies? That was creative."

A strange flush inches up my neck at the praise, to which I immediately chastise myself for seeking approval from one of *them*. But there's something about Elias that makes it hard to maintain my anger and fear.

"What is your power?"

Stars, Cassia, can you not ruin everything? Who asks that?

He glances at me with wide eyes at the direct question. "I'm a Revealer."

Ah. That explains my unease as Revealers can detect lies. I'll need to be especially careful not to let him touch me.

"That must be useful in your position." I'm going to punch myself.

He huffs a breath. "It has its applications, though it's limited. I can only tell if someone is being truthful—not what the actual truth is if they're lying."

We stop before an unmarked door, identical to most of the building. Elias faces me, and I realize I've missed something he's said.

"Ashford?" His head tilts.

"My apologies, sir," I spit out quickly. "Long day. What did you ask?"

Sir? Please, someone, shoot me.

He only laughs, eyes crinkling at the sides. "I asked if you would consider doing something for me."

My stomach drops as every thought spirals to a dark place. I'm not sure I want to know what he could ask that requires this level of privacy.

"Sure."

"As you may have observed, the men here can be... emotional at times," he says, tone slightly sardonic. "They allow baser instincts to override their better judgment, especially in close quarters like these."

That's putting it mildly. From what I've witnessed, men are constantly posturing, challenging each other, picking fights over nothing.

"I'd like you to use your ability to help defuse situations when tempers flare." I adjust my stance, interested. "Not only would it prevent unnecessary injuries, but it would give you valuable practice with your power. I'm curious to see how far you can develop it."

I blink behind the shadows of my mask, nonplussed. This is the last thing I expected. He's so impressed by my abilities that he wants me to help maintain order? I'd essentially be acting as a covert peacekeeper.

"You want me to use my power...officially?" It's impossible to keep the surprise from my tone.

"Not officially," he corrects, gesturing to the space separating us. "Between us. Your intervention should be subtle enough that others won't realize what you're doing."

I'm not upset at the request. In fact, an unexpected swell of pride that he values my abilities enough to suggest this rises. His praise feels genuine, not manipulative.

"I can do that."

Satisfied with my easy agreement, he twists the knob on the door and walks inside. "Come in, there's something I want to show you."

I follow him into the room, pausing just inside the threshold. The space is a smaller version of the training simulator from earlier—bare walls, minimal lighting, stale air. Elias walks to a wall panel and presses a square tile that's a lighter shade of gray than the others.

The tile flips open to reveal a control panel with a display screen and several buttons. His fingers move across it with practiced ease.

"Sometimes I find this place overwhelming." He doesn't look at me, but I understand his words fine. "Too many people, too many emotions, too much everything. This room helps me when I need to get away."

Before I can ask what he means, the space transforms. Bare walls fade away, replaced by a vast expanse of water stretching to the horizon. The floor beneath my boots shifts, becoming soft, yielding sand. Waves lap gently at my ankles, and I swear the water's cool touch wades through my boots. My breath catches. The simulation is incredibly realistic, far more immersive than the training scenarios. Waves thud with rhythmic crashes and birds cry in the distance. A sea breeze carries the scent of salt and something rich, organic—seaweed, perhaps. The warmth of sunlight falls across my shoulders.

It's beautiful.

More than any image I've seen in books or my own head. The water stretches endlessly, meeting a sky so vibrantly blue it makes my chest ache. The colors are more brilliant than anything I've experienced—deep azure water topped with white-capped waves, golden sand, and distant green cliffs.

"What do you think?" Elias asks, his voice cutting through my awe.

I whirl to answer and freeze, stunned by the sight of him standing there with his mask removed. His features glow in warm golden light, revealing a face far younger than I expected. His eyes are a clear hazel-green, set above high cheekbones and a straight nose. His mouth—curved in a slight smile—has a full lower lip that pairs well with the soft lines of his jaw.

"Put that back on!" I hiss, glancing frantically around for possible observers. "Someone could see you!"

His smile widens, revealing a flash of white teeth and a tiny dimple in his left cheek. Something strange and fluttery happens in my stomach at the sight.

"There are no scanners or cameras in this room." His voice is lighter, more relaxed without the mask. "That's why I come here. To breathe freely for a while."

I want to ask what he means by scanners, but his casual reference suggests it's something I should already know about. I keep my questions to myself, turning back to the simulated ocean to hide my confusion and desperation to stare.

"You can remove yours too, if you'd like," he offers. "No one will see."

"I-I'd rather not," I stammer, shifting in my stance. "In case someone walks in."

He doesn't press the issue, which I appreciate. Instead, he reaches into his pocket and pulls out a small device that resembles a flattened cylinder with a display screen.

"This is keyed to the room's controls," he explains, holding it out to me. "You can change the scenery, adjust environmental factors, even add or remove elements."

I grab the remote, our fingers brushing briefly in the exchange. An electric tingle travels through my arm at the contact, surprising me.

Stars, I never realized how much I needed my parents' hugs until now. I'm starved for any kind of connection.

"The simulation can engage all five senses," he continues, oblivious to my reaction. "You can adjust them individually. For instance, if you wanted stronger wind..." He leans in, sliding his finger across a portion of the screen. Immediately, the breeze intensifies, gusting into my mask with enough force that I raise a hand to protect my eyes. The sensation is extraordinary—I can feel the pressure, the temperature, even tiny droplets of sea spray.

A startled laugh escapes me, echoed by Elias' deeper chuckle. For a moment, we're just two people sharing a marvel, all hierarchy and suspicion temporarily suspended.

My companion moves back a few steps. "You know the way back. Don't tell anyone about this place, and try not to stay too long, but...you're welcome to use it when you need to."

I watch, my head tilting as he walks along the shore, his direction diagonal toward what should be open water. Pausing, he reaches for something I can't see, and I realize with a start that he's opening the door—which is not near where I thought it was.

"Ashford." He pauses at the threshold. "You'd be a great asset to the team. I know the Commander isn't fond of you, but keep trying. He respects effort."

Before I can formulate a response, he slips his mask back on and disappears through the doorway, leaving me alone in this simulated paradise.

Perfect I will never be. But effort? That I can give.

Focusing on the vast ocean once more, I drink in its beauty. The weight of the day's training lifts slightly from my shoulders as the waves continue their endless rhythm against the shore. With the remote in my hand, I experiment with different settings, marveling at technology that can create such vivid sensory experiences.

Is this what the world was like before the Collapse? Before the Syndicate's walls and restrictions? Did people simply walk upon beaches whenever they wished, feeling the sand between their toes and the sun upon their faces?

The injustice of it all hits me anew.

At the touch of a button, the beach dissolves, replaced by a dense forest. Towering trees stretch toward a canopy so thick the sky barely shines through. The air becomes cooler, heavy with the scent of damp earth and green growing things. Somewhere nearby, water trickles over stones.

Another press, and I stand on a mountain peak, frigid wind whipping around me, the world spread out below in a dizzying panorama of valleys and distant, snow-capped peaks. The air is so thin I find myself breathing harder, though I know it's just the simulator affecting my perceptions.

With each new scene, my resolve strengthens. This is why I'm here. Not just to gather information, but to reclaim what's been stolen from half the population. The right to enjoy these wonders. The right to breathe freely, to move through the world without fear or permission.

I will not fail. No matter what Arayik throws at me, no matter how my body aches or my mind fears discovery, I will endure.

For now, though, I allow myself a moment of peace in this simulated wilderness, storing the memory of beauty to sustain me through the trials ahead. One day, I'll stand on a real mountain, feel actual sand between my toes, breathe the air of freedom not just for myself, but for all of us who are trapped.

CHAPTER TEN

CASSIA

An hour of drinking in sights—exploring worlds beyond these dense walls.

The desert oasis with its crystalline pool reflecting perfectly symmetrical palm trees.

An ancient city of broken columns and sprawling marble steps, gilded by sunset.

The interior of what must have been a museum, with towering ceilings and paintings that stretched floor to ceiling.

A dense, misty forest where shafts of golden light broke through a canopy of magnificent green leaves.

But nothing compares to where I stand now.

My breath catches as I bask in the panoramic vista from atop another jagged mountain peak. The simulation is so real I can make out the way light plays across the expanse, casting deep purple shadows in the valleys. Snow blankets the higher elevations, pristine and untouched.

I'd initially set the tactile response to full intensity, but the biting cold had been too much. Instead of deactivating the entire scene, I'd discovered how to manipulate the temperature, allowing me to experience the majesty without the discomfort.

Smart design—another testament to how men have hoarded the best parts of the world for themselves.

The sky above me stretches endlessly, so blue it almost hurts to look at. Thin, wispy clouds trail across it like paint strokes from a delicate brush. Below, the world unfolds in waves of rocky formations, forests tucked into sheltered cervices, and in the far distance—something that makes my heart skip.

A high wall stretches across the horizon, unnaturally straight against the organic curves of the landscape. The perimeter. The boundary between Dascenia and what lies beyond.

I lean forward as though those few inches might bring clarity. Is that Ofin province I'm seeing to the northwest? Or perhaps Vinford? From this height, the territorial boundaries blur, making a mockery of the artificial divisions the Syndicate enforces with such violence.

My chest expands with a feeling I can't quite name. It's not happiness, exactly. Something sharper, more painful.

Freedom.

This is what freedom feels like—even in simulation. The vastness of the world laid out before me, choices in every direction. The ability to go anywhere, see anything, be anyone.

But also the crushing knowledge that this isn't real. Not here, anyway.

I've never even seen a proper map of our land. Just sketches in books with vague outlines of the six provinces, deliberately keeping us ignorant of our own geography. Yet I've memorized maps of the old world from history books—countries and states with borders drawn in odd zigzags, seemingly arbitrary divisions between people who were still allowed to cross them freely.

Those places had rules, yes, governments and laws, but

nothing like what we endure now. Nothing so complete in its totalitarianism, so targeted in its cruelty.

My head shakes as I force myself to take one last, lingering look at the horizon. Committing it to memory.

With reluctance, I turn away and approach the wall tile—the only thing that doesn't belong in this mountain paradise. Elias hadn't shown me how to shut it down properly, but the remote has a curved edge designed to fit back into a slot in the panel. I press it in, and with a soft click, the mountain dissolves into nothing.

The bare room feels oppressive after the open sky, its walls pressing in on all sides. The tile flips and disappears back into the uniform surface of the wall, leaving no trace of the wonders hidden behind it. I stand still for a moment, recalibrating. I should go back upstairs, but my feet don't move toward the door. Instead, I find myself staring the direction of the empty corridor that stretches beyond this room.

I'm dying to know what's in the other rooms. Elias said there were no cameras, but did he mean out there too? I walk from the space before scanning the ceiling and walls, nothing obvious standing out, but that means little. Surveillance doesn't have to announce itself to be effective.

My fingertips tingle with the urge to try the other doors, to push my luck just a little further. Information is power. And right now, I have so little of either.

But I'm not as stupid as the Commander thinks. If I'm caught snooping through restricted areas, there will be no excuse that saves me. The identity I've carefully constructed will shatter like glass, and every man in this building will know the woman hiding beneath the mask.

Not today.

As I venture back to my room, the wall-mounted clock

displays 22:47. No wonder the place feels abandoned—I lost more time in the simulation than I'd thought.

But that works in my favor now. The showers should be empty, and I desperately need to wash away two days of grime, sweat, and mud. My muscles ache with a deep, persistent throb that makes every movement a reminder of how ill-prepared my body is for this mission.

Grabbing underclothes from my room, I cringe as the door to the main bathroom hisses, revealing a row of stalls and sinks. The smell overwhelms me immediately—a potent mixture of mildew, urine, and cheap soap that has me fighting the urge to cover my nose.

Stars above. Do men really live like this?

I've used the smaller bathrooms the entire time I've been here, so this is quite the shock. I haven't showered in days and I'm certain I smell far from fresh, but this is something else entirely.

There's some grim comfort in the realization that not all male privileges are enviable.

Scurrying to the shower area, every stall is empty, and I choose the one furthest from the door, backed against the wall. With only one neighboring stall, I'm less likely to be seen if someone comes in.

Inside, I peel off my uniform with a gag, the fabric stiff with dirt and dried sweat. I should have done this yesterday, but exhaustion overtook me. I wash each piece of clothing carefully, wringing them out to dry before attending to myself.

When I finally step under the spray, I can't hold back a groan of pure pleasure. Hot water sluices over my body, carrying away days of accumulated filth, but more importantly, dissolving the tension that's kept my muscles rigid since I first put on this mask. For just a moment, I allow my vigilance to slip, closing my eyes and letting my shoulders drop.

This is the first time I've felt anything approaching comfortable since stepping out of my house. For all the wonders of the simulation room, it couldn't replicate this deep physical relief.

I scrub my hair three times, working the soap into a lather and massaging my scalp until it tingles. My body gets the same thorough treatment, with special attention to the places where armor and gear have rubbed my skin raw. By the time I'm finished, my skin is pink from heat and friction, but gloriously clean.

As I rinse one final time, fighting the urge to stay under the water forever, I hear sounds from outside the bathroom. The heavy fall of boots, followed by lighter shuffling. My muscles lock instantly, the fragile peace shattered.

No! Not now. I'd specifically waited until everyone was asleep to avoid exactly this scenario.

My fingers shut off the water quickly, grabbing my towel to dry as efficiently as possible. My clothes are still damp, but there's no help for it. I'll have to put them on wet and hope I can get back to my room without being seen.

The sounds outside grow closer—muffled voices, then a strange shuffling. There's something odd about the cadence, almost furtive. And then I hear it clearly: a ragged breath, followed by a low moan.

Oh fuck.

A soft thud against the outer wall confirms my suspicion, followed by whispered words I can't quite make out, but whose tone leaves little to the imagination.

They're...

My face heats. Two people. Together. The shuffling intensifies, punctuated by sounds that leave no ambiguity about their activities. I stand frozen, clutching my towel to my chest, unsure what protocol dictates in this situation.

Do I announce myself? I could make a run for it or just pretend I'm not here. None seem like viable options.

"Bend over," a voice commands, low and rough. "Hold onto the wall."

My jaw drops. I'd expected...actually, I don't know what I expected. But the raw directness shoots a peculiar heat through my core, followed immediately by mortification. I shouldn't be hearing this. I don't *want* to be hearing this.

Except a twisted part of me can't keep from listening.

The rhythm of bodies coming together fills the space, unmistakable in its cadence. The slap of skin on skin, guttural groans, a stream of praise and encouragement that has my heart racing for reasons I refuse to examine.

I use their distraction to my advantage, quickly pulling on my underwear and reaching for my still-wet pants. The fabric sticks to my skin, cold and clingy, but I force them on with as little movement as possible. Their noises will cover the worst of my rustling.

"You take it so well," one of them gasps, and the unexpected tenderness in his voice stops me dead.

No one will ever speak to me like that. Not with genuine desire or affection. If I'm discovered, the best I can hope for is to be purchased by someone like my father—a decent man who views women as living, worthy people. But even that is a kind of ownership. Not partnership. Not the mutual want saturating these men's voices.

The thought sucks all lingering heat from my body, replacing it with a hollow ache. I've worked hard not to feel sorry for myself. To recognize how much better I have it than women in the facilities. But sometimes the knowledge of what's been stolen from me—from all of us—threatens to suffocate me.

I'll never know what it feels like to be held by someone who wants me for myself, not just my body's utility. I'll never be touched with reverence or kissed with passion. If I'm caught, I'll become what my mother spent her life protecting me from: a numbered incubator.

These two men may hide their relationship from their peers, but they are still free to choose it. To find moments of connection in steam-filled bathrooms, to touch each other with hunger rather than clinical necessity.

Their pace quickens, the slapping sounds growing more urgent, broken gasps rising in pitch until they crescendo in twin groans. The sudden silence that follows is almost as oppressive as the sounds themselves.

I exhale slowly, relieved it's over, but uncertain what comes next. Heavy breathing filters through the space, followed by soft murmurs I can't make out. After an eternity, they shuffle again—clothes being adjusted, soft footfalls moving away.

Their departure unfreezes me. I quickly pull on my shirt, wincing as the cold, damp fabric clings to my newly clean skin. The mask is last, and oh how my soul keels over, dry heaving as the thing tumbles from my grasp in slow motion, its edge catching on the tile with an echoing clack.

I'm paralyzed, my breath stalling as I tilt my head to listen. The footsteps, which had been receding, stop. *Shit.* After a pause that squeezes my lungs flat, they return—louder, more deliberate.

No, no, no. I lunge for the mask, jamming it on my face and frantically tucking my still-wet hair into the back. My heart pounds so violently I'm sure it's audible throughout the room.

The curtain rips open with a metallic screech, and I find myself face to face with Brenner and Corin.

Brenner looms in the doorway, his massive frame nearly filling the entire space. Even with his mask on, his posture radiates menace—shoulders squared, head cocked at an angle that suggests predatory interest. He's a head taller than me, with a build that scares the weakest parts of me.

"Ashford," he drawls, the name stretched like taffy between his teeth. "Didn't know you bothered to shower."

I force a laugh that sounds more like a wheeze. My fingers curl against my thighs to keep them from trembling. I can't afford to appear weak now—showing vulnerability to men like Brenner is like signing my own death certificate.

"And I wasn't aware you two were together," I reply, aiming for casual but landing somewhere near strained.

Corin's face visibly reddens through his mask. He's smaller than Brenner, with a wiry build and nervous energy that manifests as constant fidgeting. His eyes dart between me and the floor, embarrassment radiating from him in waves my Empath abilities can feel without even trying.

But Brenner's emotional signature is something else entirely. Dark, churning anger threads through his aura, mixed with humiliation and a sharp edge of fear that makes him exponentially more dangerous. His fist clenches on the shower curtain, bunching the material until seams pop.

"And you're a little creep, too," he spits, each word dripping venom. "Do you always find places to hide to listen to others fuck? Do you even know what that means? You don't seem like the type to have ever fucked anyone before."

He's not wrong, but I stay quiet. Any excuse I make about accidentally being here will only inflame him further. His eyes fix on me with lethal focus. This isn't just about catching me in the shower—this is about the power he needs to reassert, the secret he thinks I might expose.

I glance at Corin, searching for any sign of assistance, but his discomfort is palpable. He won't intervene, not against Brenner.

Certainly not for me.

My mind races through what I know of them both. Brenner is a Charger while Corin is an Empath like me, though a weaker one—he needs physical contact and intense concentration to work his powers.

Brenner won't be able to use his abilities on me without breaking regulations, but that doesn't mean he can't hurt me in more conventional ways. And in this confined space, with my back literally against the wall, I have nowhere to run.

He seems to reach a decision, his posture shifting subtly as he lunges for my collar. Without conscious thought, my hand snaps up, catching his wrist in a grip that surprises us both with its strength.

"Touch me and the entire team, including our leaders, find out what you do when everyone else is asleep."

It's a gambit born of desperation, but I've studied enough history to know how entire groups were once ostracized for their attractions. For all the equality men enjoy compared to women, I suspect some old prejudices still linger. The way Brenner's eyes widen confirms my guess—he doesn't want this known.

His reaction flickers between shock and renewed rage. Corin tries to say something, perhaps sensing the dangerous turn in Brenner's demeanor, but the larger man brushes him off with a harsh gesture.

"Or I could just kill you and be done with it." The casual way he delivers the threat somehow makes it more terrifying. My heart hammers against each rib as my opponent barks an order to Corin. "Watch the door."

Panic wells in my chest, but with it comes a clarity I haven't felt before. Elias' words from earlier echo in my mind: *I'd like you to use your ability to help defuse situations when tempers flare.*

This certainly qualifies.

Without further hesitation, I reach out with my empathy, not bothering with subtlety as I push into both their minds. I visualize calm waters, peaceful meadows, gentle breezes—shoving these sensations into their consciousness with every ounce of concentration I can muster.

The effort to overtake Brenner's resolve makes my vision swim and knees weaken, but I don't relent. His shoulders slacken first, the tension visibly draining from his massive frame. His hand drops away from me as if too heavy to hold up. Corin, already more susceptible to emotional influence, sways on his feet.

Encouraged, I push deeper, adding layers of exhaustion to the calm. *Sleep,* I tell their bodies. *Rest. Bed. Now.*

They turn away in a daze, shuffling toward the exit without another word. The victory floods me with relief, but I maintain the connection, unwilling to let go until they're safely gone.

Just as they reach the door, Brenner pauses, swiveling with visible effort. His eyes, heavy-lidded but still dangerous, find mine. "I know you're an Empath, Ashford," he slurs, fighting my influence. "Commander will be hearing about this."

I shrug and wave him along, feigning a confidence I don't feel. I follow at a safe distance, watching as they stumble down the hallway toward their quarters. Only when the click of their door signals closing do I release my hold on their minds.

The backlash is immediate. Cold sweat breaks out across my body, and my hands shake so badly I have to press them against the wall for support. I've never exerted my power like that before, never sustained influence over multiple live targets for so long. The fact I succeeded is both thrilling and terrifying.

Back in my room, I lock the door on unsteady legs. My wet uniform clings uncomfortably, but at least it's clean now. I remove it and hang each piece on the back of the room's single chair, positioning it near the vent where warm air circulates.

The salve I prepared earlier has set to the perfect consistency—thicker than lotion but not so solid it won't spread. I scoop a generous amount onto my fingertips and begin applying it to my shoulders, working it into the knotted muscles with firm pressure.

By the time I finish, my eyelids are drooping, the combined effects of physical exhaustion, power exertion, and the day's emotional rollercoaster conspiring to pull me toward unconsciousness. I barely manage to wipe the excess salve from my hands before collapsing onto the narrow bed.

Honestly, I should be more concerned about Brenner's threat. About what tomorrow will bring when he reports me to Arayik. About whether I can survive another day of this brutal charade.

CHAPTER ELEVEN

CASSIA

Three others stand in formation with me, the biting afternoon air slicing through my lungs with each breath. My muscles scream from yesterday's drills, a persistent agony that makes even standing still torture. The training yard stretches before us, hard-packed dirt swept clean of debris, surrounded by metal hurdles and wooden training dummies that boggle my mind. Why would I fight a piece of wood? That seems quite illogical.

Training with Kellen earlier was manageable—Brenner refused to look at me, which suited me perfectly. His averted gaze meant he wouldn't notice the strain beneath my mask, wouldn't notice how I favored my right side where Arayik's combat drills had left a constellation of bruises.

But now, facing my last session with him today, cold dread pools in my stomach.

He stands at the opposite end of our semicircle, predatory energy radiating from his hulking frame. His mask points directly at me, and through the narrow slit, those baleful eyes bore into my soul. His stance is rigid. I know what he wants—to tell everyone how the freak Ashford manipulated his mind last night, how I used my power outside regulation to make him stumble away like a drunkard.

I catch his attention and give one shake of my head. The meaning is clear: keep quiet about what happened, or everyone learns what you and Corin do after dark. I'm not proud of this blackmail, but I won't apologize for it.

Brenner's mask tilts upward sharply before he turns away with a jerk, his massive shoulders bunching beneath his uniform. The air between us practically crackles with his hatred.

Every bone in my body is brittle, hollowed out by unprecedented exhaustion. I haven't slept properly since arriving, and last night's power exertion left me far more drained than I could fathom. Every step I've taken today has required conscious effort, my body moving through invisible sludge. But I can't show weakness—not with Brenner looking for any vulnerability, and not with Arayik's scrutiny falling on my every move.

"Attention," his voice cuts across the yard, and all four of us straighten. Calder and Finnick adjust their stances, feet planted wider, chins lifting.

"Commander." The other three respond in unison. I hesitate a beat too long before joining in, earning a not-so-subtle glare from Arayik which somehow conveys his disapproval despite the mask.

"Today we assess combat capability," he says, pacing before us. His movements are fluid, economical—a predator conserving energy. "You've demonstrated individual skills. Now I want to see how you function against an opponent. The field demands adaptation, quick thinking, and the ability to exploit weakness."

His movements stop, mask pointing directly at me, and a chill traces my spine.

"You will pair up. First pair takes the mats." He gestures to the center of the yard where black mats form a rough square. "Before you disperse, one of you tell me what the scan sequence is when traveling through a provincial checkpoint." My heart skips—that's the question he asked me last time.

"Sir," Finnick begins, "The sequence begins with swiping one's badge for identification. Then—" *There's more?* "—confirming the manifest code given with travel orders."

Oh. Oh, fuck me...Lachlan never mentioned that.

And Arayik didn't ask the question for any reason other than satisfying his suspicion of me.

The world spins, heat flashing through me as my hands slicken. The mask is tighter than it was a second ago, the strap biting at my head as if in punishment. A faint whine grows in my ears, the same high note that emerges before a migraine.

Don't react, Cas.

Lachlan would have known that—*I* should have known that.

Against my will, my eyes flick to the Commander, whose gaze is already trained on me. Whatever. That proves nothing; anyone could have answered the same as me, it doesn't mean they're a woman impersonating her brother to infiltrate this team of Enforcers...

Shit.

He surprisingly doesn't call me out, instead returning to our training, leaving me to stress alone. "Pair up."

Before I can even consider who might be least likely to break my neck, Brenner's voice rings out. "I'm taking Ashford."

Stars, why me?

My stomach drops. Of course I should have anticipated this. Last night's confrontation was just the prelude—he's been waiting for a sanctioned opportunity to hurt me.

"You heard him," Arayik remarks, stepping back. "Brenner and Ashford, center mat."

I have no choice now. Refusing would draw more attention than I can afford and would brand me forever as easy prey and get me kicked from the team. I need to think tactically, to use this somehow.

Perhaps this is an opportunity. If I handle Brenner properly, I might earn begrudging respect from the others. And there's something to be said for confronting a threat directly rather than waiting for it to find you unaware.

My opponent stomps toward the mat, each footfall throwing up tiny puffs of dust. His movements are aggressive, radiating violent intent. The afternoon sun catches on the metal parts of his uniform, sending brief flashes across the yard and the air feels charged, like the tense moments before a storm breaks from the sky.

Positioning myself on the mat, I stand slightly off-center opposite Brenner. I try to recall every self-defense technique I've read about and learned while here, but my mind blanks.

Yesterday, I watched him lift those forty-pound weights as if they were filled with air. His arms are twice the size of mine, his chest a barrel compared to my narrow frame. And now he wants revenge.

But there's a reason he's in this specific training with me. He's too impulsive and aggressive; he leads with his emotions, not with his head, and his weakness is being quick to rage. If I can't otherwise survive this without my powers, I can at least use that against him.

Worse still, what if my mask falls off during the fight? It's secured, but a direct hit might dislodge it. The rules permit bare faces during accidental exposure in sparring, but I can't let that happen.

The Commander approaches the edge of the mat. "Basic

rules," he says tersely. "No intentional deadly force or powers. First to three submissions or a knockout wins. Clear?"

Those are barely rules at all.

No *intentional* death leaves so much room for pain, or temporary injuries that could take weeks to heal.

"Begin."

Everything happens too fast. I make the rookie mistake of standing with my feet together, a posture so unstable that when Brenner lunges forward, his fist connects with the side of my mask before I can even think to move.

The impact is explosive. My head snaps back, vision temporarily whiting out as I'm launched backward. I land hard, skidding across the mat, hard material pressing painfully into my face. If not for the protection of my mask, my cheekbone would be shattered.

Fuck me, that hurts. My ears ring as the aching in my jaw where the impact transferred through the mask crescendos. I almost laugh at the irony—the very thing concealing my identity just saved me.

Before I can fully recover, Brenner shouts a battle cry, and I watch as his boots approach rapidly. He's going to kick me while I'm down. Pure survival instinct rises as I forgo the effort to remember everything I've read about combat. I roll sideways, enjoying the rush of air as his stomp misses my ribs by inches, slamming into the mat where I'd just been lying.

There's no time for thought, only reaction. I grab his ankle with both hands and pull with everything I have, unbalancing him just as he's shifting his weight for another kick. The unexpected counter drags him into an awkward split. He screams, clutching his groin.

This is my chance.

Scrambling to my feet, I retreat to the opposite side of the mat, putting maximum distance between us. My heart hammers as my breath comes in short, painful gasps.

I can't breathe.

Brenner pushes himself up, his head snapping toward me with murderous intensity.

"You motherfucker," he snarls, his voice thick and mucous-filled. "You're going to pay for that."

I'm already paying. My face throbs, tiny black dots still swirling at the edges of my peripheral. Both hands shake with adrenaline and fear. Is this a submission? No one has called anything, so the match must still be active.

He charges again, moving with surprising speed for someone so large. This time, I'm more prepared. I've watched enough of his movement to gather the pattern—right shoulder dropping before he strikes, weight shifting forward to his front foot, face tilted down as he focuses on his target.

It's horrifying waiting until the last possible second, yet I do before sidestepping while extending my foot. It's not a perfect execution—the force of his momentum knocks into my leg, nearly taking me with him—but it works. Brenner tumbles across the mat, his bulk working against him as he loses control and slides to a stop.

A small bubble of pride cheers inside me. I did that. Years of reading about physics and leverage, about utilizing an opponent's force against them, and I actually executed it. Maybe I'm not entirely helpless after—

The thought dies as Brenner recovers faster than I anticipated. He rolls to his knees, then launches at me with a roar. Before I can react, his bulk slams into my torso, driving me to the ground with him on top. The air rushes from my lungs in a painful whoosh. He pins me, his weight crushing.

Now I really can't breathe. Or move.

His bulk ensures I'm completely immobilized, my arms trapped at my sides as panic rises in my throat.

Then his leg shifts as he draws back for a kick aimed directly between mine. He's going for what he thinks is my most vulnerable spot. Little does he know, I don't have the same equipment he's targeting.

The kick lands, and while there's still pain—the pubic bone is sensitive regardless of anatomy—it's nothing like what he intended. I tighten my thighs, trapping his foot between my legs, and use the leverage to twist my body violently to the side. Only to slip and drop onto my opponent.

Something cracks loudly—the sound of bone giving way under pressure. Brenner's scream is immediate, a high-pitched wail that doesn't match his imposing frame. I release him at once and push myself back, watching in horror as he clutches at his leg.

The mask lifts from his face in a frantic swipe, revealing contorted features flushed with pain. His hands scrabble at his pant leg, yanking it up to expose the damage.

I'm not prepared for the visual. His tibia is visibly displaced, pushing against the skin from within. It hasn't broken through, but the unnatural bulge makes my stomach roll. The skin stretches taut over the deformity, already darkening with bruises as blood pools beneath the surface.

I did that? I didn't mean to *break his leg*—just to free myself. The realization of my own strength is...unsettling.

Brenner's face is a mess of tears and sweat, his tough facade crumbling under the wave of pain. Calder and Finnick approach with caution, looking between Brenner and Arayik as if unsure whether to help.

I should feel bad. This is a career-ending injury for an Enforcer recruit. He'll be sent away, his chances of joining the force destroyed. But all I can summon is divine relief. This man would have killed me given the opportunity, he made that clear last night. This outcome—him leaving the team with a healing leg rather than me leaving in a body bag—is the better alternative.

The Commander strides over, his movements unhurried. He kneels beside Brenner, examining the injury with clinical detachment. After a moment, he touches something on his wrist and mutters into it—a communication device of some sort.

Within a minute, two Enforcers emerge from the main building, moving with purpose toward our group. I push myself to stand, wincing at the various aches blossoming across my body. The Enforcers reach Brenner and each take one of his arms, preparing to lift him.

"No, wait," he gasps, his voice frantic and filled with pain. "I'm fine, Commander. I can stay on the team. Just need the medic to—"

"Show me," Arayik interrupts before crossing his arms. One nod to the Enforcers and they release Brenner's arms.

The moment they let go, Brenner tries to put weight on his leg and collapses with a shriek, crumpling to the ground. His face contorts, fresh tears streaming along his cheeks.

"Take him to medical," Arayik orders flatly. "He's out."

Just like that, Brenner's time as a recruit ends. The Enforcers lift him again, more carefully this time, and carry him toward the training center. Relief settles through me that Brenner is in too much pain to look back, to threaten me one final time. His departure solves multiple problems at once—one less threat to navigate.

"Styx, Crowell," Arayik commands Calder and Finnick, already moving on. "You're up."

The two remaining recruits rush to obey, taking positions

on the mat. I step to the side, grateful for the brief reprieve. My body aches everywhere—face throbbing from Brenner's punch, ribs sore from his weight, muscles coiled with tension, lingering adrenaline the only thing keeping me upright.

Finally, a moment to relax a fraction and watch as the two other recruits circle each other with more caution than Brenner showed. They're both wary and professional, testing defenses before committing to attacks. I should be watching their techniques, learning from their form, but the details blur.

"Ashford."

The sharp command jerks me back to attention. Arayik stands several yards away, motioning me toward an open patch of grass adjacent to the other recruits. My stomach drops. I thought I'd be allowed to observe the rest of the session and recover from my bout with Brenner.

No such luck.

I walk slowly, each step an effort against protesting muscles. As I approach, his posture shifts the smallest amount —feet planted wider, spine straightening, radiating authority. I stop before him, keeping a cautious distance.

For a long moment, he simply stares at me. "You're with me." I nod. "Have you ever had any physical combat training?" he continues, and I'm unsure why he wouldn't know that. Unless he's aiming to embarrass me more.

Haven't had his fill yet today.

I shake my head and answer anyway. "No. If that wasn't obvious."

"It was." The statement hangs between us, impassive and damning. "Your form and reactionary defense are terrible, and you have no offense to speak of."

Way to make a girl feel good about herself, I think, bitter. I already know all this. I don't need him to list my inadequacies again when I'm painfully aware of each one. I've spent my entire life in a house with three other people, never running, never fighting, never building more than a fraction of the strength or endurance these men take for granted.

"That's precisely why you were put in my afternoon group." Duh. "You need the most work. But I don't have time for projects, so you have one week to show improvement, or you're out."

One week? Is he fucking serious?

Seven meager days to transform from Cassia the sheltered woman to Lachlan the capable Enforcer. That's impossible.

I don't say the thoughts out loud, nodding once, not trusting my voice.

Arayik reaches behind his back and produces two staffs—long, straight poles made of some light but durable material. They're hollow in the center, which should make them easier to wield, but I suspect they'll make a terrible racket when struck together. My head already aches from Brenner's punch; I'm not looking forward to the additional assault on my senses.

"We'll start with these," he says, holding one out to me. "The staff gives you more surface area for contact, improving your chances of connecting. It also forces proper balance and teaches reactionary defense. Master this, and you'll have the foundation for any weapon."

His explanation is actually...helpful; more instructive than I expected from him. Perhaps he's not completely terrible at teaching, just impatient with those he deems unworthy of his time.

"Ready?" Why would he care?

I'm not, but I confirm anyway, gripping the staff as firmly as I can. It's almost weightless in my hands, though longer than anticipated. I mimic what I think is a defensive stance, positioning the staff diagonally across my body as I swallow heaps of bile.

The Commander doesn't give me time to second-guess my form. He moves with startling speed, his staff whistling through the air as it arcs toward me. I barely manage to lift mine in time, the impact when they connect sending painful vibrations up my arms. The sound is sharp and loud, making me wince.

His crinkled eyes suggest he wasn't even using his full strength, I realize with dismay. That was a test swing, a probing attack to assess my reflexes, and I almost missed it.

My feet stumble backward, creating space to think and plan my next move. But Arayik gives me no opportunity. His attacks come faster now, more deliberate, each one probing a different angle of my defense and hurting worse than the last. He's methodically exploiting my weaknesses, showing me exactly how exposed I am.

My mind catalogs his pattern—a slight shift in his weight before he strikes, a minute adjustment in his grip—but this knowledge doesn't translate to effective defense. My responses are too slow, arms not sturdy enough to absorb the impacts as needed.

He spins, quicker than someone his size should be able to move, feinting toward my head. I raise my staff to block, only to realize too late it's a trap. The other end of his staff sweeps low, catching behind my ankles and yanking my feet from under me.

I crash to the ground, landing hard on my back to only once again struggle for air. My attempt to inhale only triggers a coughing fit, my lungs refusing to cooperate. Panic flares, but gradually my diaphragm remembers its job, and thin sips of air make it to my starving body.

Still wheezing, I push up, only to find Arayik casually leaning on his staff, watching me struggle. I cannot discern his expression, but the relaxed posture radiates smug satisfaction. He's not exerted himself in the slightest.

The bastard.

Something hot and angry unfurls in my chest. He's playing with me—not teaching or training, just demonstrating his superiority. I'm a mouse being batted around by a particularly sadistic cat—and that pisses me off.

I am not here to be toyed with. Nor am I here to entertain his ego. I'm here for information and opportunity, to help women like my mother escape those disgusting facilities. His opinion of me means nothing as long as I achieve my goals.

Rising fully to my feet, I reclaim my staff with steadier hands. I won't give him the satisfaction of seeing me quit.

"Again," I demand, my voice rougher than I intended.

A slight tilt of his mask is the only indication of surprise before he nods once.

This time, I analyze his stance more carefully. He holds the staff with his left hand forward, right hand back, creating a fulcrum for maximum leverage. His weight rests primarily on his back foot, allowing quick pivots and direction changes.

Then he advances again, but I'm ready now.

When he moves this time, I wait until the last possible moment before reacting. Instead of meeting his strike head on, I angle my staff to deflect rather than block, redirecting the force away from my body. It's still jarring, but less painful than absorbing the direct impact.

The man presses forward with a series of quick strikes—high, low, high again—testing my adaptability. I manage to counter or duck from most of them, though each successful block feels more like luck than skill. I'm just barely keeping up, my brain working faster than my body can execute. Somewhere in this flurry of movement, I spot an opportunity. Arayik over-commits to a forward strike, leaving his right side exposed. It's probably intentional—a trap for the unwary student—but it's the only opening I've gotten.

I feign a stumble, dropping my guard just enough to make him think I've lost my balance. He takes the bait, pressing forward to exploit the weakness. At the last second, I pivot and swing my staff in a controlled path toward his exposed flank.

I don't expect to actually hit him. I just want to force him to acknowledge that I saw the opening, that I'm capable of strategic thinking even if my execution is amateur.

My staff doesn't connect—he blocks with annoying ease—but the maneuver forces him a step back to maintain his balance. A minor victory, though it feels monumental.

"Not the worst you've exhibited." His tone is begrudging, but it's enough that I'll accept it as a positive compliment.

The momentary pride is short-lived. His next attack comes with renewed intensity, as if he's decided I no longer need the infant treatment. His staff becomes a blur, striking from angles I can't anticipate, with a force I can't match.

One particularly vicious swing knocks my weapon from my hands. The staff clatters to the ground, rolling away, and before I can consider retrieving it, Arayik has circled behind me, his boot connecting square with my back. The impact launches me forward, sending me flying several feet through the air before I crash face-first into the dirt. Soil fills my mouth, gritty and bitter. My back screams with pain, and for a terrifying moment, I wonder if he's broken something vital.

I roll, my mask shifting upward on my face. I yank it back down, heart racing at the close call. I might have broken bones or crushed organs, and all I can think of is the security of my mask.

What a perfect reflection of my priorities.

"Get up," Arayik commands with venom. "Enforcers don't get breaks in the field. If you're breathing, you're fighting."

I struggle to my feet, spitting dirt from my mouth and scraping fingers through the eye slit to clear my vision. I'm so sick of eating mud and dirt.

Finnick and Calder have stopped their own match to watch us. I'm not sure how long Arayik and I have been at this, but the sun has shifted position since Brenner was carried away, creating longer shadows across the yard.

The Commander approaches, both staffs gripped in one hand. Despite his imposing size and clear physical advantage, I hold my ground. He stops before me, too close. His presence is overwhelming—a combination of physical size, unyielding authority, and the complete control he holds over my future here. It would be easy to cower, to submit to his dominance.

I am my mother's daughter, but submission has never been in my nature.

I hold his gaze, refusing to drop it despite my every instinct begging me to. Let him understand that I might be beaten, but he hasn't broken me. Not yet, at least. I fear he'll get there very soon if he keeps this momentum up.

"You've got one week to impress me. I do not have time to train anyone who doesn't want to be here."

Blood coats my teeth as I bite my tongue to keep from lashing out. Of course I want to be here—though for reasons he'd never understand.

So I simply stay silent and still, accepting his ultimatum without comment.

His eyes study me a moment longer before he straightens and strides away. Even in something as simple as walking, he demonstrates mastery.

My lungs suck in a deep, steadying breath, working to calm my racing heart—the crash after an influx of adrenaline is such an unpleasant experience.

One week. I have one week to transform myself from a

woman who's never fought a day in her life to someone Arayik deems worthy of training.

What a joke.

The odds are impossible. But then, everything about my life and presence here should be impossible.

It seems to be my specialty.

CHAPTER TWELVE

ARAYIK

A sneer forms on my face from their struggle. Three recruits, hanging from the metal bar I selected specifically for its uncomfortable width—too thick to grip easily, yet not wide enough to distribute their weight in a comfortable manner. Sweat glistens on their forearms. Their muscles tremble. This is what separates the strong from the weak.

My gaze shifts to Crowell. The skin around his eyes has flushed to a concerning shade of red, fingers slipping incrementally with each passing minute. Disappointing. As our only Adapter, his body should be conditioned to withstand physical extremes. The northern side of the perimeter is predominantly mountainous—temperatures there drop below freezing even in summer. We need someone who can function in those conditions without supplemental gear.

A flicker of movement draws my attention to Ashford. He readjusts his grip with a subtle jerk that betrays his fatigue. His mask conceals whatever grimace no doubt contorts his piss ugly face, but the tension in his shoulders tells me everything. The weakest of them all, yet somehow still hanging.

Fucking pitiful excuse of a man.

And yet, his weakness isn't just his body. Curious, when I pressed him about the checkpoint sequence, he fumbled it. Any courier worth a damn knows the order—except this one. Either he's thick headed, or he's hiding something. I haven't decided which I'd like to break open first.

My arms cross, the weight of my uniform settling across both shoulders. The fabric is a second skin to me now—black tactical material designed to intimidate as much as to protect. The mask on my face is equally familiar, the interior molded to the contours of my features through years of wear.

The band on my wrist vibrates once—a message from Syndicate Leader Rennaux demanding my presence tomorrow morning. No doubt to discuss our progress with the new squad. Or rather, his expectations for when we'll be deployment-ready. Lucian Rennaux oversees all Enforcer operations across the six provinces, his authority rarely questioned even by his fellow Syndicate leaders.

Unlike Vaughn Harridan, who manages propaganda and intelligence gathering, or Everett Montclair, who controls the economic lifeline of Dascenia, Rennaux deals in direct action. He expects results, nothing less.

The discovery of those bands of dissidents beyond the perimeter has unsettled the entire Syndicate. Three distinct groups were identified by aerial surveillance drones—one in the northeast forests, another nestled in the southern foothills, and a third moving between cave systems in the central plains. Initial estimates suggest seventy to ninety individuals total, predominantly females.

Females that should be in their respective facilities, producing more male children with powers to strengthen our ranks. Instead, they're out in the wild, uncontrolled, under-mining everything we've built.

What's most concerning is the lack of physical evidence at

the perimeter. No damaged sections or disrupted scanner networks; no signs of forced passage. It could only mean one thing: internal assistance. Someone with knowledge of the systems, access to the scanner logs, and authorization to move through checkpoints has been facilitating these escapes.

A traitor among our ranks.

That's why I volunteered to form this special unit. Every Enforcer must check in at the Center between assignments. By positioning myself here, I can personally evaluate everyone passing through. Watch for inconsistencies, behavioral anomalies, signs of divided loyalty.

So far, I've found nothing conclusive, but it's only been two weeks since we learned about the rebellion. The traitor, if they have any intelligence, will have gone to ground. Every Enforcer outpost across Dascenia received the security alert—whoever is responsible knows we're looking.

A grunt draws my attention back to the present. Styx shifts his weight, adjusting his hold. His Thermic abilities make him invaluable—being able to regulate temperature through touch means he can discreetly incapacitate targets without permanent damage. Unlike some of the more destructive powers, his is controlled and precise. Useful.

I despise training the incompetent, but even I cannot deny a certain satisfaction in this position. Watching them strain, measuring their limits, determining their worth. It's cleaner than the paperwork that consumes my days here at the hub. The endless requisition forms and petty territorial squabbles between unit commanders are agonizing. Before taking this assignment, I hadn't realized how stifling those administrative duties would become.

Kellen understood. He has the patient mind for it, but even he recognized my growing restlessness. When the opportunity to form this specialized unit arose, he and Elias didn't hesitate to join me. We've served together since we were barely out of training, our powers and approaches naturally complementing one another. My Anchor abilities ground us while Elias' Revealer talents expose lies, and Kellen's Telepath skills allow us silent coordination in the field.

We've more than earned our current ranks through years of flawless service and unwavering loyalty. And one benefit of such rank is the ability to select our own assignments. The Syndicate rewards those who prove themselves unquestioningly devoted to its cause.

Ashford slips again, recovering much to my dismay. His arms shake visibly now, though I shouldn't be surprised. His file lists only one previous employment as a messenger between provinces, but his conditioning is nonexistent. If I didn't know better, I'd think he'd spent his life confined in a cell, never dealing with proper physical exertion.

I've wanted to cut him from the team multiple times, more so after mentioning my sister Anja—something he should have never been privy to. His attitude borders on insubordination, his performance is consistently subpar, and something about him feels as though he'll never belong.

But Elias made a compelling case after our last debriefing.

"The Empath abilities he displayed are extraordinary," Elias had argued, leaning against my office wall. "Have you ever seen anyone influence emotions like that without physical contact before? And on multiple subjects?"

I hadn't. Empaths are rare enough—perhaps one in a thousand men manifests the ability. Ninety-nine percent require direct skin contact to sense emotions, let alone manipulate them. Corin Spinel, our other Empath recruit, needs both hands on a subject to achieve even basic influence.

But Ashford...

I glance at him again, studying the lean, insufficient frame beneath the uniform, my lips curling. What he lacks in physical prowess, he makes up for in his power. When we retrieve those women from beyond the perimeter, having someone who can calm them remotely will be invaluable. Females in such situations tend to resist, often injuring themselves in the process. Dead women can't repopulate. Damaged women produce fewer viable offspring.

Ashford's power could save us significant losses. It's the only reason I tolerate his continued presence.

I check my wristband. 17:08. Eight minutes past our established end time, but I'm not concerned with schedules. Training ends when I decide it ends.

"Drop," I command, disgusted at the relief that overtakes their postures. They release the bar, landing with varying degrees of grace. Styx maintains his balance perfectly—good. Crowell stumbles, which is disappointing but not unexpected given his obvious fatigue. Ashford practically collapses, his knees buckling before he catches himself.

All three stretch their shoulders and wrists, trying to restore circulation to numbed fingers. I'm finished dealing with this hopeless lot.

"Despicable," I tell them, not bothering to soften the assessment. "If you can't handle a simple endurance test, you're useless beyond the perimeter. Do better tomorrow or find another assignment."

I turn without waiting for a response. There's nothing they could say that would interest me unless it's 'yes, Commander.'

The Enforcer Training Center rises before me as I cross the yard—a massive structure of reinforced concrete and steel, its windows tinted to prevent observation from outside. To the recruits, I'm sure it appears intimidating and unwelcoming.

To me, it's simply home.

I've lived within these walls for fifteen years. First as a

recruit myself, then as an active field Enforcer, eventually ascending to leadership. I know every corridor, every room, every surveillance blind spot. The place has a rhythm to it—the shift changes, meal schedules, training rotations—that pulses through the day like a formidable heartbeat.

Inside, the familiar scent of industrial cleaner and sweat greet me. Boots stomp on polished concrete and muted conversations bounce off walls. Men move with purpose here. There's no place for aimlessness in an Enforcer's life.

In the dining hall, I nod at those who acknowledge me with the proper deference, ignoring the rest. Most Enforcers wear their masks during duty hours but remove them in designated areas. The hall is one such place, though I never take advantage of the exemption.

Mystery creates intimidation.

Kellen and Elias sit at our usual table near the door—positioned to watch the entire room while keeping our backs to a wall. It's not paranoia if the precaution has saved your life multiple times.

Kellen has already removed his mask, setting it on the table beside his tray. His features are sharp, eyes a penetrating stormy gray that miss nothing—that's fine when it's not directed at me. Dark hair cropped short frames a face that most would call handsome if they didn't know the coldness behind his calculating gaze. He's halfway through a plate of protein, with another waiting next to it.

It smells divine. My stomach tightens in response, but I ignore it. Food can always wait.

I never quite understood their comfort with removing their masks around others. To me, the mask has always been more than uniform—it's protection. It keeps others from reading my expressions and connecting the man to the Enforcer. It maintains distance. Any form of personal connection is a potential weakness, and I will not be weak.

Through fear comes compliance. Through compliance comes order. Through order comes stability.

"Training go well?" my second asks as I lower to my usual seat, his tone neutral but his eyes searching my posture for signs of my mood. He's always been perceptive, even without using his power.

Before I can answer, movement catches my attention. Ashford enters the dining hall, his uniform still showing evidence of today's training in smudges of dirt across the knees. He collects a tray, fills it with more food than his frame suggests he could possibly consume, and spins to leave.

My eyes follow him across the room, noting how he walks. There's something in his gait—a carefulness that doesn't match his supposed background. Messengers develop a looser stride from constant travel. His is stiff and deliberate.

"Why do you hate the guy so much?"

I consider deflecting, but what's the point? These two know me too well to be fooled by evasion.

My response is flat. "He's scrawny, plus physically and mentally frail. He claims some medical condition to secure private quarters, but we all know that's bullshit. I'd put him in the center bottom bunk with the rest of the recruits if I could, but he's too skilled at manipulating regulations."

Leaning back, I stretch out the tension in my neck. "He takes the easy way out of everything. When we're actually beyond the perimeter, his power will be useful enough to justify his presence, but until then, he's nothing but deadweight."

Kellen and Elias exchange looks—one of those silent communications they've perfected over the years that always leaves me excluded.

"You remember what it was like, Ry," Elias says in a careful manner. "Being thrown into training while having no choice in the matter. You never showed it, but you were scared. Lachlan is too. Out of the three of us, I'd think you could empathize with him the most." *Lachlan.* Didn't realize they were on a first name basis.

"Empathize." The word tastes bitter on my tongue. "Fuck off. You asked why I didn't like the guy, and I told you. He's about as fucking useful as a woman. Probably be a better fuck than an opponent on the mat."

Kellen's eyes narrow. "I don't think he'd be into you like that, but I'd be interested to see you ask him." Of course he would.

Elias snickers, adjusting in his seat while I glare at my third.

"What, is he your new project?" I demand. "Did I miss the directive that we're supposed to coddle recruits now?"

The man sighs. "No one's coddling anyone." His voice takes on a reasonable tone that makes me want to pummel him. "But if you're going to keep him on the squad for his powers, maybe try not looking like you want to gut him every time he enters a room. It's counterproductive."

"And what about you, Elias? You've been up Ashford's ass since you both arrived. Anything you care to share?"

A moment of silence before he answers with a creased brow. "Honestly, the guy reminds me of myself. When we first joined the force, I was scared—rightfully so." Bright eyes meet mine. "I remember what it was like to feel so overwhelmed by the training and constant chattering of everyone around us. I wish Trent had given us a little grace, so apologies if I do with a couple of the recruits who are struggling. These are our charges, Ry...we're meant to look after them and lead them, not tell them how worthless they are every chance we get. Vitriol doesn't build a good soldier—it creates a resentful one."

My mouth opens to continue the argument before I stop myself. This is pointless. We're wasting time bickering when we should be discussing strategy.

"Fine," I concede, something I will only do with these two, before leaning forward on my elbows. I glance around the dining hall, noting many of the recruits have already left. The noise level has dropped enough that private conversation is possible, though I still keep my voice low. "How are they progressing in your sessions?"

Elias shrugs, swallowing before speaking. "Better than expected, for the most part. The simulation training is revealing some interesting approaches. Forven's Clinger power gives him excellent mobility advantages, he's trained it well. And Benson can blend into shadows—very useful for recon. Rhyne is able to suppress pain, which means he'll keep functioning even when injured."

"Pax Eston's telepathic range extends farther than our initial assessments indicated," Kellen adds. "And Till's skills are developing nicely—not as refined as yours, Elias, but solid enough for field work."

"What about the two problem children?"

"You already know Brenner's out." Elias offers me a droll look. "I heard he broke his leg during training. With Ashford, of all people."

Kellen nods, scanning the room for the fifth time since I arrived. "Tibia displacement. Clean break, but he's done."

"Interesting," I murmur, reevaluating slightly. Perhaps there's more to Ashford than I thought. Brenner was a formidable recruit, though his Charger abilities were nothing special. Knocking him out of commission shows some tactical thinking, at least. *If* it was purposeful.

"Oh, and Denwick sent word," my third continues, refer-ring to the administrative coordinator who manages hub communications. "Seric from Central Tech will be here this week to upgrade the perimeter scanners."

I frown. "Why? The current ones function at 99 percent efficiency."

"Syndicate's concerned about how those women made it past the perimeter undetected. They want to increase the signal strength to ensure the chips can be picked up at greater distances."

My head shakes—what a waste of fucking resources. The chips implanted in female infants are positioned in a small pocket created in the muscle tissue over the left shoulder blade. The placement allows the device to grow with the child's body without migration. Our current scanners can detect them from fifty meters away, even through barriers.

If women are making it beyond the perimeter without triggering alarms, it's not because the scanners failed to sense the chips. It's because someone disabled the scanners or guided them through dampening their device's signal.

"Have none of them considered that the issue might not be technological?"

It's a rhetorical question, but Kellen answers anyway. "Of course. But upgrading the scanners is visible action. It looks like they're doing something decisive while the actual investigation continues quietly."

Typical Syndicate approach—public posturing while the real work happens behind closed doors. Harridan's influence, no doubt. He's always understood the value of appearances.

"Speaking of technology," Elias' starts, lowering his voice further, "have you seen the new drone footage? There's evidence of defensive structures at the northern site. Nothing sophisticated, but they've clearly been preparing for the possibility of pursuit."

I nod, processing the information. "We'll need to address that in training. Styx could be useful for disabling sentries without alerting others."

"If he can manage control at range," Kellen points out. "His precision drops significantly beyond three meters."

Disappointments. All of them.

"Then we work on that. We have maybe three weeks before Rennaux demands results. If our team isn't ready by then, he'll replace us with someone who will get the job done, regardless of collateral damage."

The implication remains unspoken between us. The Syndicate wants those women back in a facility, but they want them alive and functional. If another team is sent, they might not be so careful. Female casualties would be deemed acceptable losses.

"I'm meeting with him in the morning. He'll want a progress report."

Elias, always the optimist, offers, "We're ahead of schedule with most recruits. Focus on that."

"And emphasize Ashford's unique abilities," Kellen suggests, ignoring my scowl. "Rennaux will appreciate the strategic advantage of remote emotional manipulation for retrieval operations."

He's right, though I'm reluctant to admit it. For all my issues with Ashford, his power represents a significant asset if properly harnessed.

I stand, waving at my second and third to remain seated when they move to follow. "I need to check the office. There's bound to be a stack of bullshit waiting for my signature."

"Don't stay up all night reading requisition forms," Elias warns with a half-smile. "Remember what happened last time."

Last time, I'd gone thirty-six hours without sleep trying to process the backlog of administrative work. Nearly broke a recruit's arm during a demonstration when my concentration slipped. Not my finest moment.

But still, Elias cares too much.

And that's what I appreciate about him. He understands me to my core and will always be a loyal friend because of it.

"I'll make it quick." It's a promise we all know I won't keep. The paperwork never ends—just multiplies the moment I focus on something else.

I leave them to finish their meal, stopping briefly at the food station to collect something I can take to my quarters. As Commander, I'm entitled to eat privately, and I prefer it that way. Food is fuel, nothing more. I don't need company to consume it.

The corridors are quieter now as evening duty shifts begin. Most recruits will be in their quarters or the common areas, recovering from the day's training and preparing for tomorrow. My office is an outer corner of the administrative wing—a location I chose deliberately for its isolation.

Inside, the space is sparse but functional. Metal desk, three chairs, wall-mounted screens for communications, and a small arsenal of weapons secured in a cabinet along one wall. No personal items or decorations. Nothing to suggest the office belongs to me specifically. If I died tomorrow, someone else could step into this role without disruption.

As expected, the message queue on my terminal is full. Twenty-three new communications requiring responses, three flagged as high priority. I scan through the subjects with growing irritation.

Request for additional bunks at Outpost Seven.

Complaint about a shift supervisor in Ofin's central district.

Proposal for redistribution of patrol routes in Belken.

And on and on.

If it were permissible, I'd program an automated response telling them all to solve their own fucking problems. They're supposed to be Enforcers, not helpless children needing constant guidance. Figure it out. Adapt. Overcome. Is that not what we drill into every recruit?

But I can't. Because part of leadership is dealing with this mundane bullshit, no matter how much I despise it.

And I despise the fuck out of it.

The priority messages are answered first, addressing each with the minimum necessary words. My replies are direct, unambiguous, and leave no room for further discussion. Yes, you can have the additional bunks. No, I won't reassign the supervisor because you don't like his tone. Yes, implement the new patrol routes immediately.

By the time I finish the last message, my food has gone cold and my patience has evaporated completely. Tomorrow will bring more of the same. An endless cycle of petty problems that somehow become my responsibility despite having nothing to do with any actual mission.

I rub my eyes beneath my mask, allowing myself a brief moment of weakness in the privacy of my office. Tomorrow, I'll need to put on the Commander face again—implacable and unwavering. I'll need to impress Rennaux, push the recruits harder, maintain absolute control over every aspect of this operation.

My thoughts drift to the insubordinate recruit again. There's something off about Ashford; something that nags at my instincts.

His file is clean. Standard background, normal progression through education and early employment, no disciplinary issues or notable achievements. A completely unremarkable man who somehow possesses a remarkable power. The kind of power that could be dangerous if misused.

The kind of power that could potentially influence people to aid our females in escape.

I dismiss the thought immediately. If Ashford were behind the breaches, he wouldn't have joined this unit. He wouldn't place himself directly under my scrutiny, it would be suicide.

Still...

I'll watch him more closely. Test his reactions as I push his limits and search for inconsistencies in his behavior. If nothing else, it will force him to improve his physical capabilities or wash out trying.

Tomorrow's training will focus on combat endurance. Seven hours of continuous drills, minimal rest periods. I'll pair him against physically superior opponents, force him to adapt or break. The others won't fare much better, but Ashford will be my primary focus.

One week. That's what I told him today, and that's all he gets, useful power or not.

The sharp trill of the desk phone startles me from my stupor. I glance at the clock—nearly nine. There's only one person who uses this phone to communicate with me.

I let it ring twice more before lifting the receiver. "Leader Rennaux. I was under the impression we were meeting in the morning."

"Commander. Change of plans." The voice on the other end carries the weight of absolute authority, each syllable clipped and demanding. "Report."

My spine straightens automatically, years of conditioning taking hold despite the privacy of my office. "Sir. Training is progressing on schedule. The recruits are adapting to the phys-ical requirements, though several have been dismissed for inadequacy."

"How many?"

"Five so far, sir. We're down to fifteen active recruits."

Silence stretches through the line—he disapproves. When he speaks again, ice coats every word. "Fifteen. From an initial pool of twenty."

"Yes, sir." My voice remains steady and calm. "The standards are necessarily high for this mission. We cannot afford weak links."

"What we cannot afford, Commander, is delay." The temperature in his tone somehow drops further. "The rebel situation grows more concerning by the day. Our intelligence suggests they're mobilizing, possibly planning something significant. We need your team operational."

My jaw clenches. "Understood, sir. However, sending unprepared recruits into the field would be—"

"Your job is to prepare them, is it not?"

The words drive heat through me, but I swallow the building anger. "Of course, sir. The recruits are showing improvement. Ashford demonstrated unexpected capability during training, while Styx, Flor, Eston, and others are exceeding baseline expectations in tactical scenarios."

"Ashford." He pauses, papers rustling before he speaks again. "The one requiring special accommodations?"

Fuck. Of course he'd notice that detail in the reports. "Medical requirements that don't impact performance, sir. He's proven surprisingly effective despite initial concerns."

"Effective enough to warrant the resources we're investing in this operation?"

I almost chuckle—that's not what he wants to know. What he's really asking is if he needs to dismantle our team and find someone other than me more capable for the mission. I stare at the wall of my office, at the mission parameters pinned there in neat rows. Each recruit's progress tracked in methodical detail. "The team will be ready within the projected time-frame, sir."

"See that they are. The Syndicate's patience is not infinite, Commander. We have other options if this experiment proves unsuccessful."

Other options. The threat doesn't need elaboration—I know exactly what happens to failed operations and their commanders. "Understood, sir."

"Good, I want daily progress reports moving forward. And Commander?" His voice drops to something that might pass for conversational if not for the steel underneath. "Remember that your reputation precedes you. Do not let sentiment cloud your judgment regarding recruit selection."

The line is dead before I can respond.

I deposit the receiver with care, my knuckles white around the plastic. The urge to slam it into the cradle wars with years of disciplined control. Instead, I lean back in my chair and stare at the ceiling, allowing the fury to simmer beneath my skin for several moments.

Sentiment. As if I've ever allowed emotion to interfere with operational efficiency. As if the decisions I make aren't calculated down to the smallest detail.

But even as the anger burns, a strand of unease winds through my thoughts. The timeline is accelerating as pressure from above increases. And despite my assurances, I'm not entirely certain all fifteen remaining recruits will make the cut.

Particularly not the one who somehow managed to shatter Brenner's leg while looking like he might collapse from exhaustion.

I reach for my cold food, finally removing my mask. The air feels cool against my face, a reminder of the vulnerability that comes with exposure.

Tomorrow, the mask goes back on, and the Commander returns while the man underneath disappears.

It's the only way to maintain order—to ensure the system that protects us all continues to function.

No matter what it costs me personally.

CHAPTER THIRTEEN
CASSIA

Rain hammers against my mask, creating a deafening symphony of tiny impacts that makes it near impossible to hear anything else. I blink water from my eyelashes, struggling to focus through the narrow slit that reveals a blurred, distorted world beyond. The storm turns midday into twilight as dark, swollen clouds hang oppressively low.

It's been three days since Brenner was escorted from training. Endless sideways glances and whispered comments when I walk past other recruits. Building anxiety waiting for the Commander to call me in for punishment that never comes. I mean, I didn't intentionally break his leg, but I would think our esteemed leader would love nothing more than to kick me for ridding the team of a powerful member.

And now this—standing in the pouring rain alongside every other recruit in our special unit while Kellen gestures to a derelict urban landscape stretched out before us.

"This will test everything you've learned so far," he shouts over the storm's fury, his voice barely reaching us despite his evident effort.

I squint through the downpour, taking in the training

ground. It's a mock city—not large by real standards but impressive. Crumbling concrete structures rise four or five stories high, their windows blown out, walls scarred with simulated battle damage. Alleyways snake between buildings, some so narrow a person would need to turn sideways to navigate them. Makeshift bridges—ropes strung across gaps where buildings nearly touch—create unstable pathways above street level. Wooden planks link some rooftops, while ziplines stretch between others. The entire setup forms a three-dimensional maze designed to challenge, confuse, and test.

It's beautiful in its decay. An elaborate monument to urban warfare.

Kellen stands before us, hands clasped behind his back, seemingly unbothered by the rain soaking through his uniform. His posture remains calm; authoritative despite water cascading down his mask and shoulders. No hint of discomfort. No visible reaction to being drenched. The perfect Enforcer.

Good for him, but I won't pretend to be comfortable. I'd turn right around and sprint to the showers, soaking in their warmth, if it were permitted.

"Decision-making under pressure," he calls out. "That's the difference between success and failure in the field. Between living and dying."

I shift my weight, easing the growing ache in my lower back. We've been standing here for twenty minutes already while other Enforcers prepare. My bladder protests, and I silently curse my decision to drink extra water at breakfast. Stupid mistake.

At least the rain could be useful for something—washing away any evidence of me wetting myself and suffering through such embarrassment.

"You'll be facing multiple scenarios requiring immediate judgment," Kellen continues, not once adjusting his stance.

"When to eliminate a threat versus when to subdue or sacrifice one for the many. When to trust intelligence that might be compromised."

The rain intensifies, sheets of water now pounding against us with such force I have to widen my legs to maintain balance. My uniform, designed to repel most weather, has finally surrendered to the onslaught. Cold water seeps through at my shoulders, crawls down my spine, soaks into my boots until my toes squelch with each subtle shift of weight. Yuck.

I risk a glance over my shoulder, spotting Arayik and Elias standing beneath a hastily constructed shelter along with several senior Enforcers I don't recognize. Unlike Kellen, they've chosen to stay somewhat dry. Smart. My gaze lingers on Elias a moment longer than necessary, and I snatch it away before anyone notices. Since showing me the simulation room, he's been keeping his distance. I tell myself it's better this way.

I don't need a friend here, regardless of how lonely and overwhelmed I am.

"This exercise combines elements from all three training tracks," our third leader shouts, drawing my attention back. "For once, you won't be separated into your usual groups. Every recruit will participate together, divided into teams of three."

That explains why we're all here—even the recruits I barely know from other training rotations. Still, it feels premature. We've only been at this for what, two weeks? Most of us can handle the basic simulations, and whatever complex scenario they've constructed here is far past that. The Syndicate seems intent on pushing us faster than I hoped; something about those escapees has them rattled.

"You'll notice an audience today," Kellen continues, gesturing toward the shelter where the senior Enforcers stand. "They aren't here to observe. They're here to hunt." A ripple of tension passes through the group. Someone behind me shifts their weight, a boot scraping against wet gravel. "Each team will enter the simulation zone separately. Your primary objective is to locate and neutralize the Enforcers stationed throughout. Each one wears an orange flag attached to their back. Rip off the flag, and they're considered eliminated."

He pauses, allowing the words to sink in. "Secondary objective: find and secure the object the Enforcers are protecting. Bring it back to me to complete your mission."

A bright haze of light flashes, briefly illuminating the rain-soaked landscape. Three seconds later, thunder crashes overhead with enough force to rattle my ribcage. The storm is directly above us now.

"Sir," someone calls out—Calder, I think. "What's the object we're looking for?"

Kellen's head tilts, a subtle motion I've learned indicates mild amusement. "Finding it is part of the challenge, recruit."

Enforcers emerge from the shelter, walking toward our group with purposeful strides, causing my heart to hammer through my breastbone.

They're not here for you. You haven't been caught, this is simply training.

The inner encouragement doesn't help, and my breathing struggles for it.

Each approaching Enforcer carries two weapons—sleek, matte black pistols similar to the ones we've trained with in Elias' simulation room. I recognize the design...non-lethal but capable of delivering a painful shock on impact.

An armed man halts before me, surrendering one of his weapons without a word. The gun is heavy, cold and solid in my palm. I check the safety as we were taught, familiarizing with the weight and balance.

Not my first choice of weapon, but I'll use it if I must.

"You are permitted to employ whatever force necessary to complete your objectives." Kellen paces now, gaze snagging on each of us. "Combat is authorized." My stomach knots.

I've improved somewhat in physical readiness, but I'm still nowhere near the level of these senior Enforcers. Most of them have been doing this for years—possibly decades. We're outnumbered and outmatched.

"First team to volunteer?"

There's a moment of hesitation before Thane steps from our lineup, followed by Calder and Gage. All three stand taller than me, their naturally broader shoulders making me feel even more out of place among them. Thane's a Clinger who can adhere to any surface he touches. With Calder's Thermic power and Gage's Telepathy, they have a well-balanced team.

Kellen nods. "Excellent. The rest of you, step back."

The Enforcers with flags scatter, disappearing into the mock city like shadows melting into the night. I count fifteen of them. Fifteen against three. We're about to have our asses handed to us.

The rain continues its assault, water running in rivulets down the contours of my uniform. I shift, uncomfortable and acutely aware of my bladder's increasing, urgent signals. This is bad timing—really bad timing as I do not wish to pee on my team's feet.

I'm going to get a damn infection.

After a few minutes, Kellen signals for Thane's team to begin. The three of them check their weapons one final time before jogging into the city and disappearing between the buildings.

A holographic display springs to life, hovering above the device in our leader's hand and somehow remains stable despite the rain. The display shows six different camera angles, each revealing a new part of the city.

The device is placed on a portable stand, positioned for everyone's view. "Watch carefully," Kellen instructs, stepping back to join us. "There's much to learn from observation."

My feet shift closer, curious despite my discomfort. The cameras switch views when they detect movement, jumping from one location to another as people pass through their fields of vision. There must be hundreds of them scattered throughout the city for this kind of coverage. Impressive.

The first camera shows Thane's team moving in tight formation, backs to each other as they clear an intersection. Another camera angle catches a glimpse of an Enforcer ducking into a building, while a third shows a rooftop position where someone has established a sniper's nest. The fourth, fifth, and sixth angles switch rapidly between various locations, never remaining in one spot for more than a few seconds.

As amazing as it is, there's a disadvantage in watching this —we have no idea where these cameras are positioned. When my turn comes, this preview won't help me navigate. If anything, it only adds to my anxiety, showing me just how carefully the Enforcers have positioned themselves.

The simulation progresses fast once contact is made. Thane's team encounters resistance within minutes, exchanging fire with two Enforcers who ambush them from an alleyway.

Calder takes a hit to the shoulder, his body convulsing as the simulation gun delivers its shock. He drops to one knee but recovers with a groan, returning fire with admirable accuracy.

Gage provides cover while Thane circles behind the Enforcers, managing to flank one and rip the orange flag from his back. The 'killed' Enforcer raises his hands in surrender and moves off-camera, out of the simulation.

Over the next forty minutes, we watch as Thane's team advances methodically through the city. They work well together, communicating with hand signals and maintaining discipline even when separated. They eliminate twelve of the fifteen Enforcers, losing Gage in the process when he's ambushed by three opponents.

Finally, they locate what must be the objective—a small metal container hidden in the basement of a building near the center of the city. Calder provides cover while Thane secures the object, and they fight their way back to the entrance, eliminating the final three Enforcers along the way. When they emerge from the city, soaked and mud-splattered but triumphant, Thane raises the container. It's a plain metal box about the size of two fists, with no obvious opening mechanism. The Syndicate insignia is stamped on its surface—three interlocking hexagons representing the three founding families.

Kellen congratulates them before the eliminated Enforcers return, collecting discarded flags and repositioning them on their uniforms. They disappear back into the city to reset for the next team.

"Why did you kill them all before exiting the training?"

"Leaving enemies behind is lazy," Thane replies to Kellen without hesitation. "They could regroup and counter-attack. Complete elimination ensures mission success."

He receives a nod in response, the leader apparently satisfied with this answer before dismissing them to join the observers.

Two more teams cycle through the simulation with similar results. Both employ the same strategy: eliminating all Enforcers before extracting the objective. Both teams insist that total elimination is the only viable strategy.

My eyes remain on the screen, but I listen to the other recruits whisper among themselves, pride evident in their voices. They speak of kill counts and tactics as if discussing a game. As if the people they killed weren't real, even in simulation. The casual conversation churns my stomach.

"Ashford, Flor, Eston," Kellen calls out to me, Killian, and Pax. "You're up."

My heart sinks. This is the worst day—my bladder is nearly bursting, and I'm paired with two recruits I've barely spoken to. Killian is a Remnant who can sense impressions of past events through touch while Pax is a Telepath. Both useful powers, but we have no established teamwork or trust.

As we move toward the start point, I survey my temporary teammates. Killian stands a head taller than me, with a lean build and rigid posture that suggests much training before joining our group. I can just make out piercing blue eyes through his mask's slit when he assesses me. Pax is shorter, more compact, with a restless energy that manifests in constant small movements—fingers tapping against his thigh, weight shifting from one foot to the other.

The three of us step into the mock city, rain intensifying as I fight the urge to cross my legs against the pressure in my bladder. It's taunting me.

And there's absolutely no way for me to relieve myself here —not with cameras everywhere and teammates watching. I'll just have to endure it.

Before we can advance more than a few meters, I grab Killian's arm, bringing our small group to a halt in the shadow of the first building.

"Wait," I hiss, my voice barely audible. "We need a plan."

Blue eyes narrow. "What do you mean? We do what the others did—find the Enforcers, eliminate them, get the object."

I shake my head. "Did you watch the previous teams? They all charged in without planning and got their asses kicked before eventually winning through brute force and losses. We can be smarter."

Pax shifts, glancing around. His discomfort is palpable—whether from the rain, the delay, or something else, I can't tell. "What did you have in mind?" he asks.

I consider our strengths and limitations. None of us are powerhouses like Gage or precision fighters like Thane. We need strategy over strength.

"We split up," I suggest. "Cover more ground, find the objective faster. I'll take north, Pax west, Killian east. Use the upper levels where possible to avoid street level ambushes."

Killian seems skeptical, but our teammate nods. "Makes sense. What if one of us finds the objective?"

"Secure it if possible, but don't risk extraction alone. If you're cornered, defend your position and one of us will come when we can." I hesitate, cursing a flaw in the plan. "How do we communicate if we're separated?"

Pax taps his temple. "I can reach about fifty meters. If we stay within range of each other, I can relay messages."

That's not far—especially in a city layout—but it's better than nothing. "Good. Our primary goal is the objective, not eliminating every Enforcer. Let's move."

We separate at the first intersection, each aiming for a different direction. As I head north, it dawns on me that this is the first decision I've made as a de facto leader since arriving at the training center. It feels strange giving orders to men who would never take them from a woman. But here, behind the mask, they don't question my authority. Another bitter reminder of the Syndicate's absurd *order*.

The rain, oddly enough, works to my advantage, masking small sounds as I move and reducing visibility. I hug the walls of buildings, checking each corner before proceeding. The urban landscape is disorienting—streets bend at odd angles, debris blocks obvious paths, forcing detours through buildings or side alleys.

I chuckle; the irony isn't lost on me.

The storm darkens our landscape further, making the environment even more challenging to navigate. I use this, sticking to the dimmest shadows, moving with deliberate slowness when crossing exposed areas. My years of practicing silent motion serve me well now.

A small square between buildings rises before me just as movement catches my eye—an Enforcer positioned behind a low wall, gun trained on the approach I'm taking. I duck back just as they fire, the shot impacting the stone where my head had been seconds before.

Stars, that would have hurt.

My heart spikes, adrenaline flooding my system despite knowing the weapons aren't lethal. The danger feels real enough to trigger a fear response.

My back presses against a wall as I pant, begging my heart to slow so I can think. Why does everyone in this damn place aim for my head? Do they think I can't die any other way? I strain to detect footsteps over the rain, listening for signs the Enforcer is approaching, but the storm still drowns out most sounds. My power indicates the enemy is close, determined to take me down, but it can't pinpoint where.

Closing my eyes, I focus on my other senses. When visual information is limited, the body compensates. I've spent countless nights moving through pitch darkness, training my body to navigate without sight.

No movement. No change in the rhythm of the rain. The Enforcer must be holding position, waiting for me to make another attempt.

I hold my weapon with a tight grip, summoning courage. Without giving myself time to reconsider, I spin around the corner, gun raised, finger nestling the trigger—

But there's no one there.

Confused, I step forward, scanning for movement. Nothing. Where did they—

Something slams into my back with crushing force, driving me face-first into the wet ground. Pain explodes through my body as I impact the street, reigniting sore spots that my salve dulled, mud and grit grinding into my face where it meets the edge of my mask. Fucking hell, can everyone stop doing this?

I taste blood—my teeth cut the inner ridge of my lip. The weight on my back is immense, pinning me successfully.

Rough hands grab the back of my mask, shoving my head harder into the ground. I can't breathe, can't move, panic rising as I struggle for oxygen.

With a desperate surge of strength born from the pure need to survive, I buck my hips and twist violently to the side, creating just enough space to roll. The maneuver catches my attacker by surprise, and I manage to flip onto my back, immediately regretting it as his hips settle on my abdomen, pressing against my already full bladder.

It fucking *hurts*. And I swear a few drops escape before I stop them.

The Enforcer above me is massive—at least twice my size, with shoulders blocking what little light remains in the stormy sky. His body language radiates confidence. He knows he has me.

He reaches for his gun, which must have fallen during our struggle. I seize the moment, driving my knee upward with all the force I can muster. It catches him in the back, throwing him slightly off balance—not enough to dislodge him, but enough to buy me a second.

I grab for his uniform, fingers scrabbling for purchase on the wet fabric, trying to find the orange flag I know must be attached somewhere. He blocks my attempt with a heavy forearm across my chest, pressing until breathing becomes painful again.

My vision swims, lungs burning as dark spots encroach at the edges. I've never fought like this before—never been in a position where someone was actively trying to hurt me outside practice.

His weight shifts to grab the fallen weapon, and I exploit the momentary redistribution. Twisting my body with every ounce of strength I possess, I manage to get one arm free and reach around his torso, fingers closing on fabric that feels different from the uniform—

The flag.

I yank with everything I have, tearing it free just as he brings his weapon to bear on my head. He freezes, then curses loudly, the sound distorted by his mask and the pounding rain.

"Eliminated," I wheeze, still struggling for breath.

The Enforcer shoves off me with unnecessary force, standing to his full height and looking down at me with what I can only imagine is contempt. "Lucky shot," he mutters, then extends a hand for me.

I ignore it.

Instead, I roll to my side and push to my feet like the independent woman I am. Muscles scream in protest—each one convulsing, my face throbbing where it was ground into the street. But I won't show weakness. Not to him—or any of them.

I'm brushing mud from my uniform when he speaks again. "You didn't cut your hair before coming here?"

My body freezes, ice shooting through my veins. My hand shifts to my head on instinct and I feel nothing but horror that my hair partially escaped its tight bun, now hanging in wet strands around the edge of my mask.

It's okay. This isn't damning...I just need to remain calm.

"Yep," I respond, forcing my tone to be neutral, trying to sound masculine despite the fear constricting my throat.

"Stupid," he mutters, spinning to leave.

I stand motionless, struggling to decide whether tucking my hair back would draw more attention than leaving it. Ultimately, I choose to leave it—adjusting it now might suggest I'm self-conscious about it, which could trigger suspicion. Better to act like it's normal, like I don't care that it's fallen out.

Retrieving my weapon, I continue northward, more caution in my steps now. My body throbs from the encounter, and my bladder screams, pounding against my abdomen after having that Enforcer's weight bearing down on it. I clench my muscles, refusing to give in to the discomfort.

Truthfully, I'm surprised it hasn't burst yet.

The rain eases a bit, transitioning from torrential to merely heavy. It's enough of a change that I hear better—distant gunshots and shouting echo through the city streets.

I approach the northernmost building, a four-story structure with most of its windows intact. Logic suggests the objective might be hidden at the furthest point from the entrance, forcing teams to navigate the entire city. The building is dark, its interior a maze of collapsed walls and shredded debris. I navigate in silence, inspecting each room and discovering nothing but more dust. The sense of being watched prickles at the back of my neck, but I see no one.

Reaching the top floor, I'm about to declare the building clear when a faint scraping catches my attention. It's coming from above—the roof access must be nearby.

After a few minutes, I locate a ladder built into the wall, leading to a trapdoor in the ceiling. The sound is definitely coming from there. Someone's on the roof.

Climbing one-handed, ensuring my weapon remains ready, I edge the trapdoor open just enough to peer out. Rain immediately streams through the gap, but I can make out a figure silhouetted against the dark sky, standing with their back to me.

Guiding the trapdoor open further, wincing as it creaks, I haul myself onto the roof. The figure doesn't turn. Either they didn't hear or they're pretending not to notice, hoping to draw me into the open. My body remains crouched, weapon trained on the Enforcer's back. Standard procedure would be to announce myself and demand surrender, but this isn't a real engagement—it's a test. And I *need* to pass it.

The Commander is watching.

I advance at a neutral pace, shifting from cover to cover—air conditioning units, ventilation shafts, more piles of debris—until I'm within striking distance. The Enforcer remains facing away, seemingly unaware of my presence. It's too easy.

That's when I notice they're guarding something—a small metal container identical to the one the other teams recovered. The objective. Right there for the taking.

Without further hesitation, I lunge forward, aiming to grab both the flag and the container in one swift move. But the Enforcer reacts with inhuman speed, whirling to block my attack with ease. They're good—better than the one I encountered earlier.

We grapple, exchanging blows that the training center's combat instructors would find laughable. I'm still new at this—my form sloppy, my strikes lacking helpful force.

But what I lack in technique, I will always make up for in desperation.

I manage to land a solid hit to a shoulder, unbalancing him. My fingers brush against the flag on his back, but before I can grab it, something stops me.

The flag is a different shade of orange.

It's subtle—a deeper, more reddish hue than the standard flags. And this Enforcer was guarding the objective directly.

This isn't just another Enforcer...no, this is their lead.

In a real mission, killing him might end the engagement, but it would also eliminate a valuable intelligence asset. Someone who might have information about other hostiles, their plans, and locations.

Decision time. Eliminate or capture?

I pause long enough for the man to recover, then make my choice. Instead of going for the flag, I swing my weapon in an arc, connecting with the side of his head—not hard enough to cause real damage, but enough to stun him.

While he's disoriented, I snatch the flag I took from the first Enforcer and use it to secure this one's wrists, tying them in a butterfly knot. My father taught me knot-tying as a child, one of the only 'masculine' skills he thought might be useful regardless of gender.

"Don't move," I order, my voice low and steady in an effort to sound authoritative despite my internal shakiness. I secure the metal container, clutching it under one arm while keeping my weapon trained on my captive with the other hand.

The Enforcer glares at me through the eye slit of his mask, saying nothing.

I nod behind him before commanding, "Get up. You're coming with me."

He remains seated. Defiant.

Unlucky for him, my patience is already stretched thin by pain and the increasingly urgent demands of my bladder, and snaps. I kick him in the side—hard enough to make my point.

"I said get up," I repeat, pressing the barrel of my weapon against his temple. "Or I'll shoot you in the head until the simulated force actually causes damage."

The words stun me...they're cruel and callous, nothing like the person I think of myself being. But I know these men would show no such restraint if our positions were reversed.

The thought hardens my resolve.

"Move." The gun jabs his spine as he finally stands. We descend from the roof to the street level in tense silence. My weapon remains pressed between his shoulder blades, my finger near—but not on—the trigger. It would be embarrassing to accidentally shoot my hostage.

We begin the trek back to the main entrance, more careful now that I'm hampered by a prisoner and the objective.

About halfway there, another Enforcer steps out from an alleyway, weapon raised in our direction. My prisoner tenses, but makes no attempt to break free.

The newcomer hesitates, clearly caught off guard by the situation. "Cap, what do I do?" he calls to my prisoner. "We weren't briefed on a hostage situation."

The man in front of me grumbles something under his breath—likely cursing his subordinate for giving away his position. I was right, this is their leader.

I'm about to raise my weapon when a shot rings out from somewhere to my right. The new Enforcer jerks as the fake bullet impacts his side, then crumples to the ground. Killian emerges from the shadows, rushing forward to rip the flag from the fallen Enforcer's back.

"Ashford," he acknowledges with a nod, glancing between me and my prisoner. "How many flags have you collected?"

My reply is swift. "One." I nod toward the flag securing my prisoner's wrist before patting his shoulder. "Plus this one. You?"

"Nine," he answers, satisfaction evident in his voice. "That leaves four unaccounted for."

I do a quick mental count. Fifteen Enforcers total, minus the ones Killian has eliminated, minus my one kill and one capture...yes, four remaining.

"Take point, I'll bring up the rear with our guest." Killian isn't so happy about that plan.

After a brief argument—he wants to go back and find Pax—he reluctantly agrees, leading the way as we navigate back through the rain-slick streets. Our progress is slow, each intersection requiring careful clearing before we proceed. The rain and thunder continue to mask most sounds, making it difficult to locate approaching enemies until they're practically on top of us.

When we reach the entrance after a long, painful walk, Killian drags my prisoner out into the open area where Kellen, Arayik, Elias, and the other recruits wait. I hang back, scanning the assembled group, searching for Pax. No sign of him.

"Where's the rest of your team?" the Commander demands, stalking toward me with the predatory grace I've come to associate with him.

I glance at the city, then to the surveillance screen Kellen set up. The cameras flick between empty streets and buildings —no sign of movement. Pax should have found us by now if he was able.

"One member is unaccounted for, along with four enemies," I report. Look at me, using proper terminology. How quickly the language of oppression becomes natural when you're surrounded by it. "Permission to search for them?"

Arayik's eyes bore into mine. Even without his expression, his posture emanates disappointment. Next to him, Elias studies me with what looks like interest rather than judgment. Kellen remains unreadable as always, arms crossed, observing without comment.

No one speaks, and I take their silence as tacit approval, raising my weapon once more and preparing to re-enter the simulation.

I've only taken a few steps when a sound catches my attention—something high-pitched and repetitive, like knuckles against glass. I search upper levels for the source and finally spot movement in a third floor window of a building facing west.

Pax is there, pressed against the glass, making frantic gestures. Something's wrong.

"Shit," I mutter, breaking into a run despite my body's increasing hatred of me.

I enter the building at street level, taking the stairs two at a time, ignoring the pain that shoots through my nerves. At the third floor, I pause, weapon ready, clearing the hallway before proceeding.

The building's interior is a maze of empty rooms and collapsed walls. My feet are swift but advance cautiously, following the direction of the window I spotted Pax in. It should be on the left side at the end of the hall.

Muffled sounds guide me to a closed door. I pause, listening. It sounds like...struggling? Voices, too low to make out words.

I raise my weapon, kick the door open with far more force than necessary, and freeze at the sight greeting me.

Pax is indeed there—pressed against the glass by another Enforcer. But they aren't fighting. They're kissing, their masks discarded on the floor beside them, faces locked together in a passionate embrace that leaves no question about their intentions. The Enforcer has one hand wrapped around both his and Pax's exposed cocks, working them together in rhythmic motions.

They jump apart at my entrance, faces flushed with a mixture of arousal and surprise. My teammate's eyes widen, panic flashing across his features. The Enforcer—a man with sharp cheekbones and a day's-old stubble—reaches instinctively for his weapon before realizing the futility of his position.

I stand frozen, unable to look away despite the burning embarrassment flooding through me. I've never seen two people engaged in any sexual act before—only drawings.

This is different. Raw. Real. Two bodies finding pleasure in each other, heedless of the simulation or watching eyes.

I'm an intruder; a voyeur witnessing something deeply private. Yet I can't help noticing details—the flush spreading across Pax's chest, the way the Enforcer's abdomen tenses with each breath, the half-lidded pleasure in their eyes.

Something uncomfortable stirs in my lower abdomen—not my bladder this time, but a different kind of tension. A warmth that spreads, my skin prickling beneath its uniform.

My hand raises in wordless apology as I back out of the room, pulling the door closed before retreating. Neither man calls after me or tries to explain. I pause in the hallway, heart pounding.

A part of me envies them. Not specifically what they were doing, but the ability to reach for another person. To find something mutual and desired.

Shuffling back to the ground floor, I wonder how I explain what I found without betraying Pax's privacy? Is this like Brenner and Corin, where they'd kill another before disclosing their relationship? I wouldn't think so if neither has followed.

By the time I reach the entrance, everyone is staring at me. The Commander strides forward, his posture rigid and twitchy.

"Well?" he demands? "Where are the others?"

I glance at the surveillance screen, which still cycles through empty streets and buildings. None of the cameras show the room where Pax and the Enforcer are. A small blessing.

"I..." I begin, uncertain how to proceed.

Arayik's fingers curl at his sides. "Ashford!" he barks, his voice cutting through the rain like a blade. "Report!"

I hesitate another moment before speaking. "They're fine." The words are inadequate. "They're...occupied." That earns a chorus of snickers from the other recruits.

Someone calls out from the back, "Never seen a dick before, Ashford? You look uncomfortable."

Heat floods my face, creeping along my neck and spreading across my cheeks. I'm grateful for the mask right now, though I suspect my body language betrays my embarrassment. If my face weren't covered, everyone would know I'm not just uncomfortable—I'm mortified.

Yes, I've seen male genitalia before, but never on a real person. Never aroused and definitely never being touched by another. The image burns in my mind—Pax pressed against the glass, head thrown back in pleasure, the Enforcer's hand working both of them in rhythmic strokes.

My head shakes as I try to dislodge the thought. This line of thinking is dangerous and distracting. Inappropriate for someone in my position.

But with this being the second time I've witnessed these couplings, my mind wonders: do all the men here engage in such activities? With no women available except those purchased from breeding facilities or taken in raids, how do they satisfy themselves? Do they find comfort with each other, constructing bonds of physical intimacy alongside their professional relationships?

Does Elias...

The questions form before I can stop them. What would Elias look like in such a moment? Would his face—that handsome face I saw briefly in the simulation room—flush with pleasure? Would his stomach muscles tense and release like the Enforcer's did? Would his hands be gentle or demanding?

What would his body feel like under my touch? Would his skin be softer than it appears, or rough with the calluses of life as a soldier? Would he have hair on his chest, trailing down and down to where...

A crack of thunder directly overhead jolts me from my inappropriate reverie. The storm has intensified again, sheets of rain driving in horizontal patterns across the training ground. Kellen is speaking, ordering everyone to return to the transports. I've been lost in my thoughts like an idiot, missing whatever conclusion was reached about the exercise.

I follow the group mechanically, my mind still caught between embarrassment and unwanted arousal. There's too many things happening inside me right now, I just need to get back to the training center and sleep it off.

After I race to the bathroom, of course.

My back settles against a bench in transport two, Killian across from me, the container we recovered clutched in his hands. He's animatedly describing our strategy to the other recruits, emphasizing his kill count and failing to mention my contribution. I should be annoyed, but I'm too exhausted to care.

As the vehicle lurches into motion, I close my eyes, allowing the vibrations rumble through my aching body. Today's exercise has opened doors in my mind I'm not sure I'm ready to walk through—questions about power, agency, intimacy, and desire that have no easy answers in this broken world.

I did what I did with the captured Enforcer because I was thinking strategically. In a real combat situation, taking the enemy leader alive would be more valuable than killing them. They would have intelligence, connections, the ability to order their subordinates to surrender. One death versus the potential of many lives saved through the information they could provide.

That was my rationale, at least. But a small voice whispers that perhaps I also wanted to prove I'm different—that I don't share the same callous disregard for life these men have demonstrated.

That I can complete a mission without leaving a trail of bodies and tears in my wake.

Does that make me weak in their eyes? Or inefficient? Either way, I didn't follow the established pattern. I deviated. Made a choice that marked me as different.

And difference, in the Syndicate's world, is dangerous.

The transport lurches over a bump, and my jaw clenches as I hold in a whine. My muscles flex—hopefully we reach the training center soon. This day has been long enough without adding pissing myself to the list.

As we drive through the rumbling storm, my head wanders. I've been here many days and have gathered miniscule amounts of information on these men. It worries me. Am I any closer to reaching my goal, or am I simply being drawn deeper into their world, becoming more like them with each passing day as my priorities shift?

The thought of that terrifies me.

CHAPTER FOURTEEN

CASSIA

A frown seizes my face as the purple-black bruises marring my ribs throb with each step I take toward the training room. These past few days have been grueling, and while I'm getting better, I'm not improving fast enough for the Commander's standards, regardless that I wake early each morning, sacrificing precious sleep to go over combat maneuvers.

The corridors are nearly empty this early, populated only by a few lone Enforcers on patrol who never acknowledge me. The low hum of electricity grates my ears, not only because of how annoying I find it, but it's become a sound I associate with being watched. The entire facility is under constant surveillance. And the facility isn't the only thing monitoring me.

They are watching too. Elias, Kellen, Arayik.

They aren't watching me because I'm special...they're watching because something about me isn't *right*. Some instinct tells them I don't belong, even if they can't identify why. It's why the Commander asked me that stupid question, to confirm I'm a fraud. It's why I've felt his eyes lingering on me during training, seen Kellen studying my movements when he thinks

I'm focused elsewhere, noticed how Elias seems to appear wherever I go.

My fists clench as I exhale slowly, forcing the tension from my shoulders. Paranoia will only make me more conspicuous—I must keep behaving as normal.

Well, normal for me. Which means being an idiot who's bad at just about everything.

The moment I step inside the training room, the smell of sweat, leather, and metal overwhelms me. The vast space grumbles with grunts, slapping of flesh against mats, and clattering of practice weapons. At the far end, several recruits are already in motion—practicing hand-to-hand techniques, running through drills, or speaking in hushed voices as they prepare for another day of punishment.

Arayik hovers near the center of the room, arms crossed, feet planted wide in a stance that declares ownership of the space. He watches as Calder is slammed onto the mat by Finnick with enough force that I swear I *feel* the impact from across the room. Ouch.

"Again," the Commander orders, his voice impatient.

Calder groans, rolling onto his hands and knees before pushing himself up. Compliance is always mandatory.

I take my place with the other recruits, hands resting at my sides, trying not to appear as tense as I feel. During these non-mandatory morning trainings, I usually spend the time working alone in my room, but today I felt compelled to join the group.

The moment I'm within view, Arayik's dark gaze snaps toward me, and I cringe. Stars, why does he have to be so scary looking? Perhaps I should ignore my impulses from now on.

His second and third stand near the training equipment, watching as Arayik addresses us. The three of them form a triangle of authority—Arayik the blunt force, Kellen the calculating mind, Elias the perceptive observer. Between them, nothing escapes notice.

It's nauseating.

"You're all fucking hopeless." Great way to begin the day. "You hesitate. You think too much. You rely on orders instead of instinct." His mask turns slowly, surveying each of us. "That gets you killed."

I almost choke when his dark eyes land on me a second time. The air thickens and I know I'm about to become an example.

"Get up here, Ashford."

My heart skips and cries for help I cannot offer.

I join the Commander, careful to keep my movements measured and confident despite the tremor threatening to work its way through my legs. I stop a few feet from him, keeping enough distance that he wouldn't be able to reach out and hit me like I'm sure he aches to.

He collects a wooden staff leaning against the wall and tosses it at my feet. It clatters against the floor, the sound unnaturally loud in the sudden quiet of the room. Everyone's watching—even the Enforcers not on our team.

"Pick it up," he commands.

I hesitate only for a fraction of a second before scrambling to grab the staff. I may spend unnecessary time readjusting my grip as I recall everything from our previous session with these. Traitorous words of begging almost slip through my mouth—I do not want to do this. I'm so tired.

Unfortunately, there's really nothing helpful in those memories. Just embarrassment.

He says nothing, leaving me barely a moment before he lunges.

The attack comes without warning—a powerful, diagonal strike aimed at my shoulder. I lift the staff just in time to block, the impact jolting through my arms and into my chest. I don't know how long I'll be able to keep this up with how bad everything hurts.

But that means nothing to the Great Arayik. No, my unstoppable groans only spur him on, as if it personally offends him that not everyone is as mighty as he is.

He doesn't hesitate or pull back as he charges with another attack, a low sweep meant to surprise me. I barely manage to step back, adjusting my grip on the staff before swinging toward his exposed side.

An effortless dodge, almost lazy. As if my best performance is barely worth acknowledging.

I try again, aiming for his knee this time, putting more force behind the swing. The second attempt isn't much better than the first. He shifts his weight, and my staff connects with nothing but air.

Then he moves—a blur of violence promising endless pain.

Something strikes my legs and I slam into the ground, the impact forcing me to cough-wheeze, if that's even possible. Pain explodes through my back, the training mat doing little to cushion the fall. Is that blood I taste?

It doesn't matter, Arayik continues.

He looms above me, pressing the tip of his weapon against my sternum with just enough pressure to communicate the message: if this were real, I'd be dead. "Again."

I grit my teeth, rolling onto my side and shoving myself to stand despite the protest of every muscle. I will not let him break me. I've spent decades restricted to a single house, surviving the suffocating weight of confinement and fear. This man—this Enforcer of the system that imprisoned me—*will not* be the one to make me yield.

Fuck him for hating me this much when I've done nothing but try.

I raise the staff and charge.

This time, I'm *faster*. This time, I anticipate his block and shift at the last second, changing the angle of my attack from his torso to his legs. My staff cracks against his shin with a satisfying thud.

It's not enough to take him down—I fear I'll never be strong enough for such a feat—but it's enough to cause him pause. A small victory...the first real one I've had against him.

His expression remains emotionless, but something in his stance changes. His weight shifts minutely as his grip on the staff adjusts. He's *watching* me now, not just waiting to take me down. I've become something worth paying attention to.

That's both encouraging and terrifying.

He ambushes from an unexpected angle; not direct, but a feint that draws my defense to the left before the real strike comes from the right. I'm too slow to adjust, and the staff blows into my side. My body is airborne for a sickening moment before plunging against the mat once more.

When I land, I know I'm not getting up so fast. The pain is immediate and consuming, radiating from my ribs outward in waves that make my vision swim. Something might be cracked. I don't believe it's broken as I can still breathe without the sharp agony that would indicate a fracture, but it's certainly damaged enough to slow me.

The Commander exhales sharply through his nose, the sound distorted by his mask. "Pathetic." His favorite word.

I force myself onto my elbows, chest heaving as I try to regain control of my breathing, but I don't respond. What could I possibly say? He's right yet again.

A shadow falls over me, the scrape of calloused skin grating my mask. My blood freezes. He's going to rip it off right here, giving everyone a front row seat to my impending execution.

Fingers twitch against the seam, testing almost. Is he waiting for me to react and this is just a test?

It doesn't matter...My breath spikes, the world shrinking to that single pressure on the strap. If he pulls, it's over—

Elias interjects from where he's been watching, head tilted. "You've improved," he notes, his tone neutral but not unkind.

The Commander's hand stills, hovering at the chin of my mask before falling away. He snorts, a dismissive response. "Not enough."

Kellen finally speaks, his posture more relaxed than the other two but his attention no less focused. "Then make him better."

Have the stars fallen, or am I hallucinating?

Two of my leaders are standing up for me against theirs. I... don't know what to think about that.

The words hang in the air between them—a challenge from subordinate to superior, but delivered in a way that doesn't directly contest Arayik's authority. The subtle politics between the three fascinates me—how they navigate each other's territories without open conflict. It's clear they're friends outside official capacity, but they never question one another out in the open like this.

Arayik's neck flexes as he faces me; my eyes flicking up to maintain contact with his. The darkness behind his irises slithers inside my nerves.

"Your week is almost up, Ashford." Each word is a brick in my resolve. "And impress me, you have not." He allows that to sink in before addressing the entire group once more. "Dismissed."

The other recruits disperse quickly, eager to escape his scrutiny and prepare for their day of training. I remain on the mat for a moment longer, gathering my strength before stomping away with an obvious hunch. I need a shower and a massage to even touch an atom of this pain.

I wait until most of the others have left before making for the door. My movements are deliberate and unhurried, despite the urgency building inside me. My week is almost up, and I'm certain the Commander is going to dismiss me from the team. Send me back to a world where I don't officially exist, declaring my mission a failure.

I can't walk away with nothing.

Once the corridor by my quarters is clear, I turn on my heel and travel the opposite direction. I've only been permitted on two underground levels, but if the Enforcers keep records on anything, it will be below that. The more restricted areas will hold valuable information.

My steps move with purpose, keeping their pace steady as they descend dozens of stairs. At the seventh landing, the opportunity I've been waiting for presents itself when two Enforcers ahead of me walk through a sliding door after one presses his palm to the scanner. As the door begins its automated closing sequence, I time my approach perfectly, slipping in behind them with footsteps so silent they register nothing but the sound of the door's pneumatic hiss.

The room beyond is dim, lit by the blue glow of dozens of terminals and screens lining the walls. It's some kind of monitoring station or data hub, far more sophisticated than anything I've seen in the areas accessible to recruits. The air tastes different here—cooler, with an undertone of ozone from the electronics.

I creep through the deepest shadows, sparing glances at the Enforcers who entered before me and are focused on a console at the far end of the room. I have perhaps minutes before they turn around or someone else enters.

My eyes scan the displays quickly. Most show security

feeds, status reports, or technical jargon I don't understand. But one screen near the center of the room catches my attention, its display different from the others. Rather than scrolling data or surveillance footage, the words on the screen raise hair along my arms.

TRANSFER ORDERS — PRIORITY LEVEL 1

My stomach clenches. The following text is small but legible from where I stand.

SUBJECTS: 17 FEMALE, 3 JUVENILE
ORIGIN: HOLDING FACILITY 2, PYREM
DESTINATION: RIVERTON
DEPARTURE: 0400 HOURS, DATE CODE 1207
AUTHORIZATION: SYNDICATE DIRECTIVE 892-A

Air catches in my throat. These women are being trans-ferred to the Riverton breeding facility—the Gilded Farm. Supposedly the most humane of the facilities, though that's a miniscule comfort considering what happens within its walls.

The date code indicates tomorrow. And there's nothing I can do to aid them.

Unless...

Are there not several locations indicated for the escapee activity? If the Enforcers know their general locations, maybe I could somehow get a message to them.

But how? Even if I knew where they are, I have no way to contact anyone outside this facility, no allies I can trust with this knowledge. I could attempt contacting Lachlan, though it's not like he's able to leave the house without risking both our lives.

Pausing a moment to grieve for these women, I mentally file away every detail on the screen. Even if I can't act now, I might find a use for it later. Every piece of intelligence is a potential weapon, if wielded correctly.

A soft hiss greets my ears, and I whirl, my hand hovering the knife secured at my belt. A figure stands at the entrance, foreboding in their presence. I don't know whether to feel relieved or horrified that Elias is the one who strides into the room.

He stalks over with a slow, predatory grace that forces me to chew on my lip to keep from fidgeting. The two Enforcers at the console still haven't noticed either of us, their attention focused on their work.

Elias' golden-green eyes flicker to the screen I was just examining.

Then back to me.

I expect accusations. Demands for explanation. Perhaps even immediate arrest or dismissal.

But he doesn't say anything.

*Oh fuck he's going to kill me...*I'm so stupid.

The pressure in my chest builds as I hold a breath, suspended in a moment of uncertain fate. My mind races, calculating escape routes, excuses, potential weapons—all useless in this contained space against a trained Enforcer who outranks me.

He nods, an almost imperceptible gesture. "I won't ask what you're doing here." His voice is low enough that it doesn't carry to the others.

Then, just like that, he spins on his heel and walks away.

The door opens and closes once more, releasing him as swiftly as it had admitted him.

With a sharp exhale, I swallow around the pounding racing from my head. What just happened? Why would he see me somewhere I clearly shouldn't be, accessing information I have no authorization to view, and simply *leave*?

It's a trap. He's waiting outside to uncover what I'll do next.

Or does he genuinely not care about my unauthorized presence?

What was that saying I read about once? When life hands you lemons and all that.

Well, I'm not one to waste such an opportunity, and if the stars see fit to grant me this, then I will walk away and pretend like nothing happened.

As I rush from the room, I scan the other screens for any additional useful information, nothing standing out as immediately valuable. I have more than I came here with, and that's a start.

A poorly executed one, but a start nonetheless.

The sliding door reveals an empty landing beyond. No Elias. Convenient he found himself in the same room at the same time, though he did nothing but dismiss me before leaving.

I shake my arms out as I hurry back to my room, my mind racing with possibilities. Were those women being transferred from another facility or were they found outside the perimeter?

And the juveniles...my stomach sours. The inner workings of the facilities are widely kept secret, likely for security concerns, but I can't imagine how scared all the children must be, witnessing what happens to their mothers and knowing there's nothing they can do to stop that from happening to them when they reach a certain age.

Every day here is a challenge that pushes me further into my own insecurities, but this is what I need to keep reminding myself of. *They* are why I'm here.

But what I ignorantly didn't consider before joining this team was *how* I would help. I can gather all the information in the world, but how do I act on it, trapped within these walls, surrounded by enemies, with no connection to the outside world?

Frustration burns like acid in my veins, and I'm so absorbed in my thoughts that I almost miss the figure waiting beside my door when I finally return to the recruits' quarters.

Kellen leans against the wall opposite my room, arms crossed over his chest, insignia glinting in the light. His posture is relaxed, but there's no mistaking the deliberate nature of his presence. He's waiting for me.

My heart sinks. Did Elias report me after all?

I yearn to sprint in the opposite direction—to finally admit how foolish this whole thing was and make it back home before they catch me. Because if they do, I will face the consequences with the same defiance that brought me here in the first place.

"Ashford," Kellen acknowledges as I stop before him. "You weren't in the dining hall, so I came to inform you of a change in schedule today. Tactical room three, ten minutes." His tone reveals nothing of his thoughts.

"Yes, sir." I'm so relieved I almost sink to the floor in a puddle of stress tears.

Not an arrest, then. At least not yet.

The leader pushes from the wall, his movement fluid and controlled. He studies me for a moment longer than necessary, his gaze seeming to penetrate every bit of armor I wear. "You're improving," he remarks. "But you need to work on your defensive posture, it's a bit frantic." A pause. "And be more careful about which doors you walk through."

My blood freezes. He knows. Maybe not everything, but enough. How?

"I don't know what you mean, sir." My voice is far steadier than I feel as the walls tilt.

He makes a soft sound—not quite a laugh. "Of course not."

He steps past me, his shoulder nearly brushing mine. "Ten minutes, Ashford. Don't be late."

CHAPTER FIFTEEN
CASSIA

The sliver of sunlight cutting across my bed tells me I've slept longer than intended. I bolt upright with a gasp before remembering: free day. The rare mandatory rest period built into our training cycle. No predawn assembly in the yard, no Commander barking orders while we struggle to hold impossible-for-a-human positions, no simulation training that leaves me dizzy and dissociated.

Just a day of blessed quiet where the mask can stay off a little longer.

I slump back against the wall, cataloging each ache in my bones and muscles. These weeks of training have reshaped me—hardening soft places and creating calluses where once was smooth skin. My hands bear splits across the knuckles from blocking strikes. My thighs burn from holding squats until they tremble while my shoulders carry a perpetual tightness from hauling my weight up ropes, across beams, over walls.

Is this what being a man feels like? This constant push toward physical extremes, this endless testing of limits?

I allow myself a moment of pure rage each morning, usually dedicated to the Riverton transfer I'd discovered. Those women have been processed by now, tested for their next fertile cycle so the Enforcers know when to rape them.

A sting on my palms forces me to calm, and I pull my nails back.

Focus, Cassia. One failure doesn't end the mission.

I'm just reaching for my notebook when there's a thunderous knock at my door. "Ashford! Get your dumbass out here!"

I recognize Calder's voice immediately. Unlike most of the recruits, he's been almost friendly toward me, though 'friendly' here means he hasn't actively tried to sabotage me during training or insult me outside of it.

"What?" I call back, sliding my mask into place before cracking the door. The material is cool against my face, a now-familiar pressure I've come to associate with survival rather than constraint.

He stands in the hallway, unmasked to my surprise. His face is round and youthful despite the scruff of beard, with bright eyes that stay perpetually amused.

"We're organizing a shockball match. Need more players." He grins. "You in?"

I blink. Maybe I misheard. "A what?"

"Shockball. You know—" He gestures vaguely with his hands forming some kind of round shape. "Teams, scoring, tackling. It's a free-day tradition."

My stomach knots. A group activity is the last thing I need —especially one requiring physical coordination I do not possess. But refusing would draw attention and further mark me as different. The balance between blending in and keeping my distance has been the hardest part of my time here.

"I have plans," I reply, falling back on my usual vagueness.

Calder snorts. "What plans? Hiding in your room all day? Come on, even Elias and Kellen are playing."

Even more reason for me to stay, I don't say outloud. They've been watching me with increased interest since Elias found me the other day.

"Is...everyone going?" Shit, that didn't sound as casual as I wanted it to.

But Calder doesn't notice, shrugging. "Pretty much. Except maybe the Commander. He apparently disappears on free days. So, you coming or what?"

Refuse and seem suspicious, or go and risk exposure?

Who am I kidding, my entire life here is a risk of exposure. "Fine," I say, hating the decision even as I make it. "Give me five minutes."

When I step outside, masked and uniformed despite the casual atmosphere, I find our group of recruits and several other Enforcers milling near the main entrance. Most wear only the lower half of their uniforms with simple black undershirts instead of the reinforced tactical gear. All are unmasked, their faces exposed to the bright midday sun with an ease that makes my skin crawl.

How do they not feel vulnerable? Naked?

There's a freedom in their expressions, my throat tightening with envy and disgust—the unearned privilege of men who have never needed to hide or face consequences for simply existing.

I spot Elias and Kellen standing apart from the group, deep in conversation. Kellen's mask hangs loosely from one hand as he gestures with the other, his face animated in a way I've never seen during training. Elias laughs at something he says, the light sound gleaming across the yard. I want to hear it again.

I force myself to focus elsewhere when an uncomfortable fluttering sensation skitters through my chest, focusing on the others once more. My attraction to any of them is unacceptable.

"You're not taking your mask off?" Calder asks, falling into step beside me as the group moves toward a trail leading away from the building.

"No."

"We're not on duty, no one cares."

My response is flat toned. "I do. Someone from the Syndicate could arrive at any time, and I'm not risking disciplinary action for a game."

He raises his hands in mock surrender. "Suit yourself, Ashford. But it's over ninety degrees today. You'll cook in that thing."

He's right. By the time we've reached a clearing through the endless trees, sweat trickles down my neck and spine. I'm already panting and exhausted—this is going to be a miserable day.

Better than the alternative.

"Gather up!" Kellen's voice commands immediate attention despite its light tone. The recruits form a loose circle around him, and I position myself at the edge where I'll draw the least notice. "Standard rules," he states, rolling the sleeves of his undershirt. "Two teams, two goals, one ball." He holds up a small metallic sphere, about the size of my fist. "Field is live for tackles, but no powers. Anyone caught using abilities sits out."

He continues explaining rules that make increasingly less sense to me—something about shock zones, charge points, interference lines. I focus instead on watching others' reactions, planning to mimic their movements when the game begins.

"Alright, teams." Kellen studies the circle. "Shirts versus skins. Elias will captain shirts, I'll take the latter."

A chorus of good-natured groans and laughter ripples through the group. Several men immediately strip from their shirts, tossing them to the side with casual disregard. Others move to stand beside Elias, who's already dividing them into positions I don't understand. I have no idea what to do here.

But then my focus narrows to Kellen as he peels a shirt over his head in a single fluid motion. My breath catches as I inspect the defined planes of his chest, the ridges of muscle across his abdomen, the dusting of dark hair that narrows into a line disappearing beneath a thick waistband. His skin is several shades lighter than his face and hands, marked here and there with scars whose stories I suddenly, desperately want to know.

My tongue wets my lips. He's beautiful. I jerk my gaze away as a different kind of heat surges through my body.

Stop crushing on the men who want to kill you, idiot.

As always, my inner voice keeps me rooted in reality.

"You're with us, Ashford," Elias calls, waving me over to the shirts team. "Since you're keeping your mask on." As if that were even a question.

I join their huddle, careful to maintain appropriate distance from the others. Elias has gathered ten to his team, and they're already discussing strategy in rapid-fire terms that might as well be a foreign language.

"We'll run the double charge on their weak side," Finnick says, gesturing animatedly. "Malcolm can anchor the back line while we push for shock position."

"Darius sh-should cover the perimeter," Ronan, one of our team's Clingers, adds. "A-and we need someone on i-interference duty."

Eyes turn to me, and I realize they're waiting for my input. I stay silent, nodding as if considering their words, though I have no idea what any of it means. Just another embarrassing thing for me to process.

"Ashford can flank with me," Elias decides when I don't speak. "Keep to the outside and watch for the handoff signal." I nod again, hoping I won't need to figure out what a 'handoff signal' looks like on the spot.

The huddle breaks, and players scatter to various positions across the field. I hesitate, uncertain where to go, until Elias' hand lands on my shoulder.

"Just stay near me and follow my lead," he says, his energized voice low enough that only I can hear. "First time playing shockball?"

I consider lying, but he would know.

"Is it that obvious?"

A half-smile tugs at his mouth, lighting up his features. "A bit. Don't worry about it, it's just a game."

But nothing here is *just* anything. Everything is a test, a way to measure worthiness, to identify weaknesses. My failure to understand this simple recreation just once again reaffirms how out of place I am.

The game begins with a shrill whistle, and chaos erupts.

Bodies surge forward, men shouting and crashing into each other as they fight for position around the metallic ball Kellen tosses into center field. I freeze, overwhelmed by the sudden explosion of movement and noise.

Something catches my eye—a slight flicker around the ball, like heat distortion in summer air. As a player from Kellen's team snatches it, a small spark jumps from the metal to his hand.

It's charged somehow, I realize, awed. *That's why they call it shockball.*

The player with the ball sprints toward our team's goal, dodging and spinning around defenders with a grin plastered on his face. Two of our players converge on him, but he dives between them, rolling back to his feet in a smooth motion before flipping the ball to another teammate.

I'm supposed to be doing something, but I have no idea

what. Everyone else moves with purpose, clearly under-standing their role in this complicated mess. I stand motionless.

"Ashford!" Elias shouts, running past me. "Move up!"

I jog forward, uncertainty in my steps as I attempt to belong in this game.

A body slams into mine, hard enough to jar my teeth, and instinct takes over—I reach out, steadying us both with a hand on his bare arm. Wrong move. I hadn't closed my power off completely, and emotion slams into me harder than the impact I just took. His thrill at the violence and a sharp spike of aggres-sion flows under my skin, hijacking my pulse.

"Come on then!" I bark, shoving him harder than I mean to. The words tear out loudly, my voice not my own. The recruit stumbles, blinking at me in surprise before grinning like I've lost my mind. Laughter breaks from a few others as heat imbues my cheeks, covering both cheeks.

I'm too worked up...humiliated myself because I couldn't keep my power contained properly.

Damn idiot.

When the ball drops near me, I dodge away, earning frus-trated shouts from my teammates. Another player barrels right at me; I sidestep too late and get knocked to the ground where a rock takes residence in my shoulder blade.

Getting back up is easy, and I brush dirt from my uniform before retreating to the edge of the action, hoping to observe enough to fake competence. My team is annoyed with me—I catch multiple eye-rolls and exasperated gestures in my direction.

"What are you doing?" Malcolm hisses as he passes me. "At least *try* to block someone."

After three more disastrous attempts to participate, I fall back even further, pretending to guard some invisible boundary while actually trying to become as unnoticeable as possible.

The sun beats us without an ounce of mercy and sweat pours down my face inside the mask. I'm dizzy, overheated, and utterly humiliated, both eyes burning from something other than heat.

A shadow falls across me, and my head snaps to Elias standing beside me, breathing hard from exertion but not yet winded. Unlike most of the others, who are red-faced and soaked with sweat, he seems barely affected by the heat or physical activity.

"You going to yell at me or what?" I snap, frustration overriding caution. "I know I'm terrible."

He studies me for a moment before, unexpectedly, his expression softens. "You've really never played shockball before." Did I not tell him so already?

If Elias is bothered by my silence, he doesn't show it, instead just releasing a thoughtful sound. "Just watch for a few rounds. See how the plays develop, then join back in when you're ready."

Before I can respond, he jogs back to the action, leaving me stunned by his acceptance of my continued incompetence. I'd expected ridicule like the Commander offers, or at least disappointment—not understanding.

But I accept his advice, studying the next few rounds with curious intensity, stunned when the game becomes clearer the more I watch. The ball carries a mild electric charge that players can *shock* from one position to another on the field. Scoring happens when the ball is in a shock position and a player manages to pass it through a specific point in the opposing team's goal area. It's complex and strategic, almost like the chess I play with my father, but with the added dimension of physical prowess.

After watching three complete plays, I suck in a deep breath and rejoin. This time, when Elias signals, I move to the position he indicates, replicating the blocking stance I've seen others use. When the ball comes my way, I don't flinch back—instead, I catch it like I've seen the others do, ignoring the slight sting as the charge transfers to my hands. I pivot and pass to Malcolm, who pauses momentarily before spinning away from a defender and scoring.

"Nicely done, Ashford!" someone shouts, and a strange warmth that has nothing to do with the sun spreads through my chest.

I've always been a quick learner—my mother joked that I seemed to absorb knowledge through my skin. By my fifth rotation in the game, I'm holding my own, and by the eighth, I steal the ball from Kellen's team, earning a grudging nod of approval from Darius.

It would be easy to get lost in the simple physicality of the game, the temporary camaraderie of shared purpose. To forget, for just a moment, that these men are my enemies.

I wish.

After what must be two hours of play, Elias calls for a break. Everyone is drenched in sweat, breathing hard, many lying sprawled on the grass to recover. My own body throbs with exhaustion—legs heavy like a soaked-through towel, lungs burning, a stitch in my side sharp enough to make me wince. But beneath the discomfort is an unfamiliar feeling: satisfaction. I contributed. Learned. Adapted.

As the others discuss food and rest, I seize my opportunity and begin the trudge back to the center. I need a shower and a moment of privacy to recover my composure. More than that, I need distance from the strange mixture of disgust and attraction I feel when looking at these men with their shirts off, laughing and clapping each other on the back like they haven't dedicated their lives to oppression.

I've gone maybe thirty paces when I spot him.

Arayik stands unmoving at the edge of the tree line where the path meets the compound, arms crossed. His posture is more than rigid, though whether it's directed at me specifically or the entire gathering, I can't tell.

My first instinct is to turn around, find another way back to the compound. But he's already seen me, his head tracking my movement across the way. Avoiding him now would only earn a public scolding.

He nods toward the space in front of him—a silent command to which I comply without complaint. I bristle when he remains silent. What the hell is going on?

The Commander's eyes flick over me once, his gaze lingering on the mud streaking my uniform, before turning back to watch the forest beyond. He doesn't speak, doesn't demand explanations or issue orders. It's unnerving to be in his presence without beratement.

Gradually, other recruits begin trickling back along the path. They fall into formation beside and behind me, their excited chatter dying as they notice Arayik's presence. The atmosphere shifts from casual to formal in an instant, tension replacing relaxation.

Elias and Kellen arrive last, still engaged in conversation, shirts draped over their shoulders rather than worn. Both stop when they notice the man in front of me, exchanging a glance I can't interpret before moving to flank him. Kellen pulls his shirt back on in a smooth motion, but not before I notice a long scar across his left side, puckered and pale against his skin.

I don't dare turn my head to count, but I sense we're all here now, standing in formation before the three leaders, as the Enforcers not on our team make for the front doors.

Arayik's voice, when it finally comes, is ice wrapped in steel. "The Syndicate has issued new orders. We deploy at dawn."

Deploy? I can't have heard correctly. We've barely begun training. Most of the recruits still struggle with basic combat maneuvers, let alone the complex tactical operations we'd need for field work.

"A rebel incursion has been confirmed," he continues, voice flat and emotionless. "A location in outer Pyrem harbors one or more females and displays evidence of organized defensive capabilities." My pulse races, blood rushing in my ears. "Our mission is direct: locate to neutralize threats and retrieve viable females for processing at Riverton."

Such a dismissive way of saying kill her rescuers and send her to be bred.

"You have twelve hours to prepare. Pack only field essentials. We move out at 0500." A pause, then, "Effective immediately: all variance and transit files are now restricted to leadership only. Local terminals will display as restricted until further notice."

Arayik's gaze sweeps across our formation, landing briefly on me before continuing. "Any questions will be addressed during mission briefing at 1900 hours. Until then, you are dismissed to prepare."

This is it—the very mission I feared and hoped for in equal measure. The chance to sabotage from within; help instead of harm and make a difference.

But am I ready? Can I maintain this disguise under field conditions? Against real threats? With *real* lives at stake?

The others break formation, muttering excitedly about finally seeing action. Their eager voices make me sick—they sound like children promised a treat, not men being sent to destroy lives.

I remain rooted to the spot, mind racing through possibilities, contingencies, and dangers within them. This is happening too fast. I need more time, more information, more—

"Ashford, Spinel." Arayik's voice slices through my spiral of thoughts. "A word."

Dread pools in my stomach as the others leave me with Corin and the three leaders. Whatever this conversation is, it can't be good.

Nothing is ever good with the Commander.

"Your performances during training have been..." Arayik pauses, as if searching for the right word. "Inconsistent." Neither me or my fellow recruit offer a response, and he continues as Corin fidgets, "Under ideal circumstances, I'd remove you both from the team as you haven't improved nearly enough in the the week I gave you. Under normal circumstances, you would require at least another month of conditioning before field deployment." How does one train their voice to be so emotionless? "Neither are an option any longer."

Elias shifts, drawing my attention. His expression is unreadable, but there's a tension in his shoulders I haven't noticed before. Kellen stands perfectly still, watching the exchange without input.

"Ashford, you will serve as our Empath support during this operation." I want to roll my eyes because what the fuck else would I do? "Your ability to influence emotional states without contact will be valuable when dealing with potentially hostile females. Some may resist collection to the point of self-harm."

Collection. As if women are items to be gathered and stored. I swallow hard, forcing down a surge of rage that threatens to scream at him.

"Spinel, you will remain outside on perimeter watch. Both of you will be under direct supervision at all times," he adds, stepping closer until his mask occupies much of my vision. "Any deviation from orders, any failure to perform as required, and you *will* be removed from the team. Permanently. Is that understood?" The threat is clear: we won't be returning home if we fail this.

"Understood, Commander," I manage, unblinking as I hold his gaze. I want to scoff when Corin mumbles a yes and lowers his head.

He nods once before granting us distance. "1900 hours. Tac room one." He strides away, though his second and third do not follow.

What now...

No one speaks for several seconds, and I get the sense they're both struggling to say what they want without forming the words.

Elias is first. "Get some rest. You'll need it."

I nod, and as I turn to leave the awkward bubble, Kellen calls, "Rest in your room this time, Ashford."

My legs freeze mid-step, his cryptic warning sending ice through my veins. But when I peer back, his expression gives nothing away.

I'm so fucked.

At least they're allowing me on this mission...perhaps I can figure out how to save these people before I'm killed.

I have no idea how I'll manage it, but I have less than twelve hours to figure it out.

CHAPTER SIXTEEN
CASSIA

The convoy rumbles down a dirt road, each jolt sending vibrations through the metal frame and into my bones. Dust billows in our wake, a choking cloud that obscures the landscape behind us. I sit rigid in the back seat, my hands clenched tightly in my lap, my knuckles ache beneath their gloves. The air inside the vehicle is thick and stifling, heavy with hot metal.

My first mission. The words echo in my mind, a hollow reminder of what I've gotten myself into. Mere weeks of training, and now they're sending us to hunt women in hiding.

Women like me.

The weight of the mission seizes my lungs, making each breath a conscious effort. I distract myself with the barren landscape outside—scrubland giving way to the outskirts of Pyrem's residential district. Not far from where I grew up. Not far from the house where my parents are probably still wondering if I'm alive.

"Keep your eyes sharp," Kellen instructs from the front compartment, his voice carrying the calm authority I appreciate. Especially when frenzied butterflies invade my stomach. "We don't leave room for mistakes."

I swallow hard, grateful the tremor in my jaw is hidden. Six other recruits sit across from me, their identical masks hiding whatever thoughts might be passing through their minds. Are they excited? Nervous? Do they feel anything at all about what we're to do? I could use my power to figure that out, but I'm too wound up. I'll probably lash my terror out on someone and give myself away.

The transport slows as we enter a neighborhood of modest homes. Nothing fancy—just simple structures where ordinary people live ordinary lives. Except there's nothing ordinary about this place anymore. Not with us here, or what we've come to accomplish.

The vehicle lurches to a stop, and my stomach goes with it. The back doors swing open, flooding the dim interior with harsh sunlight. Arayik stands outside, his mask tilted toward us expectantly.

"Move," he commands.

We file out in practiced order, our boots hitting the packed gravel in near-unison. The sound is obscene with how quiet it is.

My eyes scan our surroundings, absorbing details from the cluster of small houses. They remind me of my own home—the place I left behind. My throat tightens at the thought.

Kellen gestures to a gray-stone house at the end of the street. The structure is unremarkable—worn shutters, a small garden out front with withering vegetables. Nothing about it screams *rebellion* or *harboring fugitives*.

It's just a home. Someone's sanctuary.

Just like mine was.

"Intelligence confirms one female presence," Arayik states, monotone as if discussing the weather rather than a human life. "Standard procedure. Secure the men, extract the woman."

I'm going to vomit. How in the world did I think I could do this?

I blindly stumble alongside the others in formation as we spread around the house. I'm paired with Calder, positioned at the side entrance. My pulse hammers in my ears as we take position and my power releases. I can already sense the emotions emanating from inside the house—fear, sharp and acrid like burning metal; determination, a steady undercurrent like a river flowing beneath ice in the dead of winter; and something deeper, something like resignation. They know we're here, and they know there's nothing they can do about it.

Arayik signals and the front door crashes inward under Nash's boot. Shouts erupt from inside—male voices, desperate and angry. I cringe as Kellen bark commands, biting my tongue when furniture topples.

"Go," Calder whispers, nodding toward the door beside us.

I draw the standard-issue stun weapon from my belt. It feels wrong in my hand. The weight of it makes my covered palm sweat.

Calder places his hand against the lock, and the metal changes, glowing red-hot then white. It melts inward with a soft hiss, and he kicks the door open.

We enter a small kitchen. A cracked porcelain mug rests on the counter, the handle poorly glued back in place. Pink and purple flowers outline the exterior, reminding me so much of the mug my mother uses for her tea every morning. A throat clears, and I focus on anything else. Dishes sit half-washed in a basin while a pot of something—stew, maybe—simmers on a heating element. It's so...domestic.

This is their *life*. How can we do this to them?

A crash from the front room snaps me back to the present. Calder moves and I follow, our boots creaking against the worn floorboards. Everything is magnified, each step bringing me closer to something I can't undo.

The emotions intensify as we approach the main room—fear becoming terror, determination hardening into desperation. I round the corner and freeze.

Three men kneel on the floor, hands behind their heads. Enforcers stand over them, weapons trained on their skulls. One of the men is older, gray streaking his temples. The other two seem younger—brothers, perhaps, with similar features. Their faces are etched with defiance even as their bodies tremble.

"Where is she?" Arayik demands, his voice slicing through the room.

None of the men answer. The oldest one spits at Arayik's feet, earning himself a vicious backhand that sends him sprawling.

"Search the house," Arayik orders. "Find her."

Pieces of my team disperse, tearing through rooms, upending furniture, ripping apart anything that might conceal a hiding place. I stand rooted to the spot, my mind racing. I should be helping. Playing my part. But all I can think is: *These men are going to die. They're going to die, and I'm going to watch it happen.*

A shout from the left tilts the very axis of my world. "Found her! Hidden compartment in the floor!"

The blood drains from my body.

Heavy footsteps thunder around a bend, and two recruits appear, dragging a woman between them. Her wrists are bound with thick restraints, her long, bright hair tangled around their gloved fists as they force her forward. Dirt streaks her face, mixing with tears that create clean tracks down her cheeks.

But her eyes—her eyes blaze with a fury that makes my heart stutter.

She appears nothing like the broken, submissive women I've glimpsed in the propaganda images the Syndicate displays. This woman is rage incarnate, fighting every step despite the futility.

"No!" The youngest man lunges forward, only to be slammed back to the floor by an Enforcer's boot.

"Quiet," Arayik commands, his attention on the woman. "Your identification number." She only glares, and his neck cracks from the tension. "Your identification number. And the names of any others who escaped with you."

Still, she says nothing. One of the Enforcers holding her yanks her hair, forcing her head back at a painful angle. She huffs, yet doesn't make a sound.

"We can do this the easy way," Arayik continues, his voice almost conversational now, "or we can do this while these men bleed out on the floor. Your choice."

The woman's eyes flick to her kneeling companions, and her resolve wavers. Fear for them bleeds through her anger.

"Don't tell them anything, Mira!" the older man shouts. "They'll kill us anyway—" An Enforcer's fist connects with his jaw, silencing him mid-sentence. Blood sprays across the wooden floor.

Mira flinches, but her jaw remains set. Her emotions churn—fear, rage, and beneath it all, a core of iron determination.

It's all I can do to dampen the trembling of my limbs.

Pax steps forward and raises a hand to her forehead. "Commander, permission to extract information?"

Oh, fuck. His power would allow him to manipulate things in her body; he'll make her talk, but he'll break something in her first.

"No." The word escapes my lips before I can stop it.

The room goes utterly silent. Every mask snaps in my direction, and the weight of their stares is like sludge dripping onto my uniform.

"What did you say?" Arayik's voice is stone.

I'm so stupid. My mind races—I've just made a terrible mistake, but I can't backtrack now. I need to make this sound tactical, not like I've lost my fucking mind in a fit of compassion.

"She's terrified," I remark, shrugging. "She won't give us accurate information like this. Give her space." I pause, then add, "Let me try."

He stares at me, blinking once. "You presume to give orders now, Ashford?"

"No, Commander. I'm offering a more efficient approach. My abilities can help us get what we need without resistance or harm, as you insisted yesterday."

Elias leans in, murmuring something to Arayik I cannot hear. The Commander's shoulders tense, but after a moment, he steps back with a muttered curse.

"Try, then. But if you fail, I'll let Pax have his turn." *His turn.*

Heart hammering, I approach the woman. The Enforcers holding her tighten their grip, but I motion for them to give her a little slack. Surprisingly, they comply.

I kneel before her, bringing myself to her eye level. Up close, exhaustion blankets her face, and her body trembles with the effort of remaining upright. But those eyes—they burn with a fire that agrees with the ache in my soul.

"I'm not here to hurt you," I murmur, keeping my voice low enough that only she can hear. "Just tell us what we need to know, and this can end."

Her emotions swirl around me—and beneath them all, a tiny flicker of hope. That hope startles me. It's so fragile, so easily crushed, yet it persists despite everything.

Without another thought, I reach for the hope with my power, amplifying it just enough to keep her calm. I want her to believe there's a way out of this, that cooperation might spare her some pain. It's a lie, of course. I've realized nothing I do here will save her from what's coming. But if I can make this moment easier...

"What's your number?" I ask, gentler than the foreboding presence behind me.

She searches my eyes through the slit in my mask, looking for something—humanity, perhaps. After a long moment, she whispers, "W-7249."

"And did others escape with you?"

Her eyes dart to the men on the floor, then back to me. The hope I've been nurturing flickers, threatening to extinguish.

"No." Her voice is barely audible. "Just me."

I know she's lying. I can feel it in the way her emotions shift, in the subtle tension that runs through her body. But I nod as if I believe her.

"Thank you." I mean it. I'm thanking her for her courage, for her resistance, for demonstrating what strength really looks like.

Before I can say anything else, more recruits step in, grabbing her arms and dragging her to the door. She doesn't fight them now—the hope I planted has made her more compliant.

Suddenly, I can't breathe.

I've betrayed her. Used her own emotions against her.

Bile rise in my throat.

"What about them?" Thane asks, gesturing to the three men still kneeling on the floor.

The Commander's answer is immediate and final. "Standard procedure."

My bones crystallize as Kellen and two others step forward, weapons raised. I want to look away, but I force myself to watch. I owe them that much, at least—to witness what happens to those who defy the Syndicate.

The shots are deafening in the small room. Three bodies crumple to the floor, blood pooling beneath them. It happens so fast—one moment they're breathing, the next they're gone. No ceremony or regard for their life. Just execution.

Kellen holsters his weapon as if he's done nothing more significant than swat a fly. Arayik nods once, satisfied, and turns to leave.

"Back to base," he orders. "Ashford, with me."

I follow him outside, my legs moving mechanically, eyes unseeing. The sunlight feels wrong somehow—too bright and normal for what just happened. The woman is already being loaded into a separate transport, her head bowed, shoulders slumped. The hope I gave her will die soon, replaced by the reality of what awaits her at Riverton.

I'm so sorry.

"Your approach was effective," Arayik remarks as we walk toward the main transport. "But don't ever countermand my orders again. Clear?"

"Yes, Commander." The words are ash in my mouth.

He leaves to speak with his second and third as I climb into the transport, sitting as far from the others as possible. No one speaks as we pull away from the house, abandoning the three bodies cooling on the floor and kidnapping a woman bound for a life of despair in the truck next to us.

The ride back to the training center passes in a blur. My mind keeps replaying those final moments—the sound of newly dead bodies dropping to the floor, the ache in Mira's eyes as they dragged her away. I used my power against her. I'm no better than the men I'm pretending to be.

I'm so disgusted with myself.

When we arrive, the recruits disperse, some to the dining

hall, others to their quarters. How anyone can eat after such horror, I'll never understand.

I follow the group toward the common areas anyway, but my mind is elsewhere. Mira will be processed and transported to Riverton within hours. Gone from the world forever, replaced by identification number W-7249.

Unless...

An idea emerges, dangerous and half-formed. Much like the one that led me here in the first place.

The corridors are emptying as recruits settle into their evening routines. This might be my only chance.

I slip away from the main group, striding for the lower levels. The holding cells are on sublevel four—I've seen the layout on maps during Kellen's training. If I can reach her before they transport her, maybe I can...

What? Help her escape? How? I have no plan, no resources, nothing but a desperate need to do something.

I hurry down the stairs to where the temporary detainees are held. The corridor is dimly lit, cameras positioned at regular intervals. No one guards the door at the end of the hallway as it's secured with a keypad. And yet another obstacle—I don't know the code.

Footsteps echo from around the corner, and I press myself against the wall in an attempt to appear as nonchalant as an Enforcer standing next to a prison can be.

Two men appear, deep in conversation. They barely glance at me as they pass, assuming I'm just another recruit on assignment. Once they're gone, I approach the keypad, fingers hovering over the numbers.

This is so risky. If I'm caught, it's not just me who pays the price. My family will be discovered. Mother will be sent back to a facility. Father and brother will be executed. All because I couldn't stand by and do nothing this one time.

But if I do nothing, I'm complicit. I become the exact thing I'm pretending to be.

Rolling to the tips of my feet, I peer through the cracked window on the door. It's a small antechamber with another door at the far end, likely leading to the cells themselves. A desk sits to one side, currently unmanned. On it, a tablet displays orders, luckily close enough that I can make out letters if I squint.

SUBJECT W-7249
DESTINATION: RIVERTON
DEPARTURE: 0400 HOURS

Dawn. They're moving her at dawn.

Voices emerge at the whirring of elevator doors—I need to leave. Scanning frantically, I slip into the closest room, knowing I won't make it to the stairwell before the men catch me. Their footsteps grow louder before fading a minute later. Once they're gone, I exhale a ragged breath, my back sliding against the wall to the floor.

It's only now that I can't stop the emotions from tormenting my body. Grief, rage, shame. They twist together inside me, toxic in their nature.

Those men didn't deserve to die; they were merely trying to protect someone they loved. Their only crime was basic human decency—something so rare in this world that it's punishable by death.

And Mira...

Tears slip free and coat my cheeks. Men own her body once again and will use it for pleasure and breeding. She'll never have another say or choice, never experience the freedom of smiling or sleeping in a bed where she feels safe.

I scramble to my hands and knees, rushing to a far corner of the room as I shove my mask off and retch repeatedly. Nothing but acidic bile emerges.

The convulsions don't stop until I'm heaving from the force of my sobs. It's torture to swallow around a burning throat, but I manage, shoving my mask on and rushing back to my room. I don't run into another soul, thank the stars, and wash my mouth several times until I taste nothing.

Hollow, haunted eyes catch mine in the small mirror.

Is this what becoming an Enforcer does to you? Strips away your humanity piece by piece until there's nothing left but a shell that blindly follows orders?

I hate them. I hate all of them. The Syndicate, the Enforcers, my team, my leaders, and every fucking man on this disgusting planet.

But most of all, I hate myself for not being able to do more.

My heart struggles with the weight of another failure— walking away, choosing my safety over Mira's freedom.

And I'll have to live with that choice for the rest of my pathetic life.

CHAPTER SEVENTEEN
CASSIA

The Training Center is wrong at four in the morning. The quiet sits heavy, like it's waiting for something, and my steps click against the floor as the sound runs ahead of me and returns to accuse me of things.

You don't belong here. Step. *You're an impostor.* Another step.

I shove the constant thoughts away as I count the cameras.

I know the sweep pattern now. West corridor rotates every eight seconds; the junction by the laundry is dead and has been since my first week here; the service stair on the north side breathes cold air from the lower levels as the ventilation kicks higher before shift change. I keep my head angled and my pace steady as I move, and do not peer up when a lens passes over the crown of my mask. I time my steps with that soft mechanical hum and the far throb of generators two levels below.

The showers are empty—they always are at this hour. The room smells like bleach and damp towels and metal. I slide the curtain closed, only then slipping the mask off. My cheeks are damp where the rubber sealed, the cool air relieving the sweat along my hairline as I hook the strap on the peg and turn the water.

Cold first. It shocks the skin and gives me something simple to hold on to. The pipes rattle and settle while the spray needles my scalp. Scrubbing my skin clean is no longer relaxing as the soap bites each cut along my knuckles, and my shoulder pulls as I raise my arm and stretch under the stream. The sound is steady. I breathe with it.

I try not to think about last week. I try to focus on the movements—wash, rinse, repeat—and not the transport door closing on Mira as her eyes fixed on mine like that could change anything. I still taste the sting of panic as I remember the men who pulled her away and the ones who died loving her. The question I don't say out loud washes up anyway as I scrub my arms hard enough that the skin turns pink.

Why didn't you help?

You could have tried.

The sentence lives in the hollow of my chest, dense and thrashing. The water engulfs my face and I count to five before I breathe again.

The shower is fast. I dry with a thin towel as a ceiling vent pushes in cool air, and I twist my hair into a tight knot at the base of my skull the same as every morning. The strap settles into the groove along my hairline—where I'm sure it's made a permanent dent—and the familiar pressure at my cheekbones returns. The dingy mirror outside the stalls is spotted and warped at the edges. Lachlan stares back when my eyes find their reflection. Cassia is still there behind the uniform, but there are days where I have to remind myself she exists, and this is one of them.

An hour before most of the center wakes. Enough time to try again.

I traverse the corridor and descend the back stairs as they keep me off the main cameras, pausing at each landing as I listen for the elevator's cables and the rhythm of footsteps. The smell changes as I proceed—less detergent and bodies, more cold dust and stone. My fingers go slick when I arrive at the door to Sublevel Eight.

Hovering the keypad, I enter the four-digit code I heard an Enforcer muttering to another when I had taken a leisurely walk yesterday and found myself staring at the archives. I didn't have time or opportunity to inspect anything then, but I've made time this morning. Thank the stars no one is in here when the door slides open.

Sublevel Eight isn't a series of rooms and halls like the others; no, it's a singular room, where the air inside is colder than the stairwell. It smells old—paper, dust, a faint sting of isopropyl—and the lights flicker before they settle. They must always be on.

Metal shelving runs the room in seven long rows. Boxes are stacked to shoulder height with labels in neat block letters: **BELKEN, ELESBURN, AILRIDGE, PYREM— PERSONNEL, PYREM—MECHANICAL**. A single terminal sleeps on the desk with a green light blinking slowly at the top. The chair has a slickness to it when I touch the back, and I pull my hand away to wipe my fingers on a thigh as my attention shifts to the shelves.

I don't have the time to read everything, but I don't need to. I need the outline, not every miniscule detail. Sliding two boxes onto the floor, I kneel on frigid, unforgiving concrete. **FACILITY PROTOCOLS—LOWLAND** gives me intake checklists and rotation charts along with supply ledgers that list columns of numbers that add up to lives. Rations divided by headcount, medical kits by lot numbers, restraints by type. It's all here and none of it helps right now.

When I touch a page that has writing along the bottom margin, something jumps in my heart—sharp and hot—forcing my knees to lock as a wave of fear that isn't mine pushes through paper. It diminishes quickly, but the aftertaste stays—stale breath and a thin edge of adrenaline. I drop the page before flexing my fingers until they stop trembling as I blink away the wetness fogging my eyes. That's new.

Moving on.

PERSONNEL—PYREM HUB is list after list. Names, tests, assignments, transfers. Half of it is coded and the other half reads like men reduced to rows of statistics.

Hale—fitness exemplary, discipline adequate, loyalty affirmed.

Stilen—fitness adequate, discipline poor, loyalty affirmed; assign to low-stress post.

I skim and allow the names to lodge in a place where I can retrieve them if needed. Not for today, but later.

Time is a pressure thrumming around my stomach as I move through the aisle. The ventilation deepens with the waking Enforcers somewhere above me, and water trickles through pipes, shortening my clock that much more. I put one box back, shifting attention to the next label.

TRANSIT LOGS—RIVERTON DISTRICT. The tape at the edge is newer than the rest. I lift the lid to find carbon forms with imprints that shadow through three layers. A few are stamped with the Syndicate seal in faded black. Another stack is rubber-banded and marked VARIANCES in a thinner hand, and the band bites my palm when I pull it up.

Form 17—Variance.
Route BR-6 to RVN-03.
Time 0300.
Escort detail: deviated per verbal authorization.
Receiving: RIVERTON—Annex B.

That name means nothing in the simple way names can

mean everything, and a cold spot opens in my head as I read it again. "Remember that," I whisper to myself.

Another variance is unreadable where names should be, the fields blurred by a stamp that reads ANONYMIZED PER DIRECTIVE 8. A different pen added 'Confirm with Central?' in a tight line in the margin and underlined it twice. No confirmation stamp follows. Two pages forward, the same destination appears, and someone drew a small blue five-pointed star next to it, chalky enough to smudge when my thumb passes over it.

I don't know the symbol, but I know I haven't seen it before.

The terminal remains asleep on the desk when I glance at it. Badge and ID required for entry, something I would need to steal to gain access. I'm sure all the valuable information is stored there, while everything I'm sifting through is just consid-ered busy grunt work for whoever catalogs it.

Footsteps echo through the hall, and I shove the papers back into the box before sliding the lid on as the latch of the archive door clicks in that soft way people use when they think they're being quiet.

Two voices enter, the smell of cold air and soap drifting my way. One man yawns as his boredom becomes evident; the other has the sharp scent of a new uniform and a sourness under it that makes me think he's a nasty person.

"...told you, sub-two's camera is still stuck on the blind," Bored says as a stack lands on the desk and paper rasps. "Two weeks and counting."

"Shut up about blind spots," Sour answers, a drawer squealing in his wake. "You want to keep your post? Stop stringing those two words together."

They are three steps into the room, and I am six rows back. There's no solid cover, just cardboard and chance. I slide left as

I keep my profile tight and let the shelf hide the shape of me. The metal is cold through the sleeve as I press in and slow my breathing until I'm dizzy.

"Inventory says this should've gone upstairs," Bored remarks with a scoff. "Upstairs says downstairs."

"Their problem then." Soap taps something rhythmically on the desk. "You picking up the extra watch or am I?"

"Depends on whether the morning crew keeps losing the keys to Sublevel Four." The chair creaks as he drops into it. "Who keeps misfiling transit anyway? You see this? Someone stuck Riverton returns between the vehicle logs for South Gate."

The pulse in my neck increases with those words.

"Whatever," Bored mutters. "I'll sign, you stamp, and we won't die in this room yet."

They do exactly that—two thumps of a rubber stamp, a pen scratching, a frequent sigh—and then the door hisses open again. Their footsteps retreat the way they came. The silence after feels brighter as my heartbeat slows back into something I can stand.

My mind counts to ten before allowing my body to move. I don't take anything with me—I can't. Everything returns to where I found it as a habit of erasing myself out of rooms I shouldn't be in. I'll come back another time for the missed rows.

The corridor outside is cold when I slip out, and I fold back into the path I know, matching my steps to the camera sweep and pausing at the places where the sound of voices travel. I am careful not to run and keep my head straight as a cart rattles past me in the main corridor.

Back in my room, the door clicks shut and my back rests against it as the tension runs out of my arms. My hands still shake. I clench and unclench them until the tremor edges off and stretch every limb twice over.

Eat first, then another day of training.

OUTSIDE, the yard smells of mud and fog as the morning wind sweeps the night away. The sky is a flat gray, and the air has a bite to it as the recruits gather. Our group is quiet amongst themselves while I keep to the edge like I always do, close enough to catch what's being said and far enough not to invite conversation.

Nash and Calder cackle at something Finnick said, all attention on the man telling a story about pantsing his brother in primary school. The atmosphere simmers with anticipation, each of us knowing something is different today with the change in schedule. What will our great leaders stick us with next?

The Commander stomps out of the building, Elias and Kellen flanking him as they always do—Elias quiet and contained, Kellen's head moving just enough to count us as we line up properly.

"Attention," Arayik says, and we do. Three rows, with me in the back one, between Darius and Pax. The air tightens without changing, and my jaw clenches as I stare ahead, past the three men.

"Last week's mission was a success," he says in the warmest tone I've yet heard from him. "The Syndicate is pleased."

My palms prickle as my fingers curl and the edge of a nail punctures the surrounding skin. Copper taints my tongue. Success is not even close to the word I would have used to describe that disgrace of a mission. I want to shove a fork into each of his eyes, drag them from their sockets, and stomp on them since he doesn't use them anyway. How blind can one man be? *Success?* Is he fucking kidding?

"But there's no room for complacency now." His voice carries without him needing to push it. "Our primary mission approaches. Intelligence puts the main rebel camp in the northern mountains beyond the perimeter, but there is a smaller outpost east of the wall. We leave in five days."

A ripple moves through the rows as the word beyond settles amongst us. Some of the recruits lean forward almost imperceptibly; some go still. My stomach tightens and then lurches, because this is the part I knew would come—out there is where I have to be if I want a chance to do anything but stand in rooms and listen to myself fail.

"That means a change in your schedules as you will be assessed once more. Today is combat readiness." *Stars.* "You'll be tested individually once again."

He motions with one hand, and the yard beyond makes more sense. Different stations—hurdles and walls, rope climbs, a matted square, whatever torture devices they deem necessary this time. Half the recruits break away to begin, and the rest of us stand as the wind slides across the yard and lifts the edge of my mask.

I watch. I don't want to do this. Obeying anything they command is so painful...I just witnessed Kellen murder a man simply for being human. And to them it's inconsequential behavior. But to me? Unfathomable.

How am I to look these men in the eye and hide the absolute disgust I feel each time I do? They believe me one of them, yet I'm the furthest thing from it. I'm going to give myself away if I cannot control these emotions.

"Ashford."

The sound of my family name from Arayik's mouth stings even more than usual. I angle my head toward him, hating how his attention is direct and heavy and right on me. "You're with me." Why is it always me? He spars with recruits regularly, though something tells me I'm singled out in this.

Deep breaths, Cass.

I follow him to the mat as the rustle of bodies on the course greets my ears. My heart beats at my throat as I stand square to him and keep my hands lowered.

"Attack," he instructs, nodding at me.

A puppet, I've decided. That's what I am to the Commander and his followers. A puppet to bend and mold into his version of the man he believes everyone should be.

It takes me one blink to steady the rise in my chest. I say nothing, only adjusting my stance as the air inside the mask warms. Part of me wants to sic my power on him; allow it to fill his veins before I unleash every bit of rage and torment racing through me. Watch him fall to his knees with tears streaming from those cold eyes.

"I said attack!"

I move only because disobeying will ensure my dismissal. I go for the midline and aim to make him shift his feet. He doesn't. He slides right, my elbow hitting air. The mat catches my balance fine and I reset as the sting of heat runs across my chest and away.

"Again," he says.

I go again with a feint and a step to the left. His forearm meets mine a second before the shock of contact travels through bone and lights my wrist, fizzling the nerves. He breathes evenly as if I'm a pesky bug he's killed a thousand times. A foot sweeps my leg without warning and the floor slaps my shoulder as rough material rasps my cheek from the mask.

"Up."

And I get up.

One breath to subdue the small white flare in my shoulder

and another to keep the arm as stable as I can. He launches and I can't afford to step back, so I don't. I pivot and throw an elbow into his ribs as I bring my other hand across, the hit landing on his cheek in a way that does something small to my chest—I wish it didn't feel like relief.

Because the only relief he could ever give me is by dying.

He snatches my arm and twists, forcing me to drop to one knee as a hot lance of pain slices my neck. "Better," he says without warmth. "Not enough."

We forgo words after that. He moves me where he wants me, and I try not to let him. My lungs burn and the slit of my mask burns from the sunlight, so I rely on sound and instinct to defend myself. The ring of bodies working around us is full of grunts and cheers, distracting me from the fight. Sweat runs along my spine and pools at the small of my back as my uniform sticks to every possible crevice. I'm so uncomfortable.

I block a high strike and he drops low, a fist landing in the bruise along my ribs from three days ago, dragging the air from my lungs in a noise I don't recognize as mine. My vision fuzzes at the edges for a second but sharpens again when I bite the inside of my cheek to anchor myself.

"On your feet," he demands as I fail to stand fast enough after the hardest fall I've endured yet. His voice doesn't lift, it thins. "Now."

My legs tremble as I rise and will them to hold. To stay upright because there is no version of this where I don't.

"You're at your breaking point." Duh. If it wasn't obvious I wanted to kill him before, it sure is now as I glare daggers. "This is what I've been trying to drag out of you. *This* is where I find out if you're worth carrying or cutting."

Something shimmers at the edges of my awareness—an opening I can exploit. His guard is just a hair low, and I reach; not for his skin, but for the edge of him, a tendril of emotion to unbalance him. For a breath, it's electric, and I plant a thread of doubt there. Finally, an advantage I can use—

Instead it snaps back. A white-noise roar fills my head, static behind my teeth, as a pressure I've never known drowns all thought. I stagger, my timing shredded. He doesn't notice the inner turmoil—or he does and couldn't care less—as his elbow finds my side and the air whooshes from me in an embarrassing animal sound.

It takes a few moments to reorient my head, but when I do, I'm pissed.

I lower my center and drive into him. He yields half a step, and my shoulder shrieks as it hits at the wrong angle. I almost scream when his hands grip both my shoulders and the world flips as he puts me on my back. Again. Fuck that hurts. I need to lie very still for a while, and maybe I'll have a chance of standing.

He crouches, his breath touching my eyes as he leans close. "Even after weeks of training, you're still inadequate," he says as if it's a new revelation. "I don't trust you, Ashford. But according to my men, you're worth keeping, so maybe I will keep you on the team. Just to watch you fail."

He strides away, muscling through the gathered bodies. Eyes shift away from me. No one offers a hand, and I don't expect one. I'm so close to leaving here, and that's the only reason I find the will to rise. The yard spins around me like I never stopped falling, and I make myself walk it off as my heartbeat settles into something of a normal rhythm.

When I finally make it to my room after hours of tests, my shirt lifts to the pattern of new bruises blooming like they always do—round where a knee landed, long where I hit the floor. I clean the cuts with the alcohol I hid in my pocket one day and it offers a comforting bite. My homemade salve cools the throbbing skin as my shoulder relents on its incessant twitching for the first time since this morning.

Whatever the hell they want from me, clearly getting stronger isn't going to happen in five days.

I am not their kind of fighter. But I don't need five days to make myself impossible to leave behind and not worth the trouble to cut—I've already proven how useful I can be with our last mission. I think the Commander just threatens to send me home at this point with no intention of doing so. I'm physically mediocre, but mentally everything he needs with him when looking for the escapees.

So I allow my shit performance today to float away with all my other worries. I'm not going anywhere.

The mask slides free, and I lie back very slowly as my body protests.

You're at your breaking point. I scoff. He thinks he knows me. He thinks he can break me by pushing where he's pushed a hundred men before, but he doesn't know what I'm holding inside. He doesn't know what I'm willing to do when the cost cannot be measured by the weight of my punch.

That will be his mistake.

CHAPTER EIGHTEEN
CASSIA

Arayik paces the front of our group like he owns the floor. He doesn't need to raise his voice. "There was unauthorized access in the archives yesterday at 0412—the scanner next to the door pinged when no one was scheduled to be there. So, effective immediately, all sublevels are restricted to leadership only. No one will be permitted without prior documentation." My jaw squeezes past the point of pain. A hush follows those words, then a single, clipped addition, "Now, the Syndicate has decided we've had enough time. We leave at dawn."

The room tightens. Four days gone, just like that.

Not before I'm ready, I think—and then remind myself no one asked, nor does anyone care.

My body sobs knowing the chance to heal before we leave is no longer an option. My poor muscles; even just sitting here hurts. And I now cannot visit the archives again...what a day. I don't believe they know it was me; I was precise with my movement around the cameras and I'm certain I'd be either dead or in a holding cell if they did know.

I suppose bright sides do exist.

Kellen plants his hands on the table at the front of the room. I'm seated in the front row, so the tension in his muscles is undeniable. "Recon determines the camp at roughly a day's travel beyond the southeastern perimeter. Objectives remain unchanged: secure all females of breeding age or younger for transport, and neutralize any resistance."

Secure. Neutralize. Mira's face flashes, then the men whose bodies dropped so quickly. I lock my hands at my sides.

Elias doesn't step forward so much as the room leans toward him. "You'll be assigned to squads," he adds, calm and steady. "Follow your lead without question. There is no choice beyond the perimeter. This is not training, and your actions *will* have very real consequences."

Arayik reads the list. "Ashford, Crowell, Eston, Spinel, Styx report to Elias. Amata, Flor, Hasten, Vion, Epner to Kellen. Benson, Rhyne, Forven, Rayne, Till are with me."

Relief hits hard enough I have to stiffen my body so it doesn't sag my shoulders. Not Arayik. Elias isn't safe—no one here is—but he's the best choice of the three if I'm to be stuck with any.

Kellen unrolls a map, lines and numbers identifying pre-marked spots. "I will go over this only once. There will be no time to brief you on it in the field." He pauses until every person's attention is solely on him. "Elias' squad will approach from the north while I take the east and the Commander secures the south. A river covers the west, allowing us to cover all exits before pushing their people back toward it. At which time we will complete the mission objective and return to the perimeter. Pack light. Once we're past the wall, convoys stay. We walk the remainder and will carry one drone for location confirmation."

"Signal?" asks Vito.

"Rayne, Eston, and myself will transmit necessary information when possible, but squads are expected to hold their own and reconvene by the river," Kellen answers.

I study the map. There's not much to it, which is soothing in an anxiety-inducing way. It means we don't know what we're walking in to, but it also means they know very little about the escapees or their camps. So they'll have no idea if some happen to be missing at the end of this.

"Dismissed," Arayik says, standing tall. "Pack and sleep. Be late at dawn, and I leave without you. And when I come back, I'll make sure you wish I hadn't."

We break. I'm at the door when a hand closes around my arm.

"A word," Elias murmurs when I lock eyes with him, steering me down the hall.

"Sir," I answer, neutral, as my pulse kicks.

He smells nice this close. His eyes stay on me even as they flick to our path every so often. "Are you ready for this?" he asks, low.

I expect accusation, and I get concern? That's somehow worse. And why is he only asking me? "Yes, sir." A lie, but if he catches it, he doesn't comment.

"Beyond the wall, things are far more intense. If you hesitate, someone else bleeds for it."

I nod once. "Understood."

"Pack warm," he adds. "The nights do not adhere to seasons."

DAWN IS GRAY AND FOREBODING—THE kind of gray that can make any happy person gloomy in an instant. Convoys idle at the front of the training center, engines humming low. We've been standing here for at least twenty minutes, waiting—for the Commander, of all people. Figures. "Squad two," Elias calls, and I leave formation with Finnick, Killian, Corin, and Calder. We climb into the center vehicle—narrow windows, semi-comfortable benches, air stale as can be—and I take the corner. Prison and shield, the mask presses against my cheekbones the way it always does.

The door slams before our vehicle lurches when the rest of the team is ready, and the Center shrinks behind us as the perimeter grows and grows. My heart thuds in a terrible pattern. Could it beat any faster? It tries.

The road under us falls apart fast, shifting from gravel to broken asphalt. Each crack pops the convoy and wrings a groan out of the men in unison as we lurch from our seats. Even the vehicle complains. We bounce for hours—no one speaking, just the steady breath of bodies and the dusty taste of silence—until Elias raps twice on the partition and rolls the convoy to an unsteady stop.

I peer out the window, jaw dropping at the utter expanse of the perimeter. From my position, the sky is no longer visible— nor the top of the wall.

This is...significantly larger than I'd thought.

Shedding scales of concrete run from the base up, and even surrounded by luscious trees of the forest, it's utterly intimidating.

There's a short hum of voices from the front before a long, screeching groan permeates the air. I wince from the force beating against my eardrums.

"Shit, that's fucking loud," Killian bellows, earning a backhand from Calder.

"And yelling is supposed to make it better, how?" I chuckle at that.

Before long, the convoy pitches forward. Are we driving *into* the wall? Oh, no, no, no. It's all I can do to keep my mouth shut as we pass a group of gun-wielding Enforcers before darkness surrounds us completely. I'm going to vomit.

Deep breaths. In through the nose, out through the mouth.

My father's words will not assist me here.

I'm stuck in a tiny space, where the only light is the dimmest haze offered from the front of the vehicle. What I'm able to see of the walls is even worse—they're nearly touching the vehicle on both sides. What if it collapses and we are stuck in here until we die of suffocation or dehydration? I'm no stranger to being confined to small margins, but at least there I knew *someone* would open the hatch door, even if it was an Enforcer. Now I'm stuck in here with an entire team of them.

One in, two out. Three in, four out.

I count and count as my ears grow fuzzy, my eyes aching from how hard they're scrunched closed. Time passes slow. The only thing I focus on are the number of breaths I take in line with the number of rotations from our tires. As long as the tires are moving, we're not stuck.

I'm nearing three hundred when the sound barrier spreads and my eyes spring open to the light of day once more. Given how that took forever, I'm quite curious how long it took to build this damn perimeter. I don't recall any mention of that...

Regardless, I do not want to do that again. I can manage life out here just fine, no need to go back to the training center when this is over.

"This is as far as engines go," Elias yells as we finally, blessedly come to a stop. "On foot from here."

Warm air caresses my lashes as I step out of the convoy. It smells like damp bark; wet soil instead of metal and bleach. We spill into a clearing, ensuring every person and pack is accounted for before trudging behind our leaders through blistering heat. How much sweat can my undergarments soak up before it's considered a biohazard?

I'm certain I passed that line hours ago.

Half our group is about to drop from exhaustion when Arayik barks, "We'll camp here."

There's a collective sigh.

Quiet murmurs filter through my head as I pull my assigned tent from my pack and lay it out in front of me. After some staring, Calder appears, handing me a pole, pointing with his chin. "Push the collar until it clicks."

I do. "Thank you." It's a genuine remark—stars know I would not have figured that out on my own. I watch him erect his tent, confused by how easy it seems.

It's not long before we stand near a low fire and chew rations that glue to teeth. It's not the best, but jerky is good protein and will last our entire trip. As will the crackers, though those are far dryer. My tongue quickly learns the art of consuming these with as little water as possible, knowing we need to drink it sparingly.

"Just over a day's march." Arayik pushes into our group, creating a space for himself. "Terrain will pick fights. Weather too, so rest up, we set off at first light."

"Watches," Kellen announces as the Commander retreats to his tent. "Rhyne and Till first. Forven, Vion second. Hasten, Crowell third. Ashford, Eston fourth."

Fourth watch is the black before blue. Not ideal—I'd rather have first, but it's better than second or third. I stash my gear by the tent flap before finding a place away from camp to pee. I hadn't considered how I would during the day when the other men just stand to relieve themselves...I'd soil my clothes if I try that.

A thought comes to me as I crouch behind a small bush: could I repurpose a piece of bark to work how a penis would? As long as the material wasn't necrotic, I see no reason why it wouldn't. Plus, it has to be more sanitary than baring myself to the ground like this. Clean and cunning all in one.

I'll search for a usable piece tomorrow when there's light.

I nod to Calder and Malcom when I return, practically falling into my tent. My hands lift to remove my mask out of habit, pausing at the laughter outside. The chances of someone walking in here while I'm unconscious is probable—I guess I'll be living inside this thing for the coming days.

Every bone in my body sinks into the bed roll, praising me for finally giving them a break from the pain. Sleep claims me quick.

A ROUGH SHAKE of my shoulder wakes me what feels like minutes later. "Up. Fourth watch," Pax says.

That was the least restful sleep I've ever gotten. Waking once an hour to strange noises, then to a kink in my neck, does not make for an ideal night of sleep.

Outside, the air bites. Icy dew laces the grass and the stars sit low and bright in the sky, like they're fascinated by our team and wanted a closer look.

Pax waits at the designated perimeter. "North and east are yours," he says, nodding to my left. "I'll take south and west. Check-in every fifteen."

"Understood." He prefers instructions to small conversation. Works for me.

I pace my arc as the camp breathes deeply behind me. The forest in the distance carries small sounds—little flaps of wings, branches shifting, something with four legs and a furry tail deciding we're not worth its curiosity. My power releases, and I know immediately that's what was keeping me from proper sleep. I'd built a surplus on stress and anxiety over the last day or two and haven't given it an outlet, and it's an immense relief to just let it flow where the emotions hovering idly are thin with sleep. The mask warms as I breathe and count the steps between stones.

Something shifts ahead—a deliberate movement. A shape peels from the trees and shuffles forward. A man.

My hand lands on my weapon, because that should be an Enforcer's first instinct. As should alerting the others.

And yet, my throat tightens. If I call out, he's dead. If I don't, maybe we are. I hold one breath too long.

There's an alarmed shout behind me—Pax alerting the team. The camp snaps awake with the agility of a rubber band; tents open and spit men who grip their own weapons. The figure by the trees runs. The Commander launches by me, already racing for him and the trees swallow them both after a moment.

Branches crack. A heavy thud followed by a series of grunts, with which I cannot decide if it's terrible of me that I hope the other man gives Arayik what he deserves.

"Eston." Elias' voice is at my shoulder. "Report."

"Single male, alone. He had no visible weapon, nor any obvious intention to approach our camp. Looked like he was just surveying." His words twist something dangerous inside me.

"Ashford saw him first," Pax adds like a fucking idiot.

Elias faces me, brow raised. "And why were you not the one to alert us, Ashford?" Thick sludge drags around the lump in my throat, nearly choking me.

"I—" I, what? Was going to let the man walk away? Was only planning to notify you if the man approached? I have to offer something truthful, he'll know otherwise... "I didn't realize it was a man at first."

My squad leader gazes between my eyes for several moments before the Commander stomps back toward our group.

He returns bruised, with a split lip, and it's impossible to hide the smirk. He should have gotten far worse than that. He hauls the unconscious man over his shoulder, making for the center of our camp to unceremoniously drop him between all of us. It's light enough that the scruff along his chin is visible, as are the even worse bruises Arayik gave him. I shiver at the long, angry scar running from one side of his throat to the other. His clothes don't fare much better.

"Bind him," Arayik commands, cracking his neck as his arms cross. Gage and Nash grab for spare rope and secure the man's hands at his back. "We'll ask our questions when he wakes."

Relief sways and curdles—he's alive, at least. For now.

I whirl back to my post and pace my section, securing distance from the others while it's still my watch. By the time the sky lifts to a pale seam, I've worn a path. Something disturbing dawns on me; a revelation I don't like: this is no longer a charade to me. This isn't just about surviving until I figure out the smallest ways to help.

I've seen what it's like on the inside of these men's heads— I've *lived it*. Small victories here and there will mean nothing in the grand scheme, because they will never change. They will always win because that's how they set the system up.

If the people out here could find a way to defy the Syndicate, escape the facilities, and live outside the perimeter, then there's a crack in the system running deep enough to worry our esteemed leaders. That's why they formed this Enforcer team, is it not?

They're afraid. They want these people neutralized before they can do actual damage.

I need to find that crack. Pry it open and pray to the stars it's made out of glass instead of water.

CHAPTER NINETEEN
CASSIA

Frost dusts the leaves and turns slick under boots as Arayik instructs two recruits to position the scout for interrogation. They plant him upright before shoving a tent pole between his arms, effectively keeping the man contained to one spot. Kellen pulls off the blindfold they slipped on when he was unconscious and we were instructed to pack everything. Not sure why that matters...if the man could communicate with his people, I don't think knowing we have a couple tents is a big deal.

The man blinks at our faces—counting, sorting, storing. A bruise swells high on his cheekbone where Arayik caught him, deforming his face.

"You had yourself a long walk," Arayik says, voice flat enough to pass for calm.

The scout wets a dry, cracked lip and keeps taking us in. I study him closer. He's near my age, or older if you measure years in hunger...He's far too skinny.

Elias posts to Arayik's left, Kellen to his right, all three glaring at our new camp member. The rest of us form a ring around the four of them.

"Ashford," Arayik says, eyes on the prisoner, "names, numbers, locations. I want answers, so get them."

I'm not sure if I should be relieved or terrified.

I step in and lower to one knee so I'm level with the sky-blue eyes of our guest. I couldn't care less how compromising this position is—I want to level with him when I'm inside his head. His gaze finds the slit of my mask and stays there.

The camp has a particular taste at this hour—cold metal, anxious thoughts, a thread of old smoke that doesn't blow with the wind, last night's nerves still crusted on the edges. I can't decide, but it's not pleasant.

How do you tell a man you're about to invade the most private part of him? I try to convey my sincerity through my eyes as I wouldn't dare utter it out loud; then I reach.

Fear slides through me first—acrid and sour—repressed by sheer will. Beneath it, sadness. Grief so intense I need to swallow a cry of pain. Is he grieving his family? I've no doubt they're wondering where he is by now.

"Your name," I say, pouring calming thoughts under his skin.

"Rook," he answers. A lie, I believe; there was a spike of something unrecognizable when he said it. But I keep that to myself.

"We can keep this straightforward, Rook" I tell him. "I just need some information and this is done. You talk, this is easy for everyone. But if you don't, I really don't think you'll like what these men will do to you."

He huffs, not amused. "You sound like you have no idea what will happen after you leave. Doesn't matter if I talk or not."

"You're right." His brows raise. "Either way, I will person-ally ensure the outcome is not painful if you just give us what we need." I'm not confident in that promise, but it's not a lie. I will do whatever possible to make sure they give him a quick, clean death.

He draws breath to answer. Arayik steps in and drives a knife into the man's shoulder, causing him to scream and thrash.

Who knew it was possible to hate one person this much?

I peer up with a glare so severe, heat radiates from my eyes. The meaning is clear: message received.

"Let him speak, Commander," Elias says, challenging the Anchor. Surprisingly, Arayik eases back half a pace.

The man coughs, and I lift a canteen in offering as more calm emotions leave me, a pressure building deep in my head. "Drink first. Then we talk."

He eyes the canteen like it could be a trick before drinking anyway. Water coats his chin, washes a thin line through the dirt at his throat. There's something blue peeking out from behind his ear, bright in the rising sun.

"What do your people call you?" I ask, softer.

"Rook," he says again. It still tastes wrong, but if he wishes to be called Rook, then who am I to say otherwise as a woman pretending to be her brother?

"How far is your camp?"

"Far enough," he answers.

It's at this moment I realize how selfish I am because I hope he refuses to answer my questions. He's right, Arayik will not allow this man to live after today, but he'll make it so much worse if he wastes the Commander's time. And yet, I want him to.

"How many are on watch when you sleep?"

He's careful. "Enough."

Kellen steps in a half pace, voice even. "Two? Three?"

The smallest flinch when Kellen says three. He tries to swallow it, not successfully enough to escape my notice.

"Two," he answers.

"Noted," Kellen says. His attention ticks to me, and I shift my weight to sit on both knees. He saw it, too.

Arayik crouches and snatches Rook's left foot like it's something he does often. The knife tip touches the web of skin between toes, dragging a wince from me. "Give me what I want," he says. "Cut the shit."

Rook stares at the blade, then at me. Something old and heavy moves behind those irises. "You know what you call your places?" His voice is rough. "*Facilities.* We call them white barns." His eyes slide past us as if there's one through the trees as he spits his next words. "They took my mother to one when my father died. When I got her back, there was a new number carved into her skin."

"You see, I covered up the old one. She was finally free of that prison and never wanted to be reminded of her identity in there, so I found a needle and covered the side of her neck where they place the marks. But when I got her back? There was a new fucking number on the other side. She meant nothing but money to them. You soldiers think you're so high and mighty because you can toss the rest of us around and throw our mothers away when they lose someone they love." He pauses as the knife presses just enough to make his skin blanch. Arayik doesn't need to say the threat out loud.

And still, I feel an immense sense of pride at his next words. "So no, *Enforcer*, I will not *cut the shit*. You may do what you wish with me, but you will never get anything useful from my mouth."

I want to hug him. To tell him I'm proud—that he reminds me of my father and brother. That he's a rare gem in this horrifying world.

Instead, Arayik's patience hits its ceiling. "Enough," he

shouts, shoving the tip of his blade into the crease of Rook's foot. "If he won't talk, I have no use for him."

He reaches for a small pack Finnick is already opening like he's been waiting to all morning. Shock baton, tubing, syringe, more knives. The list makes my stomach hard.

"Wait," I cry before Arayik can choose where to start, jolting from my position to stand next to him. "You'll spike adrenaline and pain before we use the only advantage we have."

"What advantage is that, Ashford?" Arayik asks, amused, without turning his head.

My voice lowers. "He thinks we're monsters. He's ready for pain and death, but he isn't ready for someone to treat him like a person. That's why he brought up his story of barns. He's anchoring himself. If I pull on that anchor, he may give us something he doesn't think is information."

A beat. Kellen's brow raises in my direction while Elias remains quiet. The Commander exhales a sound that isn't quite a laugh; a dry, fearsome sound.

"Five minutes."

That's as much space as I'm going to get.

I return to Rook and wring the rag out under the canteen mouth. I dab the cracks at his lip, not a dramatic help, but the man deserves to speak without being completely dehydrated. He startles at the gentleness.

"What's your river called?" I think of sunny days and flowing water, filling him with the peace of those images. My skull pounds as if it's going to tear from my scalp—I've been holding my power for longer than I thought. Still, I keep going.

"Old map says Kole," he answers as his eyes flutter shut. "We call it The Spine."

I pause. "Because?"

"It holds what we build; gives life to all of us that just want to live in peace." It costs him to say it, fear rising in my throat again. I share more calming feelings before continuing.

"You were counting us when we spotted you," I say, not exactly a question.

"I was deciding what you are."

"And? What are we?" I keep my voice flat to hide the excited interest I feel in speaking with this man.

He tips his chin toward Arayik without looking away from me. "It's like you said: monsters." His gaze slides to Arayik. "But that one is pure demon." Rook grins at the Commander, showcasing blood-crusted teeth.

I don't blink. "Tell me something that won't get anyone hurt."

He exhales as both shoulders drop a fraction. "We planted the kale too close in the lower bed," he mutters almost conversationally. "The kids won't thin it; they feel bad for the small ones."

"How many beds do you have?" The question leaves before I can stop it.

"Eight," he says, and also catches himself a second too late. We still have an audience.

As much as I would love to learn everything about his life and how he brought people outside the perimeter, I know my window is closing.

Reaching inside, every bit of goodness I possess gets shoved into a box as I continue. "North." No reaction. "South." Still nothing. "East—" There, a slight twitch in his eye. It appears our intelligence was correct, after all.

I know my time is exhausted when Arayik strides forward. "His camp is east," I declare for the group, holding Rook's gaze.

I'm so sorry.

Arayik's hand is already on his gun when I stand. "Good."

Elias appears at my shoulder, voice low. "Walk." And I do, my head shaking as I will the impending migraine away.

Pack heavy on my back, we step far enough that the noise of camp becomes a hum. A shrill pop spreads through the land, but I keep walking, praying to the stars it was a quick enough death.

Elias waits until my pulse has finally learned a normal rhythm again to speak. "You did good. And you kept Arayik from turning the man's hand into a lesson. That's not nothing."

"Don't make it a compliment."

I shove past him and wait for orders to move through the squads—reset packs, check straps, drink. The day is bright yet cold. Rook's lifeless eyes watch us from the ground, wrists still tied as his hair soaks in blood from the pool beneath him.

We don't walk toward him when we finally move.

We go east.

CHAPTER TWENTY

CASSIA

The forest around us shifts from peaceful to predatory in the span of a heartbeat.

One moment I'm following Finnick's steady pace through the undergrowth, my boots finding purchase on moss-covered stones and fallen logs. The next moment, the world explodes into chaos.

Gunfire erupts from three directions at once, sharp screams splitting the morning air. Voices pierce through the trees—not ours, but *theirs*. The escapees we've been hunting.

"Defense!" Arayik's voice rises above the noise, but it's too late for the careful squad divisions we'd planned. We're scattered across fifty meters of forest, caught in the open by the same people we're pursuing.

I drop behind a thick tree, bark splintering above my head as bullets tear through the air where I stood moments before. My heart slams against my ribs, the sound of my own pulse competing with the battle for dominance in my ears.

This is nothing like the simulations.

Nothing like our training.

The acrid smell of gunpowder soaked in blood greets my nostrils. Smoke drifts between the trees, mingling with the earthy scent of disturbed soil and crushed leaves. Everything is moving too fast. Too loud and real.

"Ashford!" Elias' voice reaches me from somewhere to my left. "Fire, now!"

My hands shake as I raise my weapon, finger gliding over the trigger. The gun kicks against my shoulder as I whirl and fire into the trees, aiming for the random flashes rather than clear targets—I couldn't hit anything with accuracy right now. The recoil renders my arms useless from being so sore, burning every joint for several moments.

Movement catches my attention—a figure darting between trees with a gracefulness I could only dream of possessing. And he's headed right for me. Without thinking, I break from cover to pursue my team that has shifted in a different direction. My legs pump beneath me, carrying me across roots and rocks as I run from the shadow chasing me through the forest.

As the thundering gait behind me closes in, one thing becomes clear: he's going to catch me.

And against any better judgment, I turn, finding myself face to face with a man roughly my age. His clothes are worn but clean, patched in places but well-maintained. His eyes hold no malice, only determination. This isn't a criminal or terrorist —this is someone protecting his home.

He raises his weapon, and I raise mine.

We circle each other in a small clearing, both breathing hard. Through the trees, the sounds of battle continue—shouts, gunfire, the crash of bodies through underbrush. But here, in this pocket of forest, there's only us.

"You don't have to do this," he says, his voice deep and steady despite the circumstances. "We've done nothing but try to stay away from you. None of us need to die because of it."

My lungs constrict. He's right, of course he is. I don't want to be here just as much as he doesn't want me here.

I wish it were so easy.

"It's not that simple," I manage through the thickness in my throat.

His expression hardens. "Then you're as much a monster as the rest of them."

The words hurt, only because they're true. I am a monster. I think of the woman we captured in Pyrem, of the men shot dead in front of their family. Of all the women trapped in breeding facilities while I play at being their captor.

I may be a monster, but I will never be one of *them*.

"I'm not—" I begin, but he's already moving.

He lunges forward, abandoning his gun for close combat. We grapple, his hands seeking my throat while mine fight to break his grip. He's stronger than me, but desperation lends me much needed adrenaline. I twist away from his grasp, stumbling backward.

"You came here to destroy us," he pants, advancing again. "To drag our women back to those hellholes you call facilities."

"I came here because I had to," I snap back, the words tumbling out before I can stop them.

Something in my tone makes him pause. His eyes narrow, studying the little he can glimpse of my face.

His observation terrifies me more than his physical attacks. But I let him look—will him to understand that I don't want to hurt him. For a moment I'm certain he does, but his expression hardens again before he tackles me around the waist, sending us both crashing to the forest floor.

We roll across the ground, fighting for advantage. His elbow catches my ribs, driving the air from my lungs, and I retaliate with a knee to his stomach, earning a grunt of pain. Dirt and leaves stick to our clothes as we struggle.

He gains the upper hand, pinning me beneath his weight. His hands close around my throat, and panic floods my system.

Not because I'm afraid of dying—though I am—but because if he removes my mask, anyone could appear and learn what I really am.

My vision blurs at the edges. Through the growing darkness, I see his face above mine, set with grim determination. He's not enjoying this. He's doing what he believes necessary to protect his people.

Just like I'm supposed to be doing for mine.

The thought rouses me. A drill from training plays through my mind—the Commander demonstrated turning under an opponent's weight, angling your hip so their force becomes your opening. The motions flip in my head, and I reach for the knife on my belt, my fingers closing around the handle. The blade slides free with a tone so quiet the blood funneling through my ears drowns it out.

"I'm sorry," I whisper, twisting my hip and driving it upward.

The point finds the gap between his ribs, sliding into his chest with sickening ease. His eyes widen, more in surprise than pain, before his grip loosens, hands shifting to the fresh wound.

Blood seeps between his fingers, dark and warm. The metallic smell mingles with the forest, creating a stomach-churning scent of life and death.

"Why?" he gasps, his weight settling heavier on my chest.

I have no answer that would satisfy either of us. Instead, I ease him to the side, watching as the light fades from his eyes. His last breath escapes in a small sigh, barely audible over the shouts in the distance.

I sit back on my heels, staring at what I've done.

Don't cry, don't cry.

I just killed a man. I just took a life without a second thought, as if I have any right to do so.

My hands shake as I wipe them along my pant legs, the motion automatic despite the horror coursing through me. This man died protecting his community and family. His freedom. And I killed him for it.

A heavy weight settles across my shoulders, and I don't think I'll be rid of it anytime soon. I've crossed a line I can never uncross, become something I swore I'd never be. The fact I had no choice doesn't lessen the burden—it only makes it more bitter.

Gunfire draws closer, snapping me back to the present. I need to move; rejoin the others before my absence is noted. Stars forbid my team find me here bawling over someone I was supposed to enjoy killing. I push to my feet, legs unsteady beneath me.

The battle has shifted deeper into the forest. I follow the sounds, my steps careful through the maze of trees. Shuffling drifts between the trunks, and the sour smell of more death strengthens with each step.

I emerge into a wider clearing where the main engagement is. Our forces have the escapees pinned against a rocky outcropping, but they're fighting with the desperation of people defending their homes. They know this terrain. We're just intruders.

The other recruits are spread through the terrain while Arayik crouches behind a fallen log, barking orders into his watch. Kellen has taken position on higher ground, his rifle eliminating targets with methodical precision. And Elias—

Elias moves through the chaos like a force of nature—an expert in a field of war. But his attention keeps drifting to something beyond the immediate battle, something that makes his jaw tighten.

I follow his gaze, and my blood turns to ice.

Civilians.

A group of maybe a dozen women and two children huddle behind a cluster of trees at the far edge of the clearing. They're trying to escape, to slip away while the fighters hold our attention. One of the women clutches an infant to her chest, her face pale with terror. The children can't be more than five or six years old.

Orders echo in my mind: capture the women and children. They're resources to be collected, processed, assigned to facilities or families as the Syndicate sees fit. The children will be separated by gender—boys trained as future Enforcers, girls prepared for breeding.

I raise my weapon, sighting on the group. My finger finds the trigger, applies the slightest pressure.

And freezes.

I can't do it.

I can't be the one to condemn these innocents to the fate I've spent my life hiding from. The woman with the infant appears barely older than me. The children are scared and confused, tears descending their blotchy faces while they reach for any form of comfort.

My arms waver, lowering the gun to hang at my side once more.

"Ashford!" Elias' voice cuts through my paralysis. "What are you waiting for?"

I should move. Should follow orders, complete the mission, maintain my cover. But my body refuses to obey. Every instinct screams against what I'm being asked to do.

They'll kill me for this—something I no longer care about. The Syndicate can have my life if it means those people can be free.

The moment of hesitation costs me immediately. One of the escapee fighters emerges from behind a tree to my right. His weapon swings toward me, and I know I won't be fast enough to react.

The world slows to a crawl. The muzzle flashes, the displacement of air a small comfort as the bullet passes inches from my head. Then Elias is there, his shoulder slamming into my side as he shoves me down.

My elbow slams into the ground at a bad angle, tearing a cry from me as a searing pain travels through the bone. Elias rolls us behind a thick trunk as more shots pepper the bark above us. His weight pins me down, his breathing harsh in my ear.

"Stay down," he growls, then rises to return fire.

The rebel's weapon falls silent, and I know my leader well enough to know his shot was permanent.

Elias' gaze blazes with an emotion I can't quite identify. Anger, certainly, but something else underneath. Concern? Suspicion?

"What the hell was that?" he demands, his voice a charged whisper.

"I—" The words stick in my throat. How do I explain without revealing everything? "This is our first real combat...I froze."

His stare bores into me, searching for truth behind the excuse. "Freezing gets you killed, Ashford. Gets your team killed."

"I know." The admission tastes like ash. "It won't happen again."

"It better not." He checks the mag on his weapon, then peers around our cover. "Because next time, I'm not saving your ass."

The battle is dwindling. I'm unsure of how many escaped, but by the fury in our Commander's eyes when I round the tree, I would say too many.

I watch as Kellen zip-ties the hands of a man who can't be more than twenty. Blood seeps from a gash on the prisoner's forehead, but his eyes remain on the two women next to him. Kellen tugs him forward, and he spits on the leader's feet, earning a rifle butt to the stomach that doubles him over.

The women are handled with more care, but no less firmly. They're assets now, property of the Syndicate. Tears cover their faces as Nash approaches and plastic restraints are secured around their wrists.

One of their gazes meets mine, a girl with tangled brown hair. Her eyes hold a question I can't answer—an accusation I can't deny. She doesn't understand why these masked figures have destroyed her world when she's wanted nothing but autonomy over her own body.

Unable to hold her stare a moment longer, my eyes shift away.

"Deplorable," Arayik announces as he surveys the aftermath. "We should have had them all contained in half the time. And yet *dozens of them* managed to flee!"

He's right, and we all know it. The escapees fought harder than expected, as if they were more than prepared for us. Several of our team sport wounds—nothing fatal, but enough to slow us on the journey back.

"We underestimated their capabilities," Kellen observes, dressing a cut on Ronan's arm. "They're better organized than the reports indicated."

"Better armed, too," Elias adds. He's combing through their defenses, cataloging what they've collected. "These aren't homemade weapons or basic hunting rifles. Someone's been supplying them with Enforcer-grade equipment."

Truthfully, I'm not surprised.

What did the Syndicate expect? If someone was aiding

them in leaving Dascenia, why wouldn't they also provide things they could protect themselves with?

But now they know. And if they're organized enough to mount effective resistance, then this mission is just the beginning. The Syndicate will send more forces, better equipped and less concerned with taking prisoners.

"Pack it up," the Commander orders. "We're moving out in ten minutes. I want to be back at the perimeter before dark tomorrow."

The group readies quickly while gathering useful intelligence and preparing the prisoners for transport. The dead rebels are left where they fell—a message for anyone who might find them later.

Between me and Calder, we secure the women, my hands moving automatically while my mind reels. This is what I've been training for—what the Syndicate calls the greater order. But all I see is broken families and shattered lives.

"You did good back there," Killian remarks as he passes, nodding toward the tree line where my confrontation took place. "Was a little worried when I saw the fucker chase you. Clean kill?"

I nod, not trusting my voice.

"Gets easier," he continues, mistaking my silence for something it isn't. "First one's always rough, but you'll find your rhythm."

He moves on without another word. To him, to all of them, this is just another day's work. The death I carry, the lives we've destroyed...it's all part of the job.

But as we begin the long march back to the perimeter, prisoners stumbling ahead of us under guard, I know nothing about this will ever be easy. Each step takes me further from the person I was, deeper into a role that's slowly consuming everything I once believed about myself.

The day closes around us, hiding the evidence of our battle. But the memory of what happened here will follow me long after we've returned to the *safety* of Syndicate territory. The man I killed, the families we've torn apart, the children whose innocence died today along with their protectors.

I am become death. And the worst part is that tomorrow, I'll have to do it all again.

CHAPTER TWENTY-ONE

CASSIA

T he makeshift camp settles into an uneasy quiet as the moon draws a slow path across the clear sky. Our tents are arranged in a loose perimeter around the escapees, the recruits' breathing gradually evening out as exhaustion takes hold. The prisoners sit bound against three separate trees, their forms barely visible in the dying light of our single campfire.

Having foregone a tent, I lie on my bedroll, staring through the canopy at stars I've never seen from inside the perimeter. My body aches from the day's violence, but sleep feels impossible. Each time I close my eyes, that man's face appears—the moment resignation flickered in his gaze as my blade found its mark. The burden of his blood on my hands is heavier than the tactical gear strapped to my chest.

One of the women we captured hasn't stopped crying. Soft, broken sobs that slice through the night air every few seconds. Her friend whimpers occasionally, a sound that makes my chest tighten with something I can't name. Beside her, the young man Kellen secured earlier sits with his head bowed, shoulders shaking with what might be grief or rage.

I count the minutes until the guard rotation. Darius took

first watch, his silhouette visible against the fire's glow as he patrols the camp's edge. In an hour, Nash will replace him. Then Corin.

My fingers trace the outline of my knife through the fabric of my pack. The blade that ended a life today. The same blade that might save three tonight.

The plan forms in fragments, each piece clicking into place as I sort through the various possibilities. Wait for Nash's watch. He's a Concealer which means he'll be focused on the shadows and any moving parts in the uneven terrain. His attention will be on the perimeter, not the prisoners. I can use power to cloud his judgment, make him drowsy or distracted enough to miss my movement.

I know the risks.

If I'm caught, there's not a single explanation that will save me. No story about sleepwalking or needing to relieve myself that will account for cut ties and missing prisoners. Arayik would execute me on the spot, and my family would never know what happened to their daughter who vanished one morning with nothing but a cryptic note.

Yet the alternative—watching these people get dragged back to breeding facilities or worse—feels like a suffocating betrayal of everything I am beneath this mask.

Remnants of the fire pop, sending flickering ash spiraling into the darkness. Next to me, Calder shifts in his tent, and for a moment I think he might be awake. His breathing pattern seems even. He doesn't move again, and after several tense seconds, I convince myself it's just paranoia.

Time crawls. The forest around us settles into its nocturnal rhythm as the air chills. It's going to be rather cold by morning.

When Nash finally takes his position, I force myself to wait another thirty minutes. Long enough for Darius to fall asleep and Nash to settle into his routine; for his attention to drift toward the treeline where threats might emerge. The prisoners have gone quiet, exhaustion finally claiming them despite their circumstances.

I rise slowly, every movement intentional to avoid the tell-tale creak of gear or a rustle of fabric. My boots find the soft spots between roots and leaves, years of learning ultimate silence in my family's house serving me now in ways I never imagined.

Nash stands twenty feet from the prisoners, his back partially turned as he scans the forest. Perfect.

I reach out with my empathy, feeling for the edges of his consciousness. His emotions are a steady hum of boredom and mild alertness—exactly what I need. I don't push hard, just a gentle nudge toward drowsiness. The kind of fatigue that one would sustain after a day of battle and travel, nothing that would trigger suspicion if questioned later.

His shoulders relax slightly, head tilting back to glance at the stars, and I know I have my window. He's partially asleep, enough that he won't immediately notice light sound or movement from my direction.

My feet hurry to the prisoners, the women snapping awake to stare at me with wide eyes.

"I'm not going to hurt you," I breathe. They strain to hear the words. "I'm going to free you." I receive skeptical glances, but neither of them makes a sound and I take that as my cue to get started.

The bonds are simple zip-ties, designed for speed rather than top security. My knife parts the plastic easily. The young man's eyes snap open as I touch his wrist, but I press a finger to my lips. The relief I experience when understanding flickers across his features is unmatched.

Once they're free, I gesture toward the treeline, away from

Nash's position. They move just as quiet as me, their bare feet silent on the forest floor.

But as they reach the edge of the firelight, the woman who was crying before stops. She turns back, and even in the darkness I see more tears streaming down her face, catching in the dark hair matted to her cheek. She mouths two words: "Thank you."

My knees almost buckle. This is why I'm here...not for the Syndicate's mission or Arayik's approval or even my own survival. For this moment; this small act of defiance that might mean the difference between life and death for three people who dared to dream of freedom.

They vanish into the forest, and I pray to every star they make it far before the camp notices. The stars are not on my side tonight, because as I trudge toward my bedroll, I freeze.

Elias.

He stands at the center of camp, his silhouette unmistakable even without the dying firelight to illuminate his features. My heart flips as our eyes meet across the space between us.

Time stops.

He saw everything. I'm caught, exposed, and more than finished.

My hand drifts toward my knife, though I know it's useless. Elias is faster, stronger, better trained. If he raises the alarm, I'll be dead before I can take three steps. But maybe—maybe I can take him with me. Buy the escapees enough time to get clear before the others wake.

But my squad leader doesn't move. Doesn't shout. Doesn't reach for his weapon.

He just stares at me, and in that gaze something flashes that makes my world tilt on its axis: conflict. Pain. A battle playing out behind his eyes that mirrors my own internal war as his fists clench repeatedly.

Seconds stretch into eternity, my breathing impossibly loud. Nash continues his patrol, oblivious to the drama unfolding thirty feet away. The fire crackles and pops, casting drowsy shadows that mock the stillness between Elias and me.

Then, slowly, deliberately, Elias turns his head away.

He peers into the forest where the prisoners vanished, then back at the empty trees where they should be sitting. His jaw works, as if he's having a conversation with himself. His struggle is palpable.

When he finally regards me again, there's something different in his expression. A kind of resigned understanding which forms an ache in my chest.

He knows what I've done. And he's choosing to let it happen.

Elias steps away, retreating until he's ducked into his tent once more. His presence lingers under my skin, a reminder that my secret is no longer mine alone.

I force my legs to carry me back to my bedroll, each step like walking through a lake of mud. My hands tremble as I grip rough fabric, dragging the blanket up to my chin with mechanical movements—disconnected the same way my mind is.

Elias witnessed me committing treason; watched me free prisoners that the Syndicate considers valuable assets. By all rights, he should have put a bullet in my head the moment I cut those ties.

Why didn't he?

The question gnaws at me as I stare sightlessly at the stars that lost their beauty. What does his silence mean? Sympathy? Some kind of test I don't understand? Or is he simply waiting for a better moment to expose me?

Tomorrow, when Arayik discovers the missing prisoners, I must be prepared for Elias to step forward with the truth. To describe exactly what he saw, who was responsible, and how the escape was accomplished.

The thought sours my stomach. Suddenly, the confidence I'd felt with my choice dwindles to mere threads.

But as I close my eyes and try to find sleep, I see the woman's face again. The gratitude in her eyes. That moment of hope blooming through her previously imminent despair.

It was worth it.

Whatever comes next, whatever price I have to pay, it was worth it.

I want to be scared...to fear the consequences of my actions.

Instead, I've learned change isn't something you plan for. It happens in the moments when you accept that speaking up costs more than remaining silent, but do it anyway. When you know that standing while those around you kneel is dangerous, yet still find the courage to rise and face your oppressors.

That is how change begins.

If Elias chooses to expose me tomorrow, and my time here ends in execution or worse, at least I'll know I didn't just watch.

CHAPTER TWENTY-TWO
CASSIA

Left. Right. Left. Right.

I count each step like a heartbeat, the only thing keeping me tethered to reality. Three hundred forty-seven. Three hundred forty-eight. Three hundred forty-nine.

The forest floor crunches beneath my boots, twigs snapping relentlessly. Every sound is magnified, threatening to share my secret.

Four hundred twelve. Four hundred thirteen.

I don't dare look up. Not at Elias, who walks several paces ahead, his shoulders rigid beneath his uniform. Not at Arayik, whose steps land with such force I swear the earth trembles. Not at Kellen, whose gaze I can sense on the back of my neck.

Arayik's voice slithers down my spine. "Pick up the pace. We're not on a fucking nature walk."

The group responds with a collective increase in speed, feet thudding in a rhythm that almost matches my counting. Almost, but not quite. The discord makes my teeth ache.

Five hundred twenty-six. Five hundred twenty-seven.

A branch snaps to my right, my hand flying to the weapon on my hip before I register the movement. It's just a squirrel, darting away through the underbrush. But the damage is done.

Arayik's head turns, his dark eyes finding mine through the narrow slit in his mask. I hold his gaze, forcing my shoulders to relax and my hand to lower.

Don't show weakness. Don't show fear.

"Jumpy, Ashford?" His voice is low, dangerous.

I shrug, the motion casual. "Just alert."

He glowers a moment longer before turning away. Saved for another few minutes.

Seven hundred ninety-one. Seven hundred ninety-two.

Silence stretches between the group, dense as the humid air. No one speaks. I try to focus on the mission, on the fact that we're returning with information about the rebel camp's location. We didn't capture any of the women—the rebels had moved most of them before we arrived—but we know where they're headed next. It should be considered a partial success.

But all I can think about are those three prisoners I freed. Where are they now? Did they make it to safety? Did I give them enough of a head start?

And what will happen to me when we reach the training center?

This morning was strange—to my standards, at least. Corin discovered the missing prisoners while relieving Nash of patrol duty, waking the entire camp and inciting shouts of questions and accusations.

The Commander was one second away from executing Nash for his incompetence but decided to punish him once we were back. The worst part? I would have let him. Witnessing Arayik murder someone I manipulated to release the prisoners would have been traumatizing, and still I'd have let him.

When Elias claimed he knew nothing, they'd concluded the prisoners had something sharp on their person and were able to cut themselves free. Arayik determined they weren't worth the chase as we were not *properly equipped* for such a journey, thank the stars.

One thousand forty-two. One thousand forty-three.

The perimeter rises through the trees, a stark gray line cutting through the natural world. Beyond it lies Dascenia—what they call civilization.

My steps falter for just a moment. Once we cross that threshold, I'll be back under the full weight of their surveillance.

Breathe.

Elias glances back, his eyes meeting mine for the first time since last night. There's something in his gaze I can't decipher. Not anger, surprisingly.

One thousand three hundred seventeen. One thousand three hundred eighteen.

We approach the gate, the massive structure of reinforced steel embedded in the wall. Enforcers stand at attention, their masks identical to ours, shifting when they notice the Commander.

Arayik strides forward, his voice clipped as he provides the necessary codes and identification. The Enforcers verify, stepping aside as the gate slides open with a mechanical groan, scraping against my ears same as last time.

The convoys wait for us just outside, three armored vehicles with the Syndicate's emblem emblazoned on their sides. We load in silently, and I settle in the corner, my leg bouncing the moment I sit.

I switch from counting steps to counting the rhythmic taps of my foot against the vehicle's floor. The change in pattern helps keep my mind focused, prevents it from spiraling into the endless loop of what-ifs and worst-case scenarios that threaten to overwhelm me.

The other recruits talk among themselves, their voices

mixing into a low hum of conversation. They discuss the mission, the combat, the prisoners who escaped. Nash looks miserable, head bowed, knowing he'll face punishment for failing in his duty. The others offer half-hearted reassurances, but everyone knows failure has consequences for the Enforcers on Arayik's team.

If only they knew who was really responsible for his failure.

I'm so lost in anxious thoughts that I miss the entire trip through the wall, only raising my eyes when streaks of light greet them. At least my turmoil is good for something.

Hours pass. The sun reaches its peak descending toward the horizon, and the landscape outside grows more familiar as we approach the training center. Soon, too soon, we'll return to that sterile environment of concrete and steel, where I'm likely to find my end.

Twelve thousand three hundred four. Twelve thousand three hundred five.

My family is probably sharing dinner right now in our small house. My mother setting out plates while my father tells them about his day at the library. My brother helping with the meal, unaware his identity has been borrowed for treason and murder.

Do they think about me? Do they wonder if I'm safe, if I'm succeeding in whatever mission I've set for myself? Or do they try not to think about me at all, knowing that worry will only make the waiting harder?

I'm ashamed I've done the latter. It hurts to think of them— something I cannot allow myself to acknowledge in this environment. I do miss them, though. More than they'll ever understand.

I wonder if they'll be informed of my death.

Twelve thousand six hundred ninety-one. Twelve thousand six hundred ninety-two.

The Enforcer base appears on the horizon, a lump forming at the center of my throat. My prison for the past weeks. Perhaps soon to be my grave.

No, I can't think like that. It will just make what's coming worse.

The vehicles slow as we approach a checkpoint, confirming identification to the stationed Enforcers. We pull into the central courtyard, the engines silencing with a finality that makes my heart skip.

This is it. Whatever happens next, it was still worth it.

Thirteen thousand seventeen. Thirteen thousand eighteen.

The recruits disembark in silence, falling into formation automatically. Arayik stands before us, his posture tense and angry.

"Debrief in thirty minutes," he announces, his voice spraying across the courtyard. "Dismissed."

CHAPTER TWENTY-THREE
CASSIA

Difficult couldn't come close to describing how I feel as I barely make it through my door before my legs give out. The mission weight drags at my limbs, yanking me to the floor and I lean against the wall to keep from dropping. Trembles wrack my body as I reach for my mask, desperate to welcome actual air against my skin after days of suffocation.

But I stop.

Not yet. Not until I'm certain.

Pushing myself upright, I scan my small room with frantic eyes. Nothing appears disturbed—no one has been here. At least, no one who wanted me to know.

The thought raises hairs along my arm.

I cross to the small sink in the corner and splash cold water on my mask, letting it seep through the narrow eye slit. It's not enough, but it's something. My reflection stares back at me from the dingy mirror. I was the perfect disguise...until now.

Elias saw me.

Elias *saw* me.

The memory replays in my mind with merciless clarity. Relief washed through me as the escapees disappeared into the darkness. Then the shadows shifted, revealing Elias standing there, observing me with those piercing hazel-green eyes. He didn't say a word. Didn't raise the alarm. Just...watched. And let me go.

Why?

How many times can I ask myself that question before it makes sense? I chuckle. It will never make sense.

I whirl from the mirror. Every inch of my skin prickles and there's a frantic pleading in my stomach, begging me to run. I don't know what to do.

Maybe he's waiting to gather more evidence, or he's already reported me and they're just building their case. Perhaps he's toying with me, enjoying my fear before he strikes.

Or maybe he understands, a strange voice whispers. Mine, but not.

No. He couldn't understand, and I cannot afford such hope. I have no allies here.

The bed creaks as I sit and find my notebook of lost things hidden beneath the mattress. Not my ideal choice, but where else could I put it? I flip the pages open, wanting—no, *needing* —to write anything to calm my head. I swear to the stars it's going to explode if I don't lower my blood pressure soon.

Footsteps pound in the corridor, freezing me mid-thought. Heavy, purposeful strides. Not the casual walk of recruits returning to their quarters. These footsteps belong to someone with authority, who's thoroughly angry.

No, no, no!

The steps halt outside my door.

I can't breathe.

For one stifling moment, there's silence.

Then the door slams open with such force it crashes against the wall, a long crack appearing on its surface. I jerk back instinctively as Arayik storms in, a hurricane in human form.

His entire body radiates death—mine—as his chest heaves with thunderous breaths.

He rams the door shut behind him, the lock engaging with a click that sounds a lot like I'll never be leaving this room again.

"Commander," I begin, forcing my voice steady, but he cuts me off with a sharp gesture.

"No." The single word drips with venom.

His foreboding body advances toward me, and I retreat until my back hits the furthest wall. There's nowhere left to go. My mind races through scenarios—I could duck under his arm, aim for his knee, maybe reach the door—but I know it's futile. He outmatches me in every way.

"I've watched you," he growls, his voice dangerously low. "From the first day, something was wrong."

My mouth goes dry. "I don't know what you're—"

"Do. Not. Speak!" he roars, closing the distance between us in two swift strides.

Before I can react, his hand shoots out, fingers curling around the edge of my mask. With one violent motion, he rips it away from my face, the straps snapping with a sharp crack.

Cold air caresses my newly exposed skin. I gasp, the sudden vulnerability more shocking than the physical pain.

Arayik's dark eyes widen, then narrow. "I knew it." He stares at my face with undisguised hatred. "I fucking knew it."

His hand moves with lightning speed, closing around my throat; he pulls me forward only to shove me back against the wall with such brutal force, I know I'll have a concussion. My boots scrape against the floor as he lifts me, effectively severing my air. Panic floods my system, my hands flying up to claw at his forearm.

"You think you can fool us?" he snarls, his face inches from mine. "Pretend to *be* one of us?" His grip tightens, and black spots dance at the edges of my vision. "You'll die for this."

I struggle against his hold, pushing at his arm with all my strength, but it's like trying to move a mountain. His muscles stiffen—he's using his power, making himself impossibly heavy, regardless that I couldn't fight back anyway. My arms tremble from the strain of even trying to resist.

The room darkens and narrows to a tunnel, Arayik's rage-twisted face the only thing I can see.

This is how I die, I think distantly. Not fighting for freedom, not changing the world. Just...erased. Another woman disappeared at the hands of the Syndicate's machinery.

The thought ignites something in me—a desperate, burning refusal.

Then the door bursts open behind him.

"Arayik, stop!" Elias' voice cuts through the howling in my ears. "Let him" —he pauses when he notices my face before continuing— "her go!"

The Commander doesn't turn, nor does he acknowledge the interruption. His focus is absolute, his hatred for me outweighing every other thing in his life at this moment.

"Kellen, help me!" Elias calls, and more footsteps enter the room.

The third leader appears at Arayik's side, grabbing his shoulder and gritting his teeth as he tries to pull him away. "Arayik, that's enough!"

But the man holding me won't budge. They know that. His fingers dig deeper into my throat, something puncturing the side.

I can't die...I've barely lived.

With the last of my consciousness, I focus inward, reaching for my empathy. It's harder than it's ever been—my mind clouding, control slipping—but I grasp it, heaving it to the surface with desperate strength.

I shove it outward, not in a gentle wave but in a violent surge. Fear. Panic. Pain. All of it pouring from me into him, all raw. Not just my current terror, but everything—the lifetime of hiding, of knowing I was hunted simply for existing. The horror of watching other women captured, knowing what awaited them. The helplessness. The rage.

I feel the moment it slams into him, his grip faltering slightly.

If there was ever an opportunity to seize, it's this one. I push more into him, burying it deeper. Memories of terror and grief; the crushing weight of silence in pure darkness beneath the ground. My lungs burn for air. My heart pounds against my ribs like it's trying to escape. I don't blame it.

Arayik stumbles, his brow furrowing. His hand trembles against my throat, the pressure easing just enough for me to drag in a shallow breath.

"What are you—" he manages, but I don't allow him to finish.

I let everything go. Every emotion I've ever suppressed, each piece of fear I've swallowed, all the rage I've hidden. I force it into him with all the strength I have left.

The potency of it would demolish anyone else, but Arayik remains standing.

He snarls in my face, crushing his forehead to mine. "Stop it!"

I don't. Can't. Instead, I surpass my limits and push harder until something inside him cracks—not physically, but a hairline fracture in his iron control.

His grip releases.

I crash to the floor, my legs unable to support me. My chest rattles as I cough and gasp for sweet, sweet air, each breath burning my raw throat. The room spins, sounds distorted and distant. I'm vaguely aware of movement—Elias and Kellen grabbing Arayik, dragging him back, and pinning his arms as he fights against them with feral strength.

"She's a female, a fucking traitor!" Arayik yells, his voice hoarse with rage. "Her insubordinate attitude should not be bred. The only option is death!"

"Shut up," Kellen snaps, his voice sharp.

I roll to my back, shaking uncontrollably. My hands grip the tender flesh along my throat as I wheeze, sucking air through an invisible straw. Each breath is a victory.

And there is no hiding anymore—my mask is off.

Once my lungs have calmed a bit, I force both eyes open, my vision swimming into focus. Elias and Kellen have Arayik pinned against the far wall, his struggles growing weaker as the emotional assault I unleashed continues to disorient him—I never removed the emotions, so they'll remain until he can process them on his own. His dark eyes find mine across the room, burning through my soul.

"There is only one way to deal with this, and you both know it." He's calmer now.

"That's not your decision alone to make, Ry," Elias says, his voice steady despite the strain evident in his posture.

Something passes between the three men—a current of understanding built on years of shared history. I watch it unfold, my mind still foggy, but sharp enough to recognize the power dynamics shifting before my eyes.

"You both agree to let her live? Are you fucking kidding me?"

Neither man holding him answers right away, but Kellen finally speaks, "Nobody is saying that. But we need to think this through—you cannot just kill a female, Ry." All three of them glance at me. Awkward. "We will talk about this later."

With a loud grunt, he shoves the two men away and stands to his full height. But instead of attacking me again, he turns and strides toward the door, his movements stiff.

Without a look back, he's gone, the door slamming behind him.

The silence that follows is deafening. I force myself to sit, my back against the wall for support. My legs feel like water, my hands still trembling. I'm exposed—vulnerable in a way I haven't been since I left home. My face bare, secret revealed.

Elias and Kellen shift to regard me, expressions unreadable behind their masks. For a long moment, no one speaks.

"How long have you known?" I ask, my voice a ragged whisper.

Elias shifts, arms crossing before he answers. "I suspected from day one that you had...other motivations for being here." He pauses, then adds, "I did not realize you weren't Lachlan Ashford, though."

I nod slowly, wincing at the movement. "And you?" I ask, looking at Kellen.

"Elias told me his suspicions." A slight head tilt. "I didn't believe him until now."

"What now?"

The men watch me for a moment, their eyes scrutinizing every inch of my exposed face. It's wildly uncomfortable, but I remain still, allowing them to stare

"We'll come back later to talk," Kellen says, his tone making clear the discussion is done for now.

They leave me to process the aftermath of my almost-death, a sharp hiss at the door indicating it would be futile for me to try to escape this room.

What the fuck am I going to do?

CHAPTER TWENTY-FOUR

ARAYIK

I never hesitate.

It's a discipline I've cultivated since childhood—the ability to act without second-guessing, to execute without doubt. Hesitation means weakness, and weakness is the worst quality a man can have. This is what I've built my life on. What's earned me my rank, and what keeps the order I've sworn to maintain.

But right now, I'm hesitating.

My fingers trace the security panel outside Ashford's quarters, the skin on my knuckles tight from how hard I've been clenching my fists. The corridor is empty, overhead lights dimmed for the night cycle. No witnesses to what I need to do.

Just me and the truth I've been circling for weeks. I've been testing him, pushing him, never obtaining a solid answer.

Rage unlike I've ever known boils under my skin, and I swipe a finger over the panel before kicking Ashford's door in. There's a loud crack, something I ignore in favor of the wide-eyed recruit staring back at me.

Stepping inside, I close the door to hide any would be onlookers.

"Commander," Ashford sputters in that higher-pitched whine I've come to hate.

"No." I do not want to hear another word from this monstrosity.

I waste not one more second, advancing on the dead-recruit-walking, smirking at the retreating form.

If I hadn't overheard Elias confiding in Kellen about what Ashford had done, I likely wouldn't be here. Would have sat in my hatred for this thing in our ranks, knowing I had no proof to do anything substantial. But the only proof I need is right in front of me.

"I've watched you," I growl in a voice that would have others pissing themselves. "From the first day, something was wrong."

Ashford blanches. "I don't know what you're—"

"Do. Not. Speak!" Why does this sad excuse of a human believe talking to me is acceptable?

I move faster than Ashford can react, my hand shooting out to grab the edge of the mask. With one swift motion, I rip it away, both securing straps snapping under the force.

Soft features. Wide eyes. Delicate jawline. A woman's face.

"I knew it," I growl, satisfaction surging through me like a current. Vindication tastes metallic on my tongue.

She opens her mouth—to plead, to explain, to lie again—but I don't give her the chance. My hand closes around her throat, fingers digging into the soft flesh beneath her jaw. I slam her back against the wall, lifting until her feet barely touch the ground.

"You think you can infiltrate us?" I hiss, leaning in close enough to notice the flecks of gold in her violet eyes. "Pretend to be one of us? You'll die for this."

Her hands claw at my wrist, nails digging into my skin.

She's durable for her size, but it's nothing compared to my grip. I increase the pressure, watching as panic blooms across her face.

A chuckle leaves my throat as she kicks, her boot connecting with my shin. It barely registers. I'm an Anchor—I can make myself immovable, untouchable. I shift my density, rooting myself to the spot, making my arm as heavy as stone. Her struggles grow more desperate, face flushing red.

A beep filters through the room, and my eyes roll. There's only two others in the building who could get into this room right now. I don't want to fucking deal with them—I want this done.

"Arayik, stop!" My second's voice registers in my ears, but I pay him no attention as he continues. "Let him—her go!" Ah, so he *didn't* know this thing in our ranks was a woman. "Kellen, help me!"

They each take a shoulder, yanking with everything their bodies have to give. But that will not move me; not even close. There's more yelling, more pulling, more annoyance.

Then something changes.

A sensation creeps into my mind—something foreign and invasive. At first, it's just a whisper, a faint blip of emotion that isn't mine. Then it grows, spreading through my thoughts like it's determined to overtake my being.

Fear. Not my own—hers. But I'm feeling it as if it originated in me.

"What are you—" I don't finish the words as wave after wave of terror assault my being.

I try to push it away, to focus on my rage, my duty, but more floods in. Panic. Desperation. Helplessness. A memory surfaces of a small dark space, walls pressing in, the eerie sound of heavy boots overhead. A child's terror of being discovered.

My mind recoils, but there's nowhere to retreat. More images flash through my consciousness—nightmares of a girl with long hair, hiding behind a false wall as Enforcers search her family's home. The same girl, older now, watching through a crack in the curtains as a woman is dragged screaming from a neighboring house.

"Get out of my head!" I try to scream, but my lips make no sound. My fingers attempt to tighten and halt this invasion at its source, but they don't obey me either.

She doesn't stop. Instead, everything intensifies. Loneliness envelops me—bone-deep and endless. The crushing weight of a life lived in shadows. Then anger—white-hot and righteous, burning brighter than mine. The fury of watching injustice and being powerless to stop it.

Flashes of her life strike me continuously. My hand trembles against her throat. I try to hold on to my rage, to my certainty, but it slips through my fingers like water. Something inside me fractures—a crack in the foundation of everything I've built myself on.

"Stop it!" I snarl, clenching my eyes as if it will force her out of my head.

She pushes harder, the full force of her desperation, her determination, burning through me, searing away my resolve.

My hand falls away from her throat.

The lying bitch collapses to the floor, gasping for air, one hand clutching at her neck. I stumble backward, my mind reeling from the assault. My thoughts are scattered, contaminated with her emotions, her memories. I can't separate them from my own.

I don't realize I'm being held against a wall by my own brothers until I'm screaming. "She's a female, a fucking traitor! Her insubordinate attitude should not be bred. The only option is death!"

Neither of my men moves to kill her. Why don't they understand this?

Of course they don't—they've always been too soft-hearted, even Kellen, the emotionless bastard he is. It's the exact reason I came here alone, so they wouldn't be forced to deal with the problem.

"Let's get him out," Kellen orders, his voice sharp with anger directed at me—something I'm more than familiar with.

I fight against them, but my focus is shattered. I can still feel her...her pain, fear, defiance. It clings to me like a second skin, impossible to shed.

"She's infiltrated us. She's been working against us from the beginning," I spit, jerking against their grip as they drag me toward the door.

"Shut up," Kellen growls, tightening his hold on my arm.

I laugh, the sound harsh and bitter even to my own ears. "She needs to die before the Syndicate discovers a *female* found a way into our ranks. Our reputations would be demolished."

"That's not your decision alone to make." Elias' voice surprises me, steady and calm despite his stiff posture. He doesn't defy me like this. Ever.

Fuck them. I'll come back later when they're not drooling over the cunt.

My face hardens, all emotion draining away until only cold determination remains. With a surge of strength, I break free from their hold, shoving them back. But instead of attacking the woman again, I turn and stride for the door.

At the threshold, I almost pause, ready to warn her that I'll be back.

She's not worth it.

Then I'm gone, the door slamming behind me.

She's still inside me. Her pain burns like acid under my

skin, and I will do everything to rid myself of the memory. I do not want to humanize females or view them as anything other than my duty.

Collect and deliver. Nothing more.

CHAPTER TWENTY-FIVE

KELLEN

My chair squeaks as I lean back and study the two men across from me. Arayik sits defensively, hands clenched into fists under each arm across his chest. Every line of his body screams violence he's struggling to contain as emotions flit across his face a mile a minute. Elias slouches forward, elbows on his thighs, staring at the floor like it holds answers to the questions none of us have asked.

The silence stretches between us as we remain in our curated triangle of chairs. No one wants to be the first to speak, to acknowledge what we all witnessed upstairs. But someone has to break this tension, and by all the stars of course it has to be me.

"So." My sudden voice jolts the other two. "We have a problem."

Arayik's head snaps up, his black eyes blazing. "Problem." His answering laugh is sinister. "We have a fucking infiltrator. This thing has been playing us for fools."

"She's just a woman," Elias says without looking up.

"No, she's a threat." Arayik's voice drops to a growl. "She's been gathering intelligence, sabotaging our fucking missions. She freed those rebels, Eli, you said it yourself."

Elias finally raises his head, meeting Arayik's glare. "I saw someone who couldn't stand by and watch innocent people suffer."

"Innocent?" Arayik surges to his feet, the chair scraping against concrete. My jaw tightens. "They're *criminals*. They've stolen females from all three facilities, undermined the Syndicate's authority—"

"Maybe they have good reason to."

The words are an obvious challenge—this is a disagreement they've fought over for years. Arayik stills, his expression shifting from anger to something colder and more dangerous.

"What did you just say?"

I clear my throat, drawing both their attention. "Sit down, Arayik." In here we're not Commander and third; there are no titles. We're simply three men who grew up alongside each other and do our best to complete the work we're assigned.

He doesn't move. "Did you hear what he just—"

"I heard him." My voice remains level, controlled. "And I heard you. Now sit down so we can figure this out like adults instead of children throwing tantrums."

Arayik's jaw works, muscles twitching under the flushed skin. For a moment I think he might refuse. Storm out and report us both to the Syndicate. But my sanity sighs, relieved, when he drops back into his chair with enough force to scratch the floor.

"Thank you." I fold my hands in my lap, considering my words carefully. "Now, let's start with what we know for certain. The recruit we've been calling Lachlan Ashford is not Lachlan Ashford. She's been impersonating that man in pursuit of joining our team."

"For what purpose?" Arayik demands.

"That's what we need to find out." My eyes flick between

them. "But first, we need to decide what we're going to do with her."

"Execute her." Arayik's response is immediate, though not unexpected considering the lingering emotions from the girl. "She's a spy, and a traitor to the Syndicate. The penalty is death."

"We can't kill her," Elias intones, voice quiet but firm.

"Why not?" Arayik turns on him. "Give me one good reason why we shouldn't drag her to the courtyard and put a bullet in her head right now."

Elias opens his mouth, then closes it. His hands clench and unclench several times. "We just...we can't."

"That's not a reason, that's sentiment." Arayik's voice drips with disgust. "Since when do we let emotions cloud our judgment?"

"Since we discovered that the things we know about women might be a lie," I answer.

Both men stare at me. The air in the room thickens further.

"What are you talking about?"

I lean forward, choosing my words with care. "She has power, Arayik. Or did you forget she's an Empath? A strong one, too. Stronger than most men I've seen."

"That's impossible."

"And yet it isn't." I meet his gaze steadily. "Did we not verify her power the day she arrived? We all felt what she did to you upstairs." He winces. "That wasn't some fluke or trick."

Arayik's face darkens. "Not one scanner has flagged her."

"She doesn't have a chip..." I let that sink in for a moment. "What if she's never been in the system at all?"

"How is that possible?" Elias asks.

"I don't know. That's why we need to talk to her, find out her story." I look at each of them in turn. "But I do know that killing her before we understand what she represents would be a mistake."

Arayik shakes his head. "You're both losing your minds. She's a woman. Women don't have power. It's basic biology."

"According to who?" The question slips out before I can stop it.

"According to science. According to everything we've known since the beginning of humankind." Arayik's voice rises with each word. "Are you seriously questioning the fundamental structure of our society?"

I don't answer right away. The truth is, I've been questioning a lot of things lately. The efficiency of our methods, or the necessity of some of our actions. And not only me... Elias' struggle has been far greater. He is constantly at war with himself, wanting things to change but unable to fathom not following orders. I was shocked when he informed me of what he saw, and allowed, Ashford to do with those prisoners.

Regardless, it's clear Arayik will not admit the times she has used power on him. It won't matter to him that there's no other explanation.

"I'm questioning whether we have all the facts."

Arayik stands again, pacing to the far wall. "This is insane. Who fucking cares how she managed to steal a power? The answer to all this remains the same: it's best for everyone if she's executed."

"Arayik, this immediate jump to kill her is foolish thinking." My arms cross. "I understand you're upset with her ability to deceive you, but as of right now, there is no suitable reason to do so."

Arayik stares at the wall, his expression cycling through disbelief, anger, and something sour. "I can't believe what I'm hearing. You're willing to throw away everything—our careers, our lives, our families—for some girl who's been lying to us from day one?"

"We're not throwing anything away, Ry," I remind him. This is reaching a point where he will be impossible to reason with until he calms down. "We're trying to understand—"

"No." Arayik cuts me off. "You're choosing her over us, and everything we've built together. The Syndicate will not hesitate to kill *us* if we do not kill her first."

The pain in his voice surprises me. Beneath the anger and the inflexible adherence to protocol, there's genuine hurt. We've been a team since childhood, the three of us against everyone. And now he feels like we're abandoning him.

"That's not what this is," Elias says, rising. "Arayik, we've been friends for more than twenty years. That doesn't change because we disagree about some things."

"Doesn't it?" Arayik's laugh is bitter. "You're talking about betraying everything we swore to our fathers to uphold. How is that not a betrayal of our friendship?"

I stand as well—damn this headache. "Because friendship means being honest with each other even when it's hard."

"You want honesty? Fine. I think you're both losing your fucking minds. I don't give a shit if you want to use her cunt before she dies, but if we don't deal with this quickly and decisively, *we* will end up dead."

The room falls silent again. I'm disappointed he would suggest raping the girl is why I insist we keep her alive; he knows me better than that. Elias, too.

But he's not wrong about the danger. If the Syndicate discovers what we know, what we're even considering, the consequences would be swift and final.

"What do you suggest?" I ask. I know what he's going to suggest, believing he has the upper hand in the conversation now, yet I want to hear it anyway.

"Send her to a facility if you don't want me to kill her." Arayik's voice is controlled again. "Riverton, since it's the closest. We will report that we discovered her true identity and are just following protocol, then they can deal with her."

"And if they find out she has power?" Elias asks.

Arayik shrugs. "Not our problem anymore."

"It would become our problem very quickly," I point out. "They'd want to know how we missed it, why we didn't say anything considering it's part of our training. They'd investigate our entire operation."

"Then what?" Arayik's hands wave through the air. "What's your brilliant solution, Kel? Keep her here and pretend nothing happened? Hope she doesn't kill us all in our sleep?"

I consider this. The logical part of my mind agrees with my hotheaded friend—the safest course for us is to eliminate her. But there's something I can't quite name that rebels against the logic.

Maybe it's the way she fought during training, never giving up despite being severely outmatched. Maybe it's the intelligence I saw in her eyes, the quick thinking that kept her alive and undetected for weeks. Or maybe it's something simpler— that I need to know more about her story before deciding whether her life should be ended or not.

"We talk to her." Yes, this is the right step. "We find out who she is, why she's here, what she wants. Then we make an informed decision."

"And if she refuses to talk?"

"Then we'll cross that bridge when we come to it."

Arayik shakes his head. "This is a mistake. A huge, potentially fatal mistake."

"Maybe," I acknowledge. "But it's the right thing to do."

Shit, I shouldn't have said that. He's still too worked up.

"Since when do *we* decide what the right thing is? We're Enforcers. We follow orders to maintain order—we don't question whether they're right or not, we just do it."

"Maybe it's time we started to," Elias mutters under his breath.

Arayik's expression cycles through a dozen emotions. Finally, he settles on empty calm—the Commander has taken control.

"Fine," he says. "Talk to her. Waste your time trying to understand the mind of a traitor. But when this blows up in our faces—and it will—don't expect me to go down with you."

He makes for the door, pausing with a hand on the handle. "And don't expect me to keep quiet about this forever. I have my loyalties and oaths. If I decide you've become a threat to the Syndicate...."

He doesn't finish the sentence. He doesn't need to.

The door closes behind him with a soft click, leaving Elias and me alone in the suffocating quiet of the underground room.

"Well," Elias starts after a moment. "That went better than expected."

I almost smile at that. "Did it?"

"He didn't try to kill us. I'm counting that as a win."

I sit once more, suddenly exhausted. The weight of what we're contemplating settles on my shoulders—just something else too heavy to carry.

"What do you think she'll tell us?"

Elias considers it for a long moment, staring at his wringing hands. "I think she'll tell us things we don't want to hear. Maybe things that will create questions."

"And you're okay with that?"

"No," he says honestly. "But I think it's necessary."

I nod once. He's right, of course. Whatever comfort we might find in ignorance, it's a luxury I've never cared for.

"Well, we should talk to her soon. Before Arayik changes his mind and decides to take matters into his own hands."

"You think he would?"

Elias meets my gaze. "Don't you?"

I consider this. Arayik has always been the most stubborn of the three of us, and the most devoted to protocol and hierarchy. His father's influence and sister's death run deep, shaping him into the perfect soldier. But beneath that conditioning, he's still the boy I grew up with. The one who shared his lunch when I forgot mine; the same guy who stood against bullies even when he was outnumbered.

He's scared, I know this. But that's no excuse to not face whatever this woman has to say.

CHAPTER TWENTY-SIX
CASSIA

T hirty-seven cracks mar the ceiling of my room—I've counted them seventeen times now.

I trace the bruises along my neck, memorizing each tender spot where Arayik's fingers dug into my flesh. The marks have darkened overnight, a collar of purple and blue that brands me as a traitor. My throat burns when I swallow, a constant reminder of how close I came to death.

How close I still am.

Anything to keep my mind occupied.

Footsteps echo in the hallway beyond my door—heavy boots thudding in a measured cadence I've learned by heart. Two Enforcers pass every hour, their timing so precise I could set a clock by it. If I didn't know any better, I'd think they were protecting me. But from what? They're the same men I need protection from.

Life moves on around me as if nothing has changed, and the entire foundation of the world hasn't shifted.

But it has. They know what I am now, even if they don't know what to do about it.

Laughter drifts from somewhere outside, the sound depressing and alien after the post-almost-death silence. The training yard must be active today. I wonder if they've replaced me yet...if some other recruit is struggling through Arayik's brutal conditioning while I rot in this concrete box.

They probably miss having someone to beat up.

Scrunching my eyes closed, I press a thin pillow on my face and try to remember what my mother's voice sounds like. It's been so long since I left home, but already the memory feels distant, like trying to recall a dream after waking. Does she know what happened to me yet? Does she lie awake at night wondering if I'm alive or dead?

Does she regret not stopping me?

The lock mechanism in my door clicks, and I don't bother sitting up. It's probably just Arayik coming to try again.

"Hungry?"

Elias' voice chases away my brooding, and I drop the pillow to focus on him. He stands in the doorway holding a tray awkwardly, his mask absent for once. Without it, he's younger somehow. More human. The sharp angles of his face are softened by the dim light filtering behind him.

"Depends if you'll also grace me with a trip to the bathroom," I drawl, pushing to sit against the wall. My voice comes out very rough and scratchy, still raw from Arayik's grip.

He steps in to shut the door, eyes widening considerably. Is he serious right now?

"You do know that women don't have dicks, right?" My head tilts toward the sink. "I can't just go wherever I please." I won't admit I did, in fact, pee in the sink rather than bang on the door and beg for an escort.

A girl can't hold her bladder forever, gross as it was to squat over the gritty thing. Thank the stars for soap.

The man blinks. "You're right, I'm sorry, I—" A long swallow before he speaks again. "I did not consider that. Of course you can use the bathroom."

"It's fine!" I exclaim when he reaches for the door. "I can wait."

That earns me a nod before he sets the tray on the small table beside my bed. Steam rises from what smells like actual food—not the dried-up shit that's only edible with heaps of water. "Thought you might be hungry."

I eye the plate suspiciously. "What's the catch?"

"No catch." He pulls the single chair away from the table and lowers himself, leaving space between us. "Just figured you could use a decent meal."

The smell overpowers me then—roasted meat, vegetables, something that might actually have flavor. My stomach clenches with the hunger I've been fighting to ignore. When was the last time I ate food that wasn't designed purely for nutritional efficiency? If I never saw a stick of jerky again, it would be too soon.

"You're being awfully kind for someone who's supposed to be my captor," I observe, but reach for the tray anyway. Pride won't fill my stomach.

"Am I your captor?" he asks. "Or are you mine?"

I pause with a forkful of food halfway to my mouth. "What's that supposed to mean?"

"Seems like you're the one with all the power here."

I laugh at that, but there's no humor in it. "I'm quite literally locked in a room, completely at your mercy. If that's power, I'd hate to see what powerlessness looks like."

"You made Arayik—the strongest Anchor I've ever known —release his grip on you." Elias leans forward, his speckled eyes intense. "I'd say that's power."

Ah, yes, the question I knew would be on all their minds: how does a woman have such abilities?

I bite into the meat, chewing slowly while my mind

considers his words. The food is good—better than good. It tastes like something my mother might have made.

"Is that why you didn't say anything after watching me free the prisoners?"

Both brows raise. "My point is that maybe we're not as different as we thought." Of course he won't answer.

"We're nothing alike." The words are harsh and sharp, aided by my unavoidable rasp. "You *chose* this life. You hunt women and drag them to facilities where they'll be raped and used like breeding stock. That will never be me."

"Hm." His voice is quiet, thoughtful.

He watches me eat, fingers drumming against his knee in an odd rhythm. When he finally speaks, his voice is careful and measured.

"Kellen and I would like to speak with you."

"And our dear Commander?"

"Arayik wants you dead, but he's outvoted for now."

"How democratic of you." I chew another bite, savoring the flavors. "What kind of talk are we having? The kind where you torture me to extract information, or the kind where you pretend to care about my motivations so I tell you what you want to know?"

"The kind where we try to understand what the hell we're supposed to do now."

Strange. He sounds almost torn, as if this is just as difficult for him as it is for me.

"You could always just kill me," I suggest. "Solve all your problems at once." *Shut up, Cas.*

His head tilts. "I'm starting to think killing you might create more problems than it solves."

I finish the last of the vegetables and push the tray away. My stomach feels uncomfortably full after days of minimal food, but the warmth spreading through me is worth the discomfort.

"When?" I ask.

"Now, if you're up for it."

I stand and stretch, working out the kinks from too many hours lying on an uncomfortable bed. My muscles protest, still sore from the mission and its aftermath. "Lead the way."

Elias rises and moves toward the door, then pauses. "We're not your enemies, you know."

I bark out a laugh, hurting my throat as I clutch my now cramping stomach and grab my mask. "Spare me. I don't need to be a Revealer to know that's bullshit." He doesn't answer; why would he? There's nothing he could say to counter it.

The corridor outside my room is empty, but my skin burns as if every eye in the world is tracking our movement, recording everything for posterity or evidence.

Elias leads me down a hall I haven't seen before, past doors lacking names or markings. I follow like the good soldier I am, breathing steady as we stop before a random door. His finger against a scanner unlocks it, and he pulls on the handle, gesturing for me to enter first.

The room beyond is small and windowless, dominated by a metal table and three chairs. Kellen is seated at the far end, his mask resting on the shiny surface.

The hair along my arms raises, taking with it the last of my confidence.

"Ashford," he says by way of greeting. "Sit." Do they know I'm an Ashford or are they just not sure what else to call me?

I choose the chair closest to the door—old habits die hard—and settle in. I have no weapons and am not in any shape to fight, so I'm certain my foot closer to the hallway would mean nothing if they attacked, but it's the little things.

"Is it just us?" I ask, clearing my throat, hands shaking as they remove the mask, willingly presenting my face for the first time since I left home.

Kellen confirms, then adds, "This is simply a conversation." I scoff and he almost smiles at that. "We're just three people trying to understand a very complicated situation."

I lean back in my chair, adopting the casual male posture I've perfected over weeks of pretending to be someone else. "Ask your questions, then."

Kellen and Elias exchange a look, some silent communication passing between them. Finally, the former speaks.

"What's your name?"

"Cassia." That much I can give them; they won't find it on any records.

"And who are you, Cassia?"

"You know who I am."

"We know your name. We know you're female. We know you've been impersonating Lachlan Ashford. But we don't know who you really are."

I consider the question, swallowing as it pillages in my mind like thoughts do when I'm determining how many moves I can beat my father in during chess.

Who am I? The daughter who disappointed her parents by leaving? The sister who stole her brother's identity? The woman who weaseled her way into this team of Enforcers?

"I'm someone who got tired of hiding," I answer after a few moments.

"From what?"

"From a world that pretends I don't exist, and a system that treats women like usable property."

Elias leans forward, hands clasping on the table. I meet his gaze. "So you decided to do something about it."

A shrug. "Someone had to."

"Had to what?" he presses.

I stare into his curious eyes and say nothing. Some truths are too dangerous to speak aloud, even here.

Kellen tries a different approach. "How long have you been planning this?"

"Planning what, joining your team? About five minutes before I walked out my front door."

"That's not an answer."

"It's the only answer you're getting." His mouth tightens as the other man chuckles under his breath.

The silence stretches between us as they try to read me. To understand the motivations that drove me to such extreme risk and deception.

"Who is Lachlan Ashford to you?" Elias questions, the words genuine. So they don't know...

"Someone I've met before." I wonder if Elias' power can detect half-truths? The answer isn't a lie, but it's the furthest thing from the actual truth I can say without lying. He smiles, eyes brightening.

Kellen isn't as amused, sighing deeply. "We could have just let Arayik kill you, Cassia. We do not need to be having this conversation."

"So why are you?" His stormy eyes darken; maybe he'll murder me by the time we're done.

"You see, I looked into Lachlan Ashford. It appears he is a messenger as you reported, but his supervisor confirmed his absence these last weeks." Shit. "Does he know you're here? Or did you do something to him to pilfer his identity?"

My answer is immediate, if not a little desperate. "No."

"No, what?"

"Neither are true." A dark cloud filters through my head as

I consider my options here. If I don't admit who he is to me, they'll find him at our parents' house. If I do tell them, then I'm confirming his complicity in hiding my existence. Either way, they will discover everything.

Kellen raises a brow—he's got me cornered and that's exactly what he wanted.

Unless... "I will not speak another word unless you agree to leave him and those he lives with alone. They will not be harassed, harmed, or killed for anything regarding me."

He snorts, tapping Elias' shoulder in the process. The latter simply assesses us.

"And you think you have any right to make demands of *us*, why?"

This fucker. "Because you haven't killed me or sent me off to a facility yet. You need information from me and you won't get another word unless you guarantee their safety."

The men regard one another before Elias nods. "Fine, you have our word."

"How do I know you're not lying? Is that not all men are good for?" I'm pushing my luck, but I can't help it. If it were me instead of Mira in that house, they would have killed my family and sent me to Riverton all the same without a second thought. They don't actually care. I startle when Elias' hand slides across the table, waiting palm up.

My nose scrunches at the gesture, understanding what he intends. "You think a hand shake is good enough?"

He laughs, head shaking as his hand rises. "No, I have the ability to share my power, but only if I touch you. I can show you that we're both being truthful."

My eyes stare at the offering as I ponder my options. A paper trail of contracts wouldn't be feasible, neither would an outside witness. The more I think about it, the more I realize this is the only viable option. Who would I even go to if they were lying? This way, at least I can be sure of their intentions.

My fingers rise from their place on my left arm, shifting to hover above Elias and hesitating a breath before lowering. Warm skin greets mine, my eyes snapping up when Elias' fingers close around my palm. He watches me in a way that reminds me of coaxing a scared animal—as if he knows how close I am to running away.

Then I feel it.

A simmering energy, gentle and pleasant, glides through me, and my fingers involuntarily curl to match Elias' grip. The pulse in my neck races as his power spreads, and I jolt when my mind begins to perceive the intentions of everyone in this room. I'm not certain how I can tell, but it's clear these two are being truthful with their words.

My hand pulls back the moment I confirm, not wanting anymore physical contact. It fucks with my head.

"Okay," I mutter, swallowing around my still racing heart. "I'll talk."

"Who is Lachlan Ashford to you?" Kellen repeats again.

"He's my brother." Elias sits back as his eyes widen while the other man hums to himself.

I hope I didn't just kill my entire family.

Breathe.

Elias questions me next. "Your empathy, how long have you had it?"

"Since I was a child. Turns out when you're locked away from the world, you have a lot of time to practice."

"Locked away?"

I register my mistake and almost choke on a drop of saliva, but it's too late to take it back. "Figure of speech." They won't buy that.

And they don't. Kellen's eyes sharpen. "You've been in hiding your entire life."

It's not a question, and I don't treat it like one. Instead, I examine my fingernails, noting the way they've grown since I stopped biting them out of nervousness.

"Your parents," Elias says, understanding dawning in his voice. "They hid you—*that's* why you don't have a chip."

"My parents are good people who did what they had to do to protect their daughter."

"From us."

"From the system you uphold, yes."

The weight of that admission suffocates the room, and I fear I've just triggered a different kind of interest.

"How many others?" Kellen asks.

"How many others, what?"

He's pissed, jaw clenching over and over. "How many other women are in hiding?"

I laugh, but there's no humor in it. "Why in the stars would I know that?"

"That's not what I asked."

"I don't care, I answered." I lean forward, matching Kellen's intensity. "I have been kept inside one single building my entire life. The first time I ever stepped outside was the day I met you." My eyes land on Elias, the man looking shocked at the admission. I'm not sure what they expected...it's not like I could walk around, undocumented, and live happily ever after.

The silence prickles the hairs on the back of my neck as Kellen stands, a hand swiping through his hair before he leans against the wall next to Elias.

The bruises around my neck throb with every heartbeat.

"So," Kellen finally breaks the silence, his voice deceptively calm. "Cassia Ashford."

The sound of my real name makes me flinch. Hearing it

spoken aloud in this place feels like a violation, like they've stripped away the last piece of armor I had left. It's truly over.

"Your powers," Elias interrupts, leaning against the table. "You can influence multiple people without touch...that level of control takes years to develop."

"I *had* years." The words taste bitter. "Nothing but time and books and—" I stop myself before saying too much.

"And what?" Kellen's eyes narrow. "What else?"

I meet his gaze, forcing myself to hold it. "And the knowledge that women like me are dying in those facilities while I sit safe in my room, doing nothing."

The temperature in the room drops as the men exchange a look I cannot discern.

"The facilities serve a purpose," Kellen remarks, scratching the scruff along his chin. "They maintain order and stability."

A huff leaves me, the sound harsh and broken. "You call torturing women stability?"

"They're not tortured," Elias says, but there's something in his voice—uncertainty? "The facilities provide care, protection —" Are they truly this dense?

"Protection from *what*, Elias?" I stand, anger giving me strength. "From freedom? Having their own choice and autonomy? From being a fucking human?"

Kellen takes a step forward, resting his hands next to mine on the shiny surface. "You don't understand the bigger picture. The system works—it keeps society functioning."

"For. *Who?*" My voice rises despite the danger. "For *men*. For *the Syndicate*. What about the women who never see sunlight? Who are raped like animals?"

"That's enough." Elias' command is sharp, but I'm beyond caring.

"No, it's not enough. It's never enough." My hands clench

into fists. "You want to know why I'm here? Why I risked *everything* to join this stars-forsaken team?"

They wait, watching me with the intensity of predators.

"Because I'm tired of hiding and pretending the world is acceptable when it's built on the suffering of half the population. I want that to change." My voice drops to a whisper, but it carries more weight than anything else I've said today. "I want to burn the Syndicate to the ground."

ACKNOWLEDGMENTS

Thank you for reading Daughters of Ash! I cannot tell you how honored I am that you've taken the time to give this series debut a chance. If you enjoyed the beginning to Cassia's story, please consider leaving a rating/review. They are so important to authors!

The first installment in the Bound by Order series focuses more on the characters and Cassia experiencing the world for the very first time. What a journey it is to experience it with her, right?

In the next books, we dive further into the heads of our four main characters, the world, politics, and the infamous breeding facilities. Make sure to sign up for my newsletter for first looks at the upcoming books! You can sign up at dakotamonroe.com.

The start to this series was a difficult one. As an author who normally focuses on fantasy romance, diving into a dystopian world that has almost no romance aspects at first was quite the change. I struggled to find Cassia's voice for a while, but once I did, I knew this book (and series) was going to be so important to me. Not only is it a reflection of my inner thoughts, but it's a reflection of a possible future for us and our children. Much like the Handmaid's Tale, I wanted to show what could transpire when it's too late to intervene with many of the things happening in our reality. There are also aspects of this world that directly mirror things that are currently affecting us and our neighbors. So while I hope you enjoyed this book for the characters and their stories, I also hope that you recognize the importance of the themes presented within its pages.

I want to thank the many people who have supported me throughout this journey, from an idea that sparked while watching Mulan to this completed book, and are giving me the motivation to keep going. To my husband, sister, friends, PA, and huskies...you are my everything. Thank you.

And thank you to you, my readers. Without you, stories like this wouldn't have the chance to speak. You are so appreciated.

CHARACTER GUIDE

Anja, Commander's sister
Arayik, Commander, Anchor
Brenner Choa, Recruit, Charger
Calder Styx, Recruit, Thermic
Captain Daren, Enforcer Captain for Pyrem
Cassia Ashford, Recruit, Empath
Corin Spinel, Recruit, Empath
Darius Rhyne, Recruit, Suppressant
Denwick, Hub Communications Coordinator
Easton Lesson, Hardan Lesson's son
Eliana Lesson, Hardan Lesson's wife
Elias, Commander's Second, Revealer
Everett Montclair, Syndicate Leader 3
Finnick Crowell, Recruit, Adapter
Gage Rayne, Recruit, Telepath
Hardan Lesson, Pierce's Supervisor
Kellen, Commander's Third,
Killian Flor, Recruit, Remnant
Lachlan Ashford, Cassia's twin brother
Liana Ashford, Cassia's mother
Lucian Rennaux, Syndicate Leader 1

CHARACTER GUIDE

Malcolm Till, Recruit, Revealer
Mira, Rebel
Nash Benson, Recruit, Concealer
Orson Amata, Recruit, Anchor
Pax Eston, Recruit, Telepath
Pierce Ashford, Cassia's father
Ronan Hasten, Recruit, Clinger
Rook, Rebel
Seric, Syndicate Central Technician
Silas Vion, Recruit, Thermic
Thane Epner, Recruit, Clinger
Vaughn Harridan, Syndicate Leader 2
Vito Forven, Recruit, Concealer

ALSO BY DAKOTA MONROE

ABOUT THE AUTHOR

Dakota Monroe lives in a dark world and dreams of even darker fantasies. She has been a fantasy-obsessed reader since she was a child and now brings hers to life through her writing. As a neurodivergent woman, Dakota has always felt out of place with her thoughts and ideas; but books have been her savior, and a nonjudgmental place for her to escape the colorless world we call reality. She hopes her characters, and stories, provide an outlet for others, even if just for a little while.